Big Men's Boots

Emily Barroso

"He that believes on me, as the scripture has said, out of his heart shall flow rivers of living water."
John 7 verse 38

For Simon

Also by Emily Barroso
After the Rains

Big Men's Boots

The Way

Emily Barroso

Hillman Publishing

First paperback edition printed 2013 in the United Kingdom

Published by:
Hillman Publishing
Email: books@hillmanpublishing.co.uk
Web: www.hillmanpublishing.co.uk

ISBN 978-1-909996-01-4

A Catalogue record for this book is available from the British Library.

Typset using LaTeX by Hillman Publishing

Hillman Publishing is an imprint of Coastal Peak Ltd

Introduction

Revival is a supernatural phenomenon that occurs when God pours out His Spirit (the Holy Spirit) on a people group or country, miraculously healing and transforming them; this phenomenon often spreads through the nation and across the world, as was the case with the Welsh revival of 1904–1905. The revival was characterised by supernatural phenomena and was often ushered in by the powerful songs that were sung in chapel meetings by young teenage girls as well as men and women of all ages. There have been many revivals around the world over the centuries, but nowhere more so than in Wales, 'The Land of Revivals,' where there have been revivals there since the third century. During the nineteenth century, Welsh society and culture revolved around the Nonconformist chapels where cultural meetings, not just those of a religious nature, took place in Welsh. English was spoken by the upper and middle classes, whose members were Anglican; thus a cultural chasm existed between the working class Welsh, traditionally Welsh Nonconformists, and the landowning, English speaking traditional Anglicans. Bearing these facts in mind, the Welsh outpouring of 1904–1905, took place against a background of great social and political upheaval. A young miner named Evan Roberts was one of the leaders of the revival. Roberts was believed to have had 'second sight' and claimed to have been caught up in a vision one night during which he was told by the Holy Spirit that there would be 100,000 people converted during the forthcoming revival. These statistics are documented as more than having come to pass. The 1904–1905 revival was unusual in that the Welsh as well as the national and international press covered it. Though the men and women in the first book of this trilogy are fictional, in that they are a product of my imagination, the events described are inspired by the mystical experiences that were reported in the newspapers and journals during the 1904–1905 Welsh Revival.

A Note From The Author

The novel, though a complete book, is also book one (The Way) of a trilogy that is part of the life narrative of the Christian prophet Owen Evans and the development of his prophetic gift. While Owen is a product of my imagination (he is not Evan Roberts), his experiences are inspired by Christian prophets, some of whom I have researched and some of whom I know. Owen's supernatural prophetic journey as documented in the three novels, takes him through the stages of revival: his faith is born, dies and is resurrected again.

The Bible quotations are from the King James Bible, though most of my characters would have used the Welsh Bible translated by William Morgan in 1588 (revised in 1620). 'The Lord,' as referred to by the characters in the book, is Jesus Christ. 'The Spirit,' is the Holy Spirit of God, and 'God,' or 'Father God,' is God the Father: the three of whom make up the Christian triune God: God who was on earth as man (Jesus) but still fully God (now in heaven); God the Holy Spirit who is present on the earth (and can be in man, as man chooses); and God the Father who is in heaven. All are one; each is a distinct person; each has a separate function.

The revival was widely reported by various newspapers at the time. 'The North Wales Press' and the 'South Wales Mail,' are fictional names for the purposes of poetic license. The hymn "Dyma gariad fel y moroedd" ("Here is Love Vast as the Ocean") was one of the most popular of the 1904–1905 Welsh Revival. Hence its frequent use in the latter chapters of this novel.

www.bigmensboots.com

Encarta Dictionary Definitions of Revival

1. A renewal of interest in something that results in it becoming popular once more

2. The process of bringing something back to life, consciousness or full strength

"Anfon yr Yspryd yn awr, er mwyn Jesu Grist, Amen."
("Send the Holy Spirit now, for Jesus Christ's sake, Amen.")
The plea of the people of the Welsh Revival

North Wales 1904

March

Chapter 1

It was the third day since Stephen's death: a day for rising again. Outside a newly built quarryman's cottage, made insignificant only by the mountains that rose up thousands of feet behind it, and not far from the black mounds that marked the position of the slate quarry, thirteen-year-old Owen peered surreptitiously through the window of his dead friend's bedroom. Owen's father, Jacob, and his ministry friends Martyn and Seth, loomed over the slight figure of the boy in the bed. Stephen's dark hair was splayed out on the pillow as if it had been blown by wind and his slender hands on the sheet above the blue blanket that his mother had knitted for him when she was full of hope for his birth, were waxen and stiff; his skin was the colour and density of cream; and his lips were tainted blue, as if with watercolour wash. Owen was fascinated and repelled by Stephen's ghostly fingers: these were not the fingers that had clasped at bush or scrub as they scrambled so often up the mountain, nor the hands of the boy who had playfully punched him, day in, day out since they were babies. This was a day in. There would be a day out, and then, no more days. Martyn, who had been praying near Stephen's pillow, began to call out in a loud voice: 'Father! Father! Do not forsake us, your children! We claim the resurrected power of the blood of Jesus for this child of yours! Restore him to life on this earth though he already has life everlasting through your blood!' Martyn extended his long fingered hands on either side of Stephen's head so that they hovered like wings.

'Yes Lord!' Seth, sturdy as a boxer, said, his fist punching his words in the air above his head.

'Precious Jesus intercede for us, ask our Father in heaven to send the Holy Spirit to raise him, Three in One, we are desperate for you' Jacob said.

He sounded desperate; his face was as crumpled as his clothes after three days of praying. Owen looked at the small wooden cross that hung on the wall above Stephen's bed. It did not look like an object of power, but Owen had known since he could barely speak that when God came down to earth as man, to die for mankind in their stead; and to be raised from the grave on the third day; then, that cross had become suffused with an unimaginable power that rapidly crept over the earth, irresistibly pulling life and death in its wake, as it continued to do.

Martyn continued to plead: 'Here are our hands Lord,' he raised his hands above his head and moved them back and forth.

The other two men followed suit.

'Holy Spirit of God flow through these hands and raise him as you did Lazarus!' Jacob said.

'You said we would do greater works Lord!' Seth said, his blunt fingered hands sweeping the air. 'Here is your chance!'

'Indeed you did Lord,' Jacob slapped his hand on the Welsh Bible that he was holding. 'John 14 verse 12—as you said then, you were going to the Father, and now we have the Spirit to help us do the greater works—well here we are now—let us get on with the job at hand—'

Blood. Owen thought of the last time Stephen's fingers had life in them, three days ago on the mountain. They had become blood brothers just before Stephen fell. Even as Owen looked at his dead friend, who looked something other than Stephen, he could hear Stephen's words living in his head. He forced breath down his throat to stop crying, but the tears stung and then flowed freely. Before Stephen cut into him, Owen had forced his eyes to look at the fleshy part of his hand below the thumb joint. *Just a nick*, he had said, *and then we'll be joined for all time.* Owen had initially refused the ritual, given that it seemed covenantal and Owen was sure that the only covenants he made should be before God. He had lately been disturbed by the impact of the stories that Stephen had begun reading about blood

4

sucking Vampires; but Stephen, persuasive as the smell of roasted meat to a starving man, ground Owen down, until he snapped: *All right then*. Stephen's hand had already been marked out: a bead of blood oozed from its wink of an opening. As Stephen had cut him, the thin, neat edges of the wound had blurred Owen's eyes into streaks of flesh that came back to their seams when he wiped his eyes. *You're not crying are you?* Stephen had asked, as he took Owen's hand to press it to his. Nauseated, Owen had pulled back momentarily, but his sacrificial hand was meek. *Now we are blood brothers, forever joined*, Stephen had said, as his thumb had pressed into the wedge of flesh between Owen's hand and thumb. Owen had been seduced by the wicked surfaces of the knife, and the forbidden nature of what they were doing; but as their blood mingled, his tiny hand-wound, lip-to-lip with Stephen's parted flesh had repulsed him. Afterwards, Stephen had cleaned his knife on his trousers. Now, Owen took off his woollen glove and glanced at his scabbed over hand before jamming his fists angrily into his pockets; his right leg began to shake, but not because of the cold. Doubt strangled at his heart and a haze of guilt obscured his mind. Because of Stephen's blue fingers, Owen did not believe that he would rise, but he felt bad for thinking so, given his father would like him to have faith for the desired resurrection. He glared at the mountain that had spat Stephen out; snow ran down its humps as if a vast pot of whitewash had been flung from the sky. Both of Owen's legs were juddering now. *"In you we live and breathe and have our being,"* Owen quoted Acts 17 verse 28 to God as a reminder. He pulled his fingers through his hair several times. *Please give Stephen his breath back Father God.* Jacob stood up from where he had been bending over Stephen and turned slightly, so that Owen, afraid that his father might see him, ducked beneath the window, his boot squishing a young plant that had been pushing through the rough earth and snow; Owen felt momentarily sorry that this had happened, but fearful of being seen, he got up slowly, making sure that his face emerged sideways by degrees from the side of the window. On a chair pulled up to the bed, Seth pumped his fists up and down on his thighs, as if dispelling his prayers with imaginary bellows; Owen imagined those prayers, that sounded

5

as if they were being uttered underwater, dulled slightly as they were by the window glass, travelling up to God via great gasps of air. Seth and Jacob paced up and down on either side of the bed. Martyn's head was tipped back in supplication and his splayed hands looked as though they were holding up the ceiling as well as his stacked prayers to the God who held the power of life and death. Jacob raised his Bible up and down, as he prayed. Owen imagined all the printed words in there rattling and chattering: the words about Lazarus, his stinking grave clothes uncoiling as he walked again; and those about Christ having left the tomb, cramming together with all the other words.

Martyn was pleading with God: 'Why take a child before time? What does it mean?' he collapsed his long frame into a small wooden chair and hung his head, worms of hair extended down towards his mortal lap. 'The fault cannot lie with you God. What have we not done?'

'Yes Lord, where have we believed a lie?' Seth said.

Jacob sunk to his knees on the floor, his hands clasped in his lap like a child. 'Yes, Lord, what does it mean? Is there meaning in this? There has to be a reason,' he stood up. And then, like a man realising he had the devil at his back, he swung round, and with both hands on the Bible, he shook it at the heavens, before bending over Stephen: 'In the name of Jesus, rise!' Jacob shouted.

The other men stood and raised their hands in passionate supplication. *Come on God,* COME ON*!* Owen silently urged God.

Stephen did not rise. He just lay there looking like a boneless blue boy made of paper. Outside, Owen leaned against the wall, chest heaving to suppress the pain that was a dead weight of ice within him. His back against the rough wall, he slid to crouch. Hot tears melted the snowflakes that were falling light as communion wafers on his raised face.

Chapter 2

On the day of Stephen's funeral, the sky was a searing blue and there was not a kiss of wind. The telescopic eye of the sun was withdrawn above granite mountain peaks partly hidden by cloud: their vast, drifting animal faces added to the sense that life was taking place more from above than below. Mindful that his brother would not want to be at the funeral, Huw had suggested to Owen the day before, that they have their own service on the mountain. Now, Owen chased his brother out of the back gate of the family smallholding and across the cart track towards the mountain. From the hard road that rang under Huw's hobnailed boots, they ran through soft peat bogs and splashed through streams that flowed down from the mountain, to become the wide and currently low, river nearer the base that the children of the district bathed in during the summer and slid over in the winter; the sound the water made was guttural as it trickled over moss and stone, pooling here and there when it found a receptive resting place. As he began the climb up the mountain, Owen tried to keep pace with Huw who had already begun to weave between rocks that became larger as he reached the second stage of his climb. Owen followed his brother's jagged course. A sheep skittered out of his way, before stopping on a rocky outcrop and giving Owen a dead-eyed stare that induced an image of Stephen that Owen tried to resist, but nevertheless it intruded on Owen's physical concentration: a boy's chest expiring breath. Breathing harder now, he clambered hand over boot as the steeper scramble up the mountain began. Owen pictured lungs now: grey-blue with death. Gorse pulled at his clothes as if trying to prevent him from going further. Still the images came: faster, faster, higher, higher. Failing to outpace the image of Stephen's fingers curled meekly to the sky, Owen stopped. Doubled over, he panted, his slippery hands on his knees. Above him, his brother seemed six years in distance away as well as in age. *Slick Jack, never look back,* Owen thought as his brother all but disappeared. He turned and looked down the mountain that was mostly dressed in snow apart from areas of scree, fern and heather that were revealed darkly here and there. Owen began the steep scramble upwards, focussing on the rapid movements of his boots as they slipped and gripped the unstable mountain slope. His brother was already clambering over the top of the jagged peak. Clearing the scree, Owen began his ascent up almost sheer rock to the peak; tiny shelves of rock became finger tip or foot grips, as he began hauling himself up, appreciating the strain of muscle and tendon stretching beneath his armpit, limbs working inwards and outwards like a giant black-haired insect in loose corduroy trousers. An osprey swept its wings over the sky above Owen, and Stephen's ultimate scream came crashing into Owen's mechanical marriage of body and mind so that he almost lost his grip. Stephen had fallen onto a rocky shelf, halfway up from where Owen now was. Had there not been a rock to pillow his head, he might have stood up laughing. Life was a card game: ace, ace, joker. Blood pounded in Owen's ears; he glanced behind him, but there was no reminder that a boy's body had fallen onto the scree, slipping like slate on a stack; poised momentarily between life, death and eternity. The last several yards of rock seemed impossibly sheer and Owen's arms and legs were weakened by fear rather than exertion as he pulled himself over the edge of the chimney-shaped peak; sweat soaking his woollen gloves. He rolled over on his back, panting with the twin peaks of exhaustion and the triumph of overcoming; he eyed his brother who was sitting on a slab of rock that jutted out of mountain and into sky like a diving board. Extending his arm sideways, Owen picked up a handful of grit and threw it at his brother.

'I baptise you king of the mountain,' he said as he sat up. There was a resigned note to his voice: his brother would always be faster, higher: *fearless*. The mountain crest they were on, curved outwards on either side, and then inwards to form a basin that cradled the lake below. Smaller mountains appeared to be stacked below them; gasps of cloud capped their peaks; behind them the sea was as still as a skating rink.

'It looks like God's just done this with the snow,' Owen said, shouting into the wind; he swept his hands together to form a peak and patted down his imaginary God mountains on either side.

'Actually they are more splats than streaks,' Huw shouted back.

Owen stretched his arms out wide and spun around several times. 'I'm on top of Wales!' The wind buffeted his trousers, jacket, hair and cheeks and threatened to vortex his scarf.

'Touching heaven's blue' Huw said, from his eyrie.

Owen sat down heavily a little behind his brother, the word 'heaven,' having brought him rudely down to an earth rich with thoughts of Stephen. The osprey began circling above them; so close that Owen could see the downy white feathers on its legs. Huw glanced up at the bird. 'It's because of Stephen.'

'What do you mean? Like a sign?' Owen's eye followed the osprey as it dropped behind the mountain.

'Yes, a sign of life.'

The bird reappeared and circled above them.

'Father says once you've crossed over you cannot return,' Owen said, in a mock horror voice, as he waggled his wrist near his face.

'Jesus returned from the tomb and showed himself to his disciples,' Huw looked over his shoulder at Owen through clear, green eyes.

'Dah dah!' Owen jumped up, arms outstretched in his impression of a flashy Jesus leaving the tomb.

Huw laughed as he stood up; he walked to the edge of the rock slab, to survey the opposite ridge to the one that they had ascended. 'Just as well we're not religious in the legalistic sense, in our house,' he said.

Owen balled his hands deep into his jacket and stamped his cold feet. With his arms folded, Huw stood on the edge of the rock slab, and began rocking backwards and forwards in his boots, showing his heels to more than a thousand odd feet of air. If Owen did not know him as he did, he would think he was showing off.

'He ate fish with them on the shore of Galilee,' Huw said, tucking his jacket into his trousers and wrapping his scarf over his head like a shroud. His trousers were lashed to mid shin with rags. He was not one to be concerned with appearances and would probably walk into chapel with his jacket still tucked in.

'Galilee, Galileo, Glee.' Owen said, through a ragged laugh. He imagined bits of fish, floating in the translucent body of Jesus. *Life.* Under his rough wool trousers, his knee began to shake. He could not fathom Stephen's death. Owen's eyes searched the clear blue sky; he began puffing out circles of cold air.

'There's haloes for you angels. Come and get 'em!'

'Keep joking, if it helps Owen. Let your emotions run free. There is no one here, but you and me.'

'Poetry?'

'Not intentional,' Huw said. 'I am serious Owen.' Hands in pockets, Huw stood on the edge of the slab as if waiting for a train.

Owen came up behind his brother.

'You and me and the God that snatched him,' he said into his brother's ear, before jumping backwards off the rock. He began sliding his boots side to side in the patchy snow.

'Was it a snatch or an early reward?' Huw said, facing Owen.

'Huh! A reward for his mother and father?' Owen began to pace. 'I know what you are saying Huw. Heaven is better than earth and blather, blather, blather. But what about his mother and father, his sisters and brothers? Nice reward! I'm sure they would have preferred a piece of cake.'

'There are things we don't understand Owen.'

'And things we do,' Owen said.

His body was beginning to shudder with the effort of containment; slamming his flattened right fist into his chest gave him some relief. It was impossible that they had climbed the chimney together days ago and now one of them was gone. Huw, mindful that his brother may have another attack of what the doctor called 'nervous tremors,' tried to distract him.

'I will do your chores when I get back,' Owen, 'You can curl up in front of the fire like a cat with a bowl of something good.'

'A bowl of "four days before?"' Owen said, stamping his feet, his toes were becoming numb. Huw said nothing. Owen stopped stamping and stared across at the ridge in front of him, its giant cranial fissures seemed to mock his own mortality, and he understood how someone could jump off a cliff as Mrs Thomas had: garments billowing as she fell through blue sky, the agony of the six weeks that had passed since her husband's death at the quarry trailing an invisible yet indelible message across the sky above the community below. The Thomas children still sat in school, their faces solemn, as if in homage to the woman that was brought horribly to mind every time a Thomas child was asked his times table. Twice for the Thomas': ace, ace, joker, joker. What are the chances? And not just twice, because the repercussions were like the knots in the rope that had slipped beneath him, strangling the hearts of successive generations.

'I am going to take the second ridge down,' Huw said, trying to distract Owen, whose legs had begun to shake again, the right one excessively so.

Owen did not hear Huw. He felt helpless. The actuality of death made life horrific; he felt simultaneously punched by this fate in the chest and the belly. He almost felt compelled to throw himself off the mountain rather than go on living for another moment. He laughed without amusement; trapped by the fear that his beliefs were true, and that he would slip from this life into hell for the murder of himself, were he to do what seemed the decent thing and indulge it. It was a doubly cruel fate, this sentence of life and death. Owen thought these thoughts might send him mad; or were arriving because he was indeed mad.

'There he is again,' Huw said, as the osprey reappeared. 'He is trying to tell us something.'

'Tell us what?' Owen asked. 'To jump?' he laughed again, annoyed now with his brother's usual calm.

'They'll be coming up the mountain for the service now,' Huw said, 'Did you have a prayer?'

'Life is what you make of it. Hurry, hurry, something rude

might take it' Owen began to chant. He pictured what would be happening below: men, women and children from their quarry community and the village and the town that lay further down the valley, would be streaming up the slopes in the stiff collars of their Sunday best; the men would be in their bowler hats and best suits and the women would be wearing dresses that they had spent an inappropriate amount of time mulling over, their corsets pulled so tight that their eyes would bulge beneath their stupidly large hats with ludicrous feathers. The smallish coffin would be carried on the shoulders of Stephen's father and uncles. Stephen's distraught mother would be buttressed by rock-faced older women and younger weeping women; children would stare in fearful fascination, perhaps thinking it could be them being carried like goods, no longer a person, but a *thing*, in a box.

'Owen?' Huw was looking up at him. 'Are you listening?'

'Not really, I thought I would just pray the Lord's Prayer,' Owen blew on his hands, wondering how long it would take his fingers to turn blue if he just laid them out on the mountain as an offering. In bed the previous night, Owen had pictured himself speaking passionately about Stephen, comparing his friend to his namesake, the martyr Stephen who was stoned to death in another rocky and desolate landscape a biblical time ago. Now he pictured Stephen the martyr's beatific face being pulverised by rocks; and he pictured Stephen his friend, his body that would soon be in the ground, blue and then eaten away. He pulled his fingers through his hair, his legs juddering.

'Easy brother.' Huw put his hand on his brother's forearm.

Now, shamed by the cold stare of the mountains, Owen felt that he could not conduct himself, much less anything else.

Huw had been wondering whether the union strikers that had not returned to work at the quarry as Stephen's father had, would stand shoulder to shoulder as part of the community they had once been or would they stay away, divided still, unto death, even the death of a child?

'Shall we do the communion?' Huw said. His voice was low and warm, with just the faintest crack in it that seduced the ear.

'We do not have the bread and the wine.' Owen's voice was deeper and more rugged than his older brother's, though he was six years younger, and it was not yet broken, but it pitched itself now and again causing his family to make a show of not noticing its peaks and troughs.

'Do we not? Huw produced a little bottle of red wine and some bread from his pocket.

Owen ran his fingers through his hair and it sprung up in fright with each raking. 'It would not feel right.'

The wine in the bottle quivered like the blob of blood on his cut hand had. Today Owen did not believe in the resurrection power of the blood and the bottle was an offense to him.

Huw understood and put the bottle back in his pocket.

'Shall I say the Lord's Prayer then? You could follow with something?' Huw stood up. Owen caught a whiff of his brother, a faint pepperiness, laced with honey.

Owen made no objection, so Huw began: 'Our Father, who art in heaven, hallowed be thy name...'

A vast bank of cloud had blocked out the sun. Huw raised his brows as the sky darkened and a great shadow appeared on the face of the mountain, but Owen glowered so he said nothing. The sun came back with a shock, just as Huw came to 'for thine is the Kingdom, the power and the glory for ever and ever...' As Huw said 'Amen' the osprey appeared from the other side of the mountain.

'See?' Huw said. 'He has come to say 'amen.'

Owen rolled his eyes at this statement of cheese, but they both watched the osprey spiral up to the heavens and then drop down again, only to climb back up and hover.

Huw figured that the procession down below would be shuffling into the chapel now.

'I will go back down now,' he said, his eyes on the mountain ridge below them. 'I am going to round that buttress over there,' Huw pointed to a ring of rock circling part of the ridge below. There was hardly anything to grip, but Owen knew that it was the lack of grip that was attracting Huw.

'I will leave you to contemplate and say your goodbyes.'

Owen did not know whether to feel annoyed that Huw was leaving so abruptly, given the occasion, or relieved, because his conversation was making him irritable. Huw took out a small paper-wrapped parcel containing some of their mother's bara brith cake and his tea bottle from the cloth bag that he had tied to his waist, and thrust them at his brother.

'Here. For whatever communion you choose to make.'

Huw began to walk away, but then he turned abruptly and came back.

'Owen? Mother and Father will not be pleased with me for leaving you on your own, but I have a feeling that it will be good for you,' Huw gripped him by the shoulders. 'You are a warrior Owen—like David. You can slay Goliath if you put your heart and mind in focus.'

But Owen had had enough of words. He watched Huw as he disappeared rapidly down the pinnacle. His whole being was concentrating on working out the route over the mountain. He disappeared around the buttress for a while, but soon after, Owen observed his brother picking his way over the jagged rock of the ridge as if traversing the spiny back of a dinosaur. Before long he dropped out of sight as he came off the ridge and descended the north face of the mountain. Owen imagined him digging his boots sideways into the loose scree as he jump descended sideways. He would be at the main road on the lower slopes in half the time it took him to climb up. Lately the idea that his attraction for the mountains was born out of partial terror had begun to rise in Owen; the mountains possessed a magnetism that drew him up in spite of himself; he was in awe of them and he wanted to be embraced by their coldness as Huw was. Owen was conscious that his mother, Anwen and Huw saw his fear. *Quite a beast to overcome*, Anwen had said when Owen returned from his first encounter with the Devil's Ridge. Though pleased, Owen had squirmed, because on the ridge that day, there had been a moment of such acute fear, that he had almost allowed himself to fall rather than continue in terror. Now, at a loss as to what to do next, Owen walked to the opposite side of the mountain and sat down. The sea in the distance was a flat metallic sheet, mirroring the lower edges of the cumulous clouds that separated sky from sea. A familiar fear descended like the inevitability of dusk. He felt alone in his spirit, alone in his mind, as well as physically alone. Frozen and fog-framed by his breath, he contemplated staying there until he froze to death, until he noticed the osprey circling in the sky above him again. The bird flew with deep, slow wing beats, suspending them now and again to glide; the wing beats of the bird calmed the rapid beating of Owen's heart. As he watched the long tapered wings and fanned tail of the bird, he imagined painted lines drawing the flight pattern of the bird in the sky; he kept drawing the flight pattern in his mind, even setting it to imagined music, until he was sure that *it*, whatever it was that stalked him, was not going to come and force him to leap off the edge of the mountain. Anxiety worried at his edges, until, mounting a surge of sudden feeling, Owen turned suddenly and took off, running as fast as he could, down a slope until he came to the flat rock in the place where he had last faced Stephen and held out his hand to be cut. As he sat there he began sensing that he was not alone, but he was not afraid. Without thinking he turned and sat exactly where Stephen had sat; strangely, he felt comforted sitting there. He stared down at the dip in the rock where Stephen had laid his pocket knife; Stephen's laughter filled his mind; which acted like a trigger. He felt a roar coming up from his depths, causing him jump off the rock; the force within him took him over the edge of the mountain and down to the spot where Stephen had lain.

'Stephen!' he screamed at the sky. 'You were my best friend!' He doubled over panting, his hands on his knees. Then he felt himself rise up again.

'I love you Stephen!'

Owen began beating his chest and screaming, but this time not with pain. After a time, it seemed that the roar within him quietened; he lay splayed on scree on the mountain slope, wondering whether the inner screaming had gone and whether it would come back. He laughed for some time before wondering again whether he was mad and then reasoning that if he were, he would not *wonder* about being mad, he would just *be* mad. As he lay there looking up at the sky, the osprey reappeared and began making wider and wider circles until it circled up higher and higher and became a black dot that became a speck before vanishing in to the blue.

Chapter 3

In the queer light of approaching darkness, Owen walked with his parents from the schoolhouse, up a slate strewn track towards the cottage. He felt that the mountains that the road cut through were encroaching, threatening to squeeze the life out of him. On the side of the road, a rowan tree stretched out sideways from a rock fissure, its naked branches like a shock of witch's hair rooted in a mossy green face.

'Easy my boy,' Jacob said, putting his jacket around Owen's shoulders.

No one spoke of Stephen at school, he had already become taboo, but the teachers made comments: *His father tried to revive him;* he saw Miss Robert's shake her head; children walked past him and he heard their whispering. Stephen's empty desk stood in front of him; in the absence of Stephen it seemed to be expanding and breathing, ever present in his peripheral vision. During dictation, he pictured his friend sitting in front of him so clearly that he almost heard him say 'the room smelled of boggy-boiled-cabbage,' when the teacher said 'the room smelled of freshly baked bread.'

He must be alive somewhere, Owen had thought so desperately that his hands had begun to sweat and his heart to beat so rapidly he was afraid it would fly out of him like a red bird. *It is impossible that he is gone completely.* At the entrance to the quarry, the hacked out parts of the mountain, looked like giant cubes of fibrous meat: grey and visceral, they glistened on the lenses of Owen's eyes. From the mouth of the quarry, a black regurgitation of rocks spilled onto the valley road. A straggle of men appeared from behind the rubble trolleys, their faces shrouded with dust, their eyes glowing in the vanishing light; they stopped in front of Jacob and shook his hand one by one.

'Thank you for doing your best, now we must do our best,' Stephen's father Thomas said, his dusty bowler hat in his hands. Life had beaten him so hard on the back that his shoulders had caved inwards; his dead men's arms hung limply by his sides. Cadwy Jones had been one of the leaders of the recent strike, but had ended up cap in hand, begging for his job back so that his family would not starve. *Blackleg* he was called, by men that were prepared to starve for their beliefs if necessary. He had incurred the wrath of union and most of the community treated him like a sulphurous smell. *Blackleg*, Owen turned the word over in his mind and wondered how Stephen's father felt now, about all the *trying*. Trying to get the quarry bosses to pay the men properly; trying to get compensation for the widows; *trying* to save his son. Owen did not remember the time period before leaving his friend's still warm body on the mountain and being put to bed in his brother's room after a cup of warm milk and brandy, because he could not climb the ladder to the crog loft. The postman was the first live human being he had encountered, and so the news was given, though Owen did not remember uttering it. Cadwy Jones had carried his last-born son down like a baby swaddled in his arms with his coat. Most of the community had stood in vigil, and they parted like the red sea when he came down the mountain, so that Thomas could walk through with his youngest son. Now, Stephen's father put his hands on Owen's shoulders and applied gentle pressure. The wings of Thomas's own shoulders pointed backwards. Owen slid his eyes from Stephen's father's face, to the ground. *He is like a dog that having been shot, is nevertheless still alive*, Owen thought.

'Do not carry anything, Owen,' Cadwy Jones said, his hands still on Owen's shoulders. 'You must lay your burdens down,' he said, not looking at all like a man that had laid his burdens down, though he was still standing, which was remarkable. Stephen's father's hand, now hanging by his dusty black jacket, was large and bony, void of flesh and rivered with the veins of time. Anwen gripped Stephen's father's hands with her ivory-skinned ones, and with her eyes looking deeply into his, spoke words of comfort. Afterwards, the three stood for a while and watched the men disappear over the mountain track. Stretching her shawl out to envelop Owen, Anwen pulled him to her side. When Owen raised the side of his face from her linen-covered ribcage, he saw tears on her pale cheek. The road became cart tracks as it stretched over the mountain and down towards the sea; the Evans smallholding could now be seen: a long stone cottage with slate roof that faced the sea, a scullery and outhouse attached to one end and barns and pens arranged behind it, facing the mountains; fields on either side and a steep one in front, when viewed from below, the front wall appeared as a line above which the sheep looked to be stuck on sideways; a track above led over the carved mountains to the quarry and barracks where some of the quarrymen lived and then sloped downwards to the village with its collection of shops and the pub and inn; a road below that ran all the way down to the town and the sea beyond. Near the quarry barracks, twelve cottages came into view six on either side of the road. Newly slated and painted an innocent white, these homes were spat at with indignation. Oil lamps gleamed in the windows, but there were no signs stating 'Not traitor,' in these windows and the doors would be barred shut from the inside. Never had the building of new cottages caused such murderous dissent, though Stephen's death had brought some peace to a community that had been divided since some of the men had taken up Lord Penhurst's offer to return to work, bribing them, some said, with the new cottages. The returned men did not receive the fairer pay or better working conditions that they had all gone on strike for in the few years preceding: what they received was a wage, new cottages to live in, though the quarry steward would be a monkey on their backs for rent; and a divided community. Lately, and due to his loss, Stephen's father had been left alone. The men that had returned to work following the strike, had moved into the cottages over the past week and most chose to go to the local chapel near the quarry barracks where Jacob was minister, rather than venture down the valley to the village chapel that many of them had grown up in, for fear of the local families: the families of those that had *set their faces like flint* were braying for the blood of those that had crumbled, though perhaps not as loudly as before. There had been many strikes in these parts in recent history, but none so long and so acrimonious as the one that had ended in practise only recently: for some the end was a beginning; for others a turning back: a turning they would neither forget nor be allowed to forget.

In the cottage Anwen piled more peat onto the coals and pumped the bellows until the fire burned fiercely behind the grate; she put a blanket on Owen's shoulders and pulled the settle he sat on closer to the fire. She fetched Owen a slate and pencil and handed them to Owen, who shook his head, so she left them on the settle opposite him. Sipping hot sweet tea, Owen stared at the devouring flames. He no longer heard the laughter of his friend in his head, but he was tormented by images of him in death. In his desolation he doubted; and he was afraid of his doubt. Without God, life had no meaning, with God, he was forced to endure the eternal mind that countenanced the death of children. He picked up the slate and began to draw. At the range, Anwen set the water on to boil before sitting down at the kitchen table next to the range, to peel the potatoes into a basin. She sang as she peeled and watched Owen draw without making it obvious that she was doing so. As soon as his child's hand could manipulate the chiselled rock, Owen had begun to draw on the slate on the steps and on the path outside the back door. Anwen encouraged his drawing by giving him what materials she could lay hold of and soon he had graduated from slate to lead and paper, ink and pen, though he still drew on slate; as was evident all around the back door and on the walls of the milking shed. Each detailed drawing of family, smallholding, mountain animal and bird, found on slate, stone, wall or paper, was a joyful discovery for Anwen; the years of slates that he had drawn on were stacked along the back wall of the sheep pen and occasionally a visiting farmer or a child would go through these slates and if they had the mind for it, they could trace the story of Owen from when he was only several years old until now; the slates more a record of his life than anything Anwen had carefully recorded in the margins of her housekeeping book: *Owen took his first step today, he is only nine months.* When Owen drew himself, he was always seated or standing away from the objects that he had drawn as if observing his creation. Huw was more physical and gave her 'heart bumps' of a different variety as she put it. From the age of seven, Huw was climbing the mountain with the older boys of the district. Often, he would disappear from the cottage, and Anwen would find him climbing the slopes; by eleven, there was not a mountain in the area whose ridges had not experienced Huw's fingertips or his elasticised feet. As he grew, he unsettled his parents by speaking of the mountains as if they were living beings. He began to argue with his father about spiritual matters from the age of about eight; at twelve he read aloud to him the verse from Isaiah, *For ye shall go out with joy, and be led forth with peace: the mountains and the hills shall break forth before you into singing, and all the trees of the field shall clap their hands.* He said, *The mountains sing when I am on them, Father. They sing beneath my feet.* Anwen reassured her husband that it was a good thing that the mountains helped Huw focus on spiritual matters, but to Jacob, Huw's attraction to the mountains was a dangerous thing. *But do the mountains not speak of God?* Anwen had asked. Anwen placed the last peeled potato in the basin and looked out across the front field where the sheep were grazing and beyond, out to sea. The tide would be out and the mussels would be clinging to the rocks; the mussel men would likely be out in their boats with their long rakes, dredging mussels from their beds. Anwen would have liked to gather mussels before the end of the season, but now she might have to wait until September, which set up an instant craving within her. She recalled sitting on the beach with her mother and the other women deep into the night as they gathered and sorted mussels by lantern light, while her father was out on the boats. She thought of the mussels, oysters and clams that her mother used to cawl with potatoes and of the herrings that she was fond of pickling in the late summer months and of the infinite variety of fish available in the rich waters surrounding North Wales. Now that she lived on the mountain rather than in her childhood home nearer the sea, her cawls were usually made with mutton, which was satisfying in a different way; now, across the years of time, she could almost hear her mother calling her to supper and the taste of her long gone mother's fish stew, came back to her potently; her eyes stung with emotion and so she thought of the rich yellow butter in the pantry, freshly churned by her this morning, and of the milk still warm in the pail in the scullery, and a surge of joy at the wonder of life rose up in her, and she thanked God for the life she had had across her history, for the parents she had loved, and for her husband and children and for the fact that there was a good dinner to be given them that night. Still gazing at the sea, she prayed for the women whose men had gone to work in the coalmines of the south rather than return cap in hand to the quarry following the strike and she prayed for the women whose husbands had returned to work so that they could put food on the tables for their families and a good slate roof over their heads.

Chapter 4

Huw, recently returned from the quarry, leaned against the old oak dresser, chatting to Anwen as she sliced the potatoes for the five-minute potatoes and bacon.

'The men are skittish,' Mother. 'They want an outlet. I am afraid there will be violence.'

'We must pray against it Huw,' Anwen said as she began frying the bacon on the skillet. She felt uneasy about Huw working at the quarry given that feelings were running so high since the quarry reopened, but she knew she must not give way to the fear that occasionally brushed at her like the fabric of her skirt at her ankles.

'There is more support for the unions, Mother, though I suspect some are paying up for the sake of appearances,' he shifted, placing a socked foot on the wall behind him and folding his arms. 'And the preachers they prefer are the ones that speak of social justice.'

'If they came to the fellowship meetings we could discuss these things and if they attended the prayer meetings, we could pray—the young seem to have forgotten that self-sacrifice leads to fruition, it's a basic Biblical principle—I suspect they are more interested in reading The Clarion than the Bible nowadays.' Anwen sighed as she turned the pale pink and white top layer of bacon to expose the sizzling brown sides below, working the crisp bits off the base of the skillet; a rich smell filled the cottage. 'We need another revival to bring the changes that will heal from within and have lasting consequences without,' she said, gesturing to Huw to get the plates.

'The enemy of God is sowing tares amongst the wheat, encouraging people into other belief systems when there is but one way—the wicked one is the adulterer of thoughts and he works in the dark. Ignorance is his playing field.'

Huw, his mouth watering in anticipation of the bacon that he could already taste, took the cutlery from the drawer and began setting the table. 'Truth be told Mother, The Clarion is something of a socialist Bible to working men nowadays, but some of the men are saying that the chapel is no longer relevant to the needs of society.'

Anwen slid the potatoes and onions from her chopping board into the skillet. 'It is not relevant because they do not attend and therefore they do not throw their needs—or those of others—into the debate—and contend for them—before God and man. There needs to be fellowship for the church to be the living thing that God intended.' Anwen turned the potatoes and onions with her wooden spoon. 'The building is the shelter; the people are the stuff of it, if they do not come how can they be built into God's plan? I wonder if they pray at all,' she poured a cup of water into the skillet and picked a few sprigs of wild thyme from the branch that was hanging above the range into the water along with half a teaspoon of salt, before scraping the meat vigorously from the base of the pan with her wooden spoon to create a stock. 'They have no staying power—though I agree that the meetings should be relevant,' she said, bending to stoke the flames in the grate. 'God is always relevant.'

'The world is changing and the chapel needs to be relevant. God is not boring mother,' Huw turned from laying down the forks. 'He is infinitely creative, we need to be creative too—what say you brother?' Huw called over to Owen, who was sitting by the fire drawing.

'Well God did tell Adam to name the animals so I suppose we are meant to be creative with what he gives us,' Owen said without looking up from his slate.

'There you are Mother, *out of the mouths of babes*,' Huw went and kissed his mother on the cheek.

'And how have the babes been instructing you now?' Jacob

said as he came through the door. He took off his hat, and ran his fingers through his hair that was rain-wet on the ends. Meg was jumping all over him. 'There girl, down girl, you are a wet little sheepdog are you not?'

Meg responded by shaking her fur in his face. Jacob rubbed the dog briskly on both sides of her face while making growling noises.

'Our eldest was telling me that the chapel is becoming irrelevant to some of the men,' Anwen was lighting the oil lamp for the table. 'It is God that will entice them back, Huw,' she reached up and hung the lamp on the hook suspended from the ceiling, 'though we need to make sure they are included in the debates.'

'Well if that is the case we must pray for the relevance of the truth that is Christ Jesus to assist us—and them,' Jacob shook the rain from his coat before hanging the shoulder parts over several wooden hooks by the door to dry.

'We need something new Father. The churches need their fire back. The young need a new religious experience and the politically minded need to see more being done to assist the community,' Huw took the supper dish his mother handed him to the table while his father acknowledged his mother's raised brow with a wry smile.

'Ah yes. We do need more workers in the field Huw, or how are we to conduct the work,' he winked at his son. 'But, this socialism—this new philosophy is not new.' Jacob picked up the Bible from the dresser. 'What did Christ preach if it was not socialism? The parable of the Good Samaritan is socialism. We need good Samaritans and a philosophy is not going to create them. The power of the Holy Spirit come to live within people and transforming them from the inside out is true socialism,' Jacob went to the scullery to fetch a mug of water.

'Yes, Father,' Huw called from where he sat at the table. 'Jesus came to write the law on our hearts, but the young are not seeing the work so much these days.'

'Really?' Jacob said, mug in hand. 'They should get out more. Jacob said. He gulped water. 'I, and many like me are worked to the bone - good preaching, though son - you should consider the ministry,' he wiped his mouth and smiled as he rubbed his hands together. 'Well, there we have it. Where's the youngest?'

Anwen and Huw smiled at each other as Jacob went over to the settle to see Owen.

'I saw that, my lovely,' Jacob said to Anwen who had just mimed *'Well there we have it,'* at Huw.

Jacob looked over Owen's shoulder at the slate. 'That's a fine piece, my son. Is that the hand of God?'

'Yes,' Owen said. It's the hand of death.'

Jacob crouched in front of his son. Owen continued to draw. What was already represented on the slate was the mountain. A large hand, palm facing, appeared to be making ready to scoop up the lake.

'Anger can be like a cold hand squeezing the life out of your heart son,' Jacob said, his hand gripping air to demonstrate.

'Yes, but who caused the anger?' Owen said.

'Well there are only two sources.' Jacob stood up. 'You are entitled to your feelings. Only work them out. It is a strenuous business being angry with God. To say nothing of it being a losing battle.'

'What if I don't like him today?' Owen said, scratching lines onto the palm of the hand of God.

'It is best to like Him every day, given He is your creator and understands you best. Pour your heart out to him though, son, as David did. He knows how you feel anyway but it will get it off your chest,' he rose and kissed his son on his head.

'Where is my pretty wife,' Jacob said getting up completely. 'And my great, hulking useless son,' he said, smiling at Anwen and Huw. Huw laughed and went to his bedroom to use the jug and basin before supper. He felt for his brother: death was just the thing to scupper ones faith.

The angel had a very handsome appearance. He was about eight feet tall, with massive wings that stretched up a foot high behind him, their tips almost reached the floor; everything about him was human looking, only oversized and somehow magnified: his eyes were larger, and set further apart than Owen was used to seeing in human beings; his shoulder-length hair was of a bronzy-gold colour that appeared to be undulating and he wore a long white robe with a gold sash. The angel's expression changed as he raised his hand. Owen could not articulate in his mind the expression on the angel's face: he looked kind, but stern at the same time. He pointed, and as he did so, Owen saw fire raging over land. As he watched, the fire rapidly consumed the vegetation beneath it, before appearing to consume itself. Bright shards of lime green grass shot up from the black ground where the fire had been. *It is not the end, but a beginning*, the angel said. *Do not fear*. Owen woke up in his crog loft bedroom. There was a palpable presence in the room, and his hands were shaking as he felt for the matches. Once the candle was lit he jumped out of bed and looked over the edge of the loft. The doors to his parents and Huw's bedrooms were closed. In the main room below him, everything was in its place: through the window opposite, the moon cast light over the Bible and papers on his father's desk on the far side of the living room; and the twin settles were like dark wooden arms stretching out to him from the still glowing eyes of the coal in the grate; the table in the centre of the room was bare but for the jug of daffodils his mother had placed next to the lamp. He got back into bed and leaned against the wall looking out of the small window above his bed at the mist on the field that obscured the view of the sea. He lay rigid in his bed, trying to understand the meaning of the dream that had been as real to him as the sweat that ran from his hands onto the sheet. The fear was not unlike the time that Stephen and Owen had spent too long on the mountain and the mist had descended so thickly with the gathering darkness, that draped in cloud, they had had to feel their way downwards: a fear so primal that he had become acutely aware of his own humanity. He was so much at the mercy of the mountain and the elements that interacted with it, that he was sure he was only lumps of flesh, puddles of blood and piles of bones. They had found their way down the mountain, by accident, Owen thought, though according to Anwen it was by design, as she had begun getting a sense that something was wrong that afternoon and had begun to pray for his protection then. Owen was looking at the slate that he had finished drawing earlier that was now propped against the wall opposite him.

26

His heart began to pound: in the large hand that he had drawn, another hand had been perfectly drawn. The blunt thumb was unmistakeable. It was Stephen's hand.

In the morning, when he heard his mother go outside to do the milking, he picked the slate up and ran outside with it. He put it behind some slates that he had drawn some years previously. As he pulled his singlet and long johns on he thought: How does one not fear when one is afraid? When he put the question to Anwen later that day, she said that God had told Joshua not to fear when he went into the Promised Land. She said that it was a command and therefore we are capable of obeying that command if we put our heart to it, and ask God to give us the grace to obey. Anwen often spoke of putting one's heart to something rather than one's mind. What she meant was that one was supposed to put their essential self, their spiritual self into something. She said that when that heart shift had occurred the mind could follow. *There was no use putting your mind to something, unless your heart was in it first.* Owen had found that although some of his fear had dissipated as he had looked into the angel's eyes, when the angel left the room, the fear had returned. When Owen focussed on the words again, *do not fear*, he found the fear would disappear again. In the weeks following, he returned to those words in his mind over and over again. As he meditated on them, they did indeed become part of him. *Was this the word made flesh?* he asked his brother. *I do not see why not,* his brother had replied. *I have long argued that the Bible is a miracle working text that has one universal meaning, as well as a plethora of individual meanings at any one time.*

Anwen waved Jacob and her sons off from the back door as they made their way up the mountain track; they were going to chapel to practise for the upcoming Eisteddfod, in which they all sang in the choir. Afterwards she stood on the back step with her cup of tea for a long time watching the stars appear as she prayed and communed with God: thanking Him as she did several times a day for Jacob and Huw and Owen, and for the little one that went home. Anwen was also praying as to whether to put Owen forward for the scholarship to the town school. Her main concern was that the cares of the world would stifle his faith given its rigorous intellectual reputation for the sciences. In her mind, religion and science were compatible, but she knew one of the masters at the school and to say he was of a spiritual bent would be to bend him over entirely. The local school was harsh, but Anwen was able to cleanse her son from ill feeling when he returned distressed on occasion. Anwen listened to the shuffling of the sheep in their pen. One of the ewes would lamb any day now and Anwen sympathised with her inability to get comfortable. In the final weeks before she gave birth to Owen she would get up in the night to pace, hoping her walking would rock her kicking child to sleep. She thought that he would be a wanderer then, but it was Huw who wandered all over the mountains, though Owen followed when he was older. Owen wandered in his mind. He was the wonderer. She had a sense that his wondering would one day take him far away from her and she was grateful that his restlessness and his adventures did not take him from her yet. Owen did not often talk of these adventures, or of the dreams that he had, except occasionally when he cried out at night, and even then, he only seemed to spill their contents because he was caught between that world and this and was not aware of his mumblings; but she had long been aware of his gift of second sight. At first she thought that the gift was an imaginative one given his sensitivity and his creativity, but when Owen began to predict things that came to pass, she spoke to Anna, a known prophet from the district, who told Anwen that the child was prophetic, and that his sensitivity and creativity in the physical realm corresponded to his gifting in the spiritual realm. Jacob and Anwen had discussed this and decided to pray for their son and to watch over him but to try not to stifle him by interfering too much; they wanted him to have a normal boyhood as much as possible. Vast and vivid, the evening star was displaying its majesty, Anwen thought of the three wise men that followed the star that led the way to Christ in Bethlehem and from there to the eternal God. A lamb bleated in the field beside her and Anwen pulled her shawl tighter as the air cooled; she also thought of the words of Psalm 19 verse 1: *The heavens declare the glory of God; the skies proclaim the work of his hands.* 'We are, as St Paul said, without excuse, Father, she said out loud. The works of your hands are everywhere.'

April

Chapter 5

Little wonder these houses were known as 'the pits,' Owen thought as he followed his mother down the steps to the cellar house. The odour that came up from the windowless single room that they were descending was of soiled nappies and human excrement melded with the odour of overcooked vegetables and damp. Holding the bag of Anwen's late season apples that they had taken from the barn loft that morning in a blaze of sunshine, he followed his mother down the steps into the gloom. Owen's eyes adjusted slowly to the darkness. A candle burnt on a table against a wall. On one side of the room were two shallow cots for children; a ladder was propped against the wall below the crog loft, where Rhys and Mary Davies slept. The focal point of the room was the open hearth. The fire in the grate was as sparse as Mrs Davies herself who was attacking the contents of a huge pot near the grate with a dolly stick. A tin bath was on the floor next to her.

'Every time I boil these I feel sure there will be nothing left of them, though they come out clean, thanks to the soda, you see. Off out the lot of you!' she shouted. There was a scuffling sound and three figures jumped off a wooden platform in the corner of the room.

'The other seven are all working now, you see' Mary Davies said. 'Four boys in the quarries—living in the barracks, you see, thank the Lord. Three of the girls are serving in the big houses—who would have thought—their fingers on fine linen, Annie. That leaves these three scallywags—shoo! Out the house, the lot of you.'

Two little girls and a boy shot up the stairs like cats caught raiding.

'I count myself lucky that I have ten living and only three dead,' said Mrs Davies.

'God is gracious,' Anwen said, putting her basket on the table. 'Oh wait a while,' she turned and called up after the children. She glanced at Mrs Davies. 'I have something for them. Owen give the children the apples.'

Owen handed red and orange skinned apples to the children. Skinny and unsmiling, their eyes loomed up at him from the sunken depths of poverty. The smallest girl, Betsey, snatched hers and ran to the corner of the room where she ravaged the apple until her mother shooed her outside. One by one, flour, potatoes, carrots and turnips were produced from Anwen's basket; she laid this bounty on the table. The candle spluttered and went out.

'Ah, yes,' Anwen said, as she took six candles bound with string from her basket.

'I had one more, though I am grateful to you, Annie.'

Anwen felt dreadful. Pride was all Mary had and now she had snatched that from her too.

'I make them last, you see,' Mrs Davies said, 'so that I can learn my reading after the children have gone to bed. My letters are ready for you to look at, Annie,' Mary said, nodding in the direction of the hearth.

Mrs Davies large letters, scratched white against the dark slate, lay on the hearth.

What must it take for this woman, worn to the quick, by childbearing and housework, to take out her slate—yet how invaluable, to learn to read, for herself?' Anwen thought.

'Have you not been able to find any other work Mary? I hate to see you washing all those nappies.'

'I washed my own children's nappies for more years than I can remember Annie. It's work you see, and it puts the food on the table. People will always want their nappies washed.'

Why must I always say the wrong thing? Anwen thought. She struggled in her efforts to help but not to patronise.

'Have you had any word from him Mary?'

'The last word I had was that he was going to Conwy to fight—he was drunk at the time though,' Mary laughed unhappily as she attacked the contents of the pot with the stick. 'I don't know which is worse, you see—wondering when he will come home and in what state, or knowing he has gone or what he has gone and done. I am sick to the quick of the union—'

Mary's tone became lighter. 'I would rather he went south—then I would not need to boil his clothes, you see, the children's clothes are so much smaller than his, and mine seem to go much longer without getting all smelly you see. Oh Annie I used to dread washday when he was still at the quarry.'

Anwen laughed at Mary's joking. 'I hate the washday Monday too, Mary. Shall we pray for washing angels to descend and just do it for us?'

'I'm serious, Annie, you see, praying hasn't helped me,' she said, both hands gripping the stick, wet tendrils of hair slicking her face. 'Will praying bring my dead children back to life or bring my husband back sober and no longer married to the union? Will it give him a job—outside the quarry of course?'

'I came to see you as well as pray for you, Mary,' Anwen said, moving towards Mary and holding out her hands. 'You praised God for so many alive—we must continue to pray with faith. I know the eternal God who answers prayers and so do you. Your father was healed in the revival of '79. We all forget so quickly. Our God is the God of Lazarus—of your father Mary. Do you want Rhys to come back?'

'I'm sure I don't know, I've stopped caring about where he goes. Every time there is trouble connected to the quarry he disappears,' Mary laughed. 'It's so obvious the foolish man.'

Anwen smiled with commiseration. Rhys was good at leaving a trail of disaster behind him.

'I have prayed he would never come back, you see,' she balanced a nappy on the end of the dolly stick to lose some of the heat. 'I am so sick of hearing about the quarry and about those houses. I wish he were not so bitter. His bitterness is like poison and it's infecting all of us. I'm tired of the fighting—the union kind and the bare knuckled kind'

'Well maybe God answered your prayers then.' Anwen smiled.

'How can we do more, Mary? What can we pray for?'

Mary laughed as she squeezed the water out of a nappy with her red hands and dropped it into a tin bath.

'Eilwen tells me Miss Morgan is leaving to be married. Eilwen is devastated, Annie you see. Can't you lobby? Why should a woman not teach when she is married—at least until she has children? That way you see, she will not have to do the washing!'

Anwen laughed, though she knew Mary was diverting.

'And scrubbing on Tuesdays, and all the rest,' Mary said. 'I don't even know what to pray for any more, you see,' Mary said. 'I don't want my children to fall into the scalding tub, like the Hughes child, or be lost walking home from school or be taken by the fevers like little Bronwen across the way. I don't want them to live in a cellar house when they grow up—it's not a house, Annie is it? Do you think those prayers might be answered, Annie?'

'I believe they can and they will, Mary. Can you sit a while? I will make some tea—Owen fetch the water please.'

'Tea? I haven't had any for a week. Oh you are a saint to a sinner like me Annie,' Mary said, sitting down with her legs splayed out in front of her, she tipped her head back and sighed. 'Oh Annie I miss having a baby on my lap.' She raised her head. 'Though I would never want another.' She got up quickly. 'These nappies will not wash themselves Annie.'

Anwen thought of the child that Mary had lost; of the evening she had spent with Mary, coaxing the ailing infant to live. She could feel the rough fabric of the swaddled child against her cheek even now. *He won't take my baby will he Annie?*

'No.' Anwen said, reaching for the dolly. 'They will not wash themselves. I will wash them, while you sit at this table and tell me what your life was like when you were a girl and drink hot, sweet tea with me.'

'Oh, away with you Annie, I can't let you do that. I am paid for the work.'

'You will be doing me a favour. I have a mind to do it and a desire to hear you tell me of your past,' Anwen tucked tendrils of dark hair into her plain white cotton cap and retied her apron in readiness.

Mary Davies laughed. 'If I was a girl I can't remember. Oh

34

what will happen if I remember? But hot sweet, tea. Oh that sounds nice, like, Annie.'

Outside, Owen inhaled the sweet air. He walked the short distance to the end of the track where the cellar houses stopped and filled the kettle for the women at the pump. The sound of blasting at the quarry could be heard in the distance. On the way back from delivering the kettle, he found two of the three children playing with stones in the dirt.

'Where's your sister?' Owen asked.

'Don't know,' said Gwilm without looking up from the small metal box that he was filling with dirt. His cap was lying in the dirt.

'Don't care about Catrin,' said little Betsey. She had a pile of stones in her pinafore. Her flat cap, the same as her brother's also lay in the dirt. Owen noticed a rainbow beetle heading for the cap. He picked it up and cupped it in his hands.

'What do you think I have here Betsey?' Owen said.

'Let me see,' Gwilm said abandoning his box.

Owen opened his hands carefully. The beetle's antennae searched the unfamiliar terrain of Owen's palm.

'Those colours don't look real,' Gwilm said.

'What do you mean?' Owen asked examining the shades of purple, orange and green on the beetle's iridescent back.

'It looks like it comes from another planet like.'

Owen laughed. 'I know what you mean. The colours are like something beyond this world.'

Betsey held out her hands and Owen tipped the beetle into her palm. 'Ooh it's itchy scratchy tickly wickly,' she said.

'Those aren't words,' Gwilm said. 'She's always making up words that aren't words.'

'But surely if they are words to her they are words?' Owen said. 'You called them words.'

Betsey gave Owen the beetle back and smiled and skipped off to the field on the side of the track. 'I will make a daisy crown for my head,' she said.

Gwilm went back to his box. 'It's all just a load of nonsense,' he said.

Owen pondered their words. Life was just nonsense if the

meaning of it was not understood. People were just feeling their way in the dark like the rainbow beetle without the light of understanding. He watched Betsey skipping across the field to a clump of wild daisies. She plonked herself down and began picking them. She may live in a dark room, Owen thought, but she has a magnificent playground out here, as good as any childs. He felt a rush of brotherly affection for the children and began praying inwardly for them. He prayed for Mary too. And then, he prayed for Rhys as well, that he would stop the bare knuckle fighting and the going off away from the family and leaving them alone—though as he prayed this he thought that it might not be so bad, him going off all the time, given what the community knew of his violence. When he had finished, he looked up and spotted Catrin swinging on the gate to the farmer's field a little way up the track.

'Would you like to see our beetle?' Owen called.

'I don't like creepy crawly things,' Catrin called back, as she continued to swing. 'How about some hot, sweet tea?' Owen called, setting the beetle free. It ambled off up the dirt track, the sun shining on its back, sending sparks of light off its rainbow wings like something from another planet.

'I don't drink tea.' Catrin shouted. 'Can I have water?' she stood up on the farm gate and balanced on it, the tips of her black boots pointing up at the sky then down at the ground like batty blackbirds as she balanced. She jumped off the top of the gate, giving Owen, who thought she might break her neck, a start.

'I am going to run away and join the circus,' she said, coming up beside him and cupping her hands. Owen laughed, 'What are you doing?'

'Making a cup from my hands.'

Owen began to pour water, noticing the dirt on her hands as he did so. He stopped pouring.

'Wash them a little first.'

Catrin gave him a strange look and immediately Owen felt convicted for drawing attention to her grubbiness; simultaneously he heard the words from Matthew's gospel in his thoughts, *And if anyone gives even a cup of cold water to one of these little ones*

36

because he is my disciple, I tell you the truth, he will certainly not lose his reward.

He began pouring, and she drank six, seven handfuls, spilling plenty on the ground. *My cup runneth over.* As Owen watched the splashes fall to the earth, the land around them seemed to become greener and the grasses on the side of the dirt track appeared to undulate. Crystal drops of water shivered separately on the ground, refusing to dissipate; miniature oceans of vivid colour swam in their singular worlds. Owen's hands began to sweat and his stomach to swarm. He looked up to steady himself. A single cloud was moving rapidly over the mountains, their surfaces rich panels of jade and mauve beneath the clear sky. He closed his eyes tightly and concentrated on pouring. When he had poured the final handful, he looked down again at the splashes and all appeared normal. His heart was beating rapidly. 'Water tastes better out of hand cups doesn't it?'

Catrin nodded. Her head tilted sideways at him, her large eyes curious. 'You look worried, like.'

'Do you like sugar?' Owen asked, covering his anxiety with words. 'I am sure my mother has some in her basket.'

'Is it a magic basket?' Catrin asked. She laughed as she pushed away the blonde hair that kept draping her eyes.

Owen laughed. He was about to say no, before thinking again and saying, 'It's better than magic. She has a special kind of food that never runs out.'

'What kind of food?' Catrin sniffed and wiped her wet nose with the back of her hand.

'It's the kind of food that feeds you for ever.'

'Until you get very fat, like?' Catrin asked.

'Yes, very fat, so fat you could just float up to the sky like a giant balloon.'

'I would like to float up to the sky—to escape.'

The words made Owen feel like crying, so he changed the subject back to sugar. Catrin slipped her hand into his. Owen felt a little uncomfortable; he had never had his hand held by a girl before.

'Can I have two sugar lumps?' Catrin smiled at him.

'You can have four,' Owen said.

37

Later, Mary called out to them as Anwen and Owen made their way up the track towards the mountain path. 'Can you imagine Miss Morgan washing the long johns and the singlets Annie? Oh do lobby so she can keep her white gloves on a little longer!'

'It's hard Mother, leaving them to live like this,' Owen said as they walked.

Anwen put her arm around her son. 'God is close to the poor and the broken hearted,' she said. 'He is the rescuer, but we can help in the turning of the tide.' Owen thought of what happened when he was giving Catrin the water and he had the peculiar sensation of water beginning to trickle inside him.

Anwen sat down at her husband's desk and began to write her weekly article for *The Women's Voice* magazine. Every now and again she glanced through the window where she could see Owen helping his father with the sheep: one of the lambs was poorly and not feeding. Owen picked up the lamb from where it was bleating weakly by the stone wall and took it to its mother who had already taken a few hesitant steps towards it. Jacob and Owen laid the mother on her side and Owen placed the lamb on its mother's teat; after a few attempts, he managed to get it to suck. Anwen watched with vicarious pleasure as her husband put his arm around his son. *Life affirming*, she thought as she began to write. It is hardly surprising that Welsh women are dying before time. Many of us are living in crowded and damp conditions that are a breeding ground for sickness and accidents, it is little wonder that tuberculosis and typhoid are rife. If a woman needs to see a doctor, she must pay for it, if she has the time to go at all, given the relentless toil of her labours—unpaid of course. As we know, with a few exceptions, women are denied the educational opportunities that men enjoy. Thank the Lord for the chapels and our various meetings, debates and discourses! Should a woman wish to work, her options are limited. One of our beloved teachers will shortly be wed, which means, in this supposedly enlightened age (enlightened as a coal pit!), that she must give up the job she loves. Our children must give up the teacher they love. Let us hope she loves her homework as much as she has loved her schoolwork. Could she not work part time and keep house the other half? Or perhaps earn the money to pay a local girl to help while she is away? Just thoughts. If you have anything to say on this matter please try to write in though of course we understand that is not easy. I will endeavour to take your thoughts further. Bethan as ever will be door knocking in your area to take your votes on various matters. As you know, Bethan has zeal to take them to the highest offices in the land. Just picture it ladies! Your voice heard in the highest offices of the land. Do take part so that your part can be taken—and not by someone else! Anwen added a note about the Literary Society meeting on Thursday evenings before leaning back in her chair, with her pen in her mouth. After a while she crossed out the words 'enlightened as a coal pit!' so as not to appear too strident and perhaps offend some of her readers; then she sat back and watched dark clouds bank over a yellowy sky; the sun fell on the stone floors in blocks of light as she enjoyed the brief time she had alone with her thoughts before her evenings work began.

Chapter 6

'Father?' Owen said through mouthfuls of porridge, some weeks later at breakfast. 'Mary was a prostitute was she not?'

'That is true son.'

Anwen took a slight inward breath and held the porridge ladle aloft as if contemplating scooping Owen's words up with it. Like steam, they hung in the air.

'Can you explain to me Father. What exactly is a prostitute?' Owen put a huge spoonful of porridge and cream in his mouth.

Huw looked up at Owen, one eyebrow raised. 'Why do you ask?' he was taking his blackened boots off the fender where they had been propped by Anwen the night before, following their soaking by the rain and their subsequent blackening and greasing.

'Aled Matthews was asking whether you consorted with prostitutes as well as blacklegs, like Jesus did, Father,' Owen said. 'The lads entered into a debate about what sort of woman a prostitute is and whether there were any in the town,' Owen crunched the sugar on his porridge. 'Or the village.'

'Well I never—' Anwen said. 'I don't recall mention of blacklegs in the New Testament. Eat up now Owen, and off to school,' she said as she carried a basin full of dishes to the scullery.

'Well they are ignorant of these things Mother,' Owen said.

Jacob smiled at his wife. 'A prostitute, my son is a woman who has intimate relations with a man who is not her husband,' Jacob said as he began to open the envelopes of his letters with a butter knife.

'Like an adulterer?'

'No an adulterer is a woman who is married and has intimate relations with a man other than her husband,' said Huw.

'Oh,' said Owen like kissing and suchlike.'

'Yes, kissing and suchlike.' Huw said.

'Can you explain the suchlike?'

Anwen set her own porridge on the range to keep warm.

'Owen!' she said a little more excitedly than she would have liked. 'Must you question so?'

'It is alright Anwen,' Jacob said. 'It is better he knows the facts. Might I have another cup of tea?'

Anwen nodded and picked up the kettle. At the water urn, she wondered whether she would ever have asked her own parents such a question. No, she would have tried to look it up and if she had failed she would have prayed for someone to give her the answer and the answer would probably have been supplied by Sally, who delighted in shocking the other girls and who became known as sailor Sally, soon after she left school. Far more shocking to the seaside town than her prostitution, was Sally's conversion at a revival meeting by Mother Roberts, a travelling preacher, and her subsequent ministry to the poor.

'A prostitute son, is a woman who has intimate relations—'

'Like with a man and wife.'

'But not with the love.' Huw interrupted, scraping the last of his porridge from his bowl.

'Yes, not necessarily with the love—' Jacob said.

'But why not?' Owen asked. 'Why would a man be intimate with a woman without the love?' his words mumbled slightly due to his mouth being filled with porridge.

'Sometimes son, a man is lonely and feels the need for the company of a woman and because he does not know her very well—'

'But what if he does know her?'

'Usually son, a man will seek out a woman that he does not know, so that there are not any complications—'

'What complications?'

'The complication of relationship.' Jacob said eyeing Huw in warning so that he did not complicate matters further.

'Are all relationships complicated?' Owen asked.

'Certainly they can be,' Jacob said, settling back into his chair and crossing his right leg over his left.

'But not when there is a prostitute?'

'When a man uses a prostitute, brother,' Huw said, putting a slab of yellow butter on a piece of bread, 'the relationship is less complicated because the man pays the woman to be intimate with him.'

Anwen came back into the room. She pointed her washing cloth at Owen. 'The word 'uses' is right Owen. He does not see who God created her to be,' Anwen's voice began to crack. 'He sees her as a body, an object—it's heart-breaking,' Anwen's eyes filled with tears and she went back to the scullery.

'Oh,' said Owen, 'I see.' He set about eating again, before pausing to say, 'How strange.' His father picked up the newspaper and his brother smiled.

'But what about if the woman is not married and she is intimate with a man?' Owen asked, quieter now, so as not to alert Anwen.

'And she is not a prostitute?' asked Huw from the corner of his bread stuffed mouth.

'Yes,' whispered Owen. 'And she is not a prostitute, but someone he knows but is not married to?'

'Ah,' says Jacob. 'Now that is another matter son. The Bible is very clear on this.'

'Yes,' said Huw chewing his bread. 'Thou shalt not commit fornication.'

Anwen set Jacob's tea before him and then picked up Owen's jacket from the back of the settle. 'We should remember that one of Jesus' best friends was a former prostitute,' Owen, Anwen said, helping him into his jacket. 'And no sin is greater than another.'

'Oh,' said Owen. That is not a commandment I know. I only know, *Thou shalt not commit adultery.*

'Hurry up now Owen. It is time for school. 'Anwen kissed Owen on the forehead.

'Perhaps it is a commandment your brother knows as the Lord has written it upon his heart,' Jacob said.

In the bedroom, where she had begun stripping the beds, Anwen sighed. Her son seemed too young to be having conversations about prostitutes, but she was glad that he felt that he could. She would never have had the temerity to speak the word 'prostitute' in front of her mother, let alone her father.

'Now there brother, you have begun a new debate,' Huw said, pulling his boots on. 'It is as I said, Jesus came to write the laws upon our hearts through the Holy Spirit, so that we would have the law quicken in our consciences through love and not through the punishment of Old Testament law that required trying in our own strength.'

'All scripture is useful for correction son,' Jacob said.

'This is a matter of doctrine is it not?' Owen said.

'Yes indeed Owen.' Jacob looked at Huw, an eyebrow raised.

'Now,' Jacob said to his younger son. 'Let us end the matter for today. If a man is intimate with a woman who is not a prostitute—'

'And not an adulteress,' said Huw.

'And not his wife,' said Owen.

'Yes,' Jacob said patiently, crossing one leg over the other and leaning further back in his chair. 'All of the above—'

'And not an angel—' Owen said.

'Yes and definitely not an angel,' Huw laughed.

Anwen came out of the bedroom, swathes of sheets in her arms. 'It seems the subject, which is a serious one, is becoming amusing.'

'Then,' Jacob said, 'the man and woman are committing the sin of fornication, which is a grave error in God's sight,' he tapped the table with his fingertips for emphasis.

Huw got up from his chair, and took his tea bottle and lunch bag from his mother's proffered hand. 'Sorry, Mother—come brother,' he said. 'Let us send you off to school, where you can receive further education.'

'Is the sin of fornication worse than the other sins?' Owen asked in a raised voice as Huw steered him out the door by the shoulders.

'Only in father's eyes,' Huw said quietly so only Owen caught it.

'All sin is an abomination in God's eyes!' Jacob shouted through the doorway as he snapped the newspaper open again.

'And stinks in the nostrils of heaven!' Huw said at precisely the same time as his father uttered the words. He placed Owen's cap on his head and playfully pulled it over his eyes.

Later that day, Owen raced down the track, scattering sheep in his wake. On the front field, his mother's sheets snapped at the wind that threatened to sail them across the Irish Sea. He burst through the door of the cottage and flung his satchel on the floor as Meg leapt up at him. Anwen was rubbing flour and butter together in a mixing bowl. 'Keep Meg outside please, Owen, it took me half the morning to clean the floor. And I found plenty of crumbs under your bed,' Anwen said. She noticed a trace of dried blood below Owen's nostril. 'What happened, Owen?'

'Aled Matthews hit me for father allowing the miners to come to chapel yesterday.'

'Not Aled Matthews again in this house—does he expect us to bar them?'

'He said his father has to live in the coal mines and he will never see him, and the men who aren't with them are against them,' Owen patted his legs and Meg leapt into his arms.

'Put that dog down! You speak like a train, carriage after carriage after carriage, puff, puff, puff. Take a breath. They don't live in the coal mines in the south, though it might feel like it,' Anwen said. 'And did you hit him back?'

'Only to defend myself.'

'You know we don't believe in fighting Owen,' Anwen said, beginning to knead the mixture in her bowl.

'Not even the good fight—with all your might?' Owen pinched some of the raw dough from the bowl and put it in his mouth.

Anwen suppressed a smile. 'Not with our fists—did you get a caning?'

'Yes. But Matthews did not, even though he began it—I finished it though,' He patted his thighs again and Meg jumped into his arms; he staggered back with the weight of her. 'He was the one on the floor,' Owen said, laughing through the licks that

Meg was painting his face with.

'That dog is too big for that now Owen—how many times must I say so?'

Anwen rubbed her forehead with the back of her hand. 'Why must my head itch when I cannot scratch it? When you've spread the hay for the pigs, Owen, and given them the peelings, see if the hens have another egg or two for me will you,' Anwen shouted at Owen's retreating back as he followed the sheepdog out of the back door. 'What will your father say to your fighting?' she said more to herself than to Owen as she shaped the mixture into round cakes with her hands. She stoked the fire to get it up again, before placing the cakes on the bakestone. As she turned the cakes she thought, *Sometimes we need to be zealous in fighting for what we believe, unless evil is to prevail.*

Outside, the pear trees wore their blossoms like wedding dresses. Owen fetched the hay from the cowshed, before spreading it on the earth floor of the sty. Mama pig had her back curved into the corner, she had her eyes closed, and one velvety grey ear flopped forward on her head; she looked like she was grinning at Owen. Six piglets suckled at her side, three were plain pink, and the other three had their mothers black patching. He felt a rush of love for her.

'You stink mama pig,' he said as he tossed the vegetable peelings. As usual he had to resist the urge to lift a piglet into his arms. *It won't help you to cuddle them, they must leave when they are ready,* his father often said. Instead of unwelcome bacon thoughts, he welcomed to his mind again the thwumping sound his fist had made as it sunk into Aled Matthews' stomach, and tasted again the satisfaction of seeing Matthews stagger and then drop, winded, to his knees. The looks of admiration from some of the tougher boys had made the caning worth it. In the henhouse the hens clucked and brooded. He tried not to think of his headmaster's words but they swirled in his mind like scum on a bucket of milk. Owen's thoughts turned from victory to discomfort as he remembered the faces of some of the boys who had supported Aled. *Get him, Matthews, get him for his bloody blackleg supporter father.* Owen felt under the warm bodies of the hens for eggs and collected several that he took inside to Anwen. Bess, the milk cow, was grazing in the backfield. *The sins of the father will be visited on the son,* words became welts more painful than the ones that creased his backside; he wrapped his arms around Bess's thick, white neck and hugged her fat bulk as he murmured in her ear. Her tail flicked and the serpent's hiss of his headmaster's next words struck him again. *Will you be a preacher like your father?* His rump stung as he tried to banish the words that were delivered more sharply than the cane. He pulled Bess's unyielding body by her rope harness and began leading her to the cowshed; each step caused him pain, and each step stoked his anger a little more. Why should he be blamed for his father's actions? He carried Bess's water pail to the water pump near the gate and tossed the remaining water as hard as he could onto the innocent potato patch. His father did not take sides anyway. Owen pumped water into the pail and brought it back to the shed and set it in the corner. Finally he split a sack of coarse bran and placed it near the pail.

Later that evening, Owen discovered that the welts across his backside made it difficult for him to sit down properly for long, so he crouched in front of the fire, leaning rather than sitting on the settle to finish drawing his ship.

'What no tea? No cakes?' Huw joked to his mother, as he kicked the door open with his booted foot. 'Fine welcome for a man on bargain letting day.' Huw took his boots off by the door and placed them against the lower bar of the range. Why are you crouching there like a Hottentot?' Huw asked. 'Nice sails—is it a clipper?'

But Owen, in the depths of concentration, continued to curve his pencil over the stern of his ship without hearing anything. Huw rolled his eyes fondly.

'Well? Did you negotiate a good price for the bargain—and is it good rock to work?' Anwen said, as Huw came over and kissed her on the cheek.

'Good? It was good for the steward and the English lord, but we will all eat.'

'Are you working on the mountain or in the sheds?' Owen asked, sharpening his pencil with a blade.

'On the mountain of course,' Huw said, pushing Owen's head

playfully.

'Do you have ropes and chains?' Owen asked.

'Of course—like Houdini—all paid for by my good self—and my tools—that you will not use for carving or drawing with little brother. I pay for their sharpening out of my wages.' Huw tore the blackened crust off the bread on the table and stuffed it into his mouth.

'I wish I could work there and never again go to school,' Owen said.

Huw laughed at his brother as he sat down at the table and took a slice of bread and butter from a plate his mother put in front of him.

'I thought you were going to be a missionary and sail the seven seas?' he said, chewing with the left side of his mouth. 'The village is still simmering, Mother. One of the new cottages was visited last night.'

Anwen came and sat down next to him at the table, a mug of tea in her hand. 'Not the Jones place—was anyone hurt?'

'It was the new place—they left a cold warning—leave or face the consequences. They were out at chapel, but Miss Morgan confronted them on the road as they left and she returned. I hear she put them to shame. Father will no doubt be visiting each place in turn on the way home.'

'He'll be late again then—they didn't—*she* didn't!' Anwen said. 'That's outrageous behaviour. The authorities should be called. But good for Miss Morgan—a woman of mettle indeed! Her pupils ought to be proud of her.'

'Miss Morgan from school—what did she do?' Owen asked.

Huw rubbed the area between his brows with his thumb and forefinger. 'Apparently she told them they ought to be ashamed of themselves.'

'Too right as well,' Anwen said

'Her father was the first man to take up Lord Penhurst's offer—Rhys Davies sees him as an instigator. Evan Morgan is a fine man,' Huw yawned as he spoke. 'But I am afraid he has been singled out and Rhys Davies is a single minded man.'

'As his wife has discovered to her cost,' Anwen said, nursing her cup with both hands as she sipped her strong tea.

'They say Rhys Davies is the greatest fighter in the district and he is to take on the champion of Cardiff—the man that they call The Bull.'

Huw went over to his brother and began skipping from side to side in the manner of boxer as he play punched his brother who ducked away from him.

'Owen returned with a bloody nose today due to your father preaching to the quarrymen,' Anwen said.

'And what was your response, Owen?' Huw said, reaching for a second slice of bread.

'I felled him,' Owen said getting up carefully to join his brother at the table.

Huw laughed.

'There is no glory in fighting Huw,' Anwen said, putting the kettle back on its crane over the fire. 'Don't encourage him, Huw,' she said pouring more tea.

Owen lowered himself onto the chair to sit more on his hip than his backside.

'There can be glory mother,' Huw swallowed, 'depending on the cause. Sometimes a man has no option but to defend himself,' he took the cup of tea his mother gave him.

'But at what cost?' Anwen said.

'Sometimes the expense is worth it mother,' Huw said, taking another large bite of bread.

Owen grinned at his mother, before grimacing in pain.

'The tub Owen,' his mother said. 'Huw, water please, and plenty of it. Warm water and salt will soothe your aching body.'

'No Mother, I will have to sit down!' Owen said.

'You can kneel,' Anwen said.

'Yes,' said Huw getting up. 'And pray for strength at the same time,' he winked at his brother.

Chapter 7

Anwen glanced at the clock on the dresser as she sat down with her cup of tea to knit by the fire. Owen sat at the table drawing with an ink pen. It was after nine in the evening and her husband's neck of lamb and vegetables were drying out in the oven. Jacob had spent the last week riding around the district with fellow ministers, going from house to house, pleading for forgiveness and reconciliation as he had been doing for months now. In the evenings he was exhausted and fell in to a deep sleep as soon as his head touched the pillow, leaving Anwen to stare out of the window wondering at the inner struggles that he usually spoke to her about as they lay in bed. Anwen jumped up as eagerly as a girl when she heard the door scrape.

'Hello my love—is that the kettle on to boil?' Jacob said as he came through the door. 'My mouth could do with wetting. It is dry from talking and coaxing,' he reached out to ruffle Owen's hair.

'Give Rosie some hay and a brush down,' my lad.

'Oh it's good to be home,' he sighed. He went and kissed Anwen.

'Any progress?' Anwen asked, taking his hat and coat.

'I am afraid that this bitterness has set in like dry rot, Annie. The men are very bitter about the cottages. It has reopened wounds and reignited feeling. It is just as it was when the men went back to work—like waiting for the sound of gunfire. I have pleaded with them, but to no avail. You would not think that they were Christian men Annie. When I spoke about forgiving them, Rhys Davies spat on the floor and threatened to fell me with his great knuckle head.'

'He never!' Anwen said. I will have words with him about that when I see him. What will Mary say?'

'She'd say save your spit no doubt,' Jacob laughed. 'He is wedded to his cause—I expect she's noticed.'

'Did he try to fight you father?' Owen asked, putting on his boots. 'Imagine a bare knuckle fighter taking on a minister.'

Jacob laughed. 'I wouldn't have fought him,' Owen.

'Well you can't just stand there and take it father,' Owen said.

Jacob sat down at the dining table to chat through the events of the day.

'I am afraid to tell you our youngest was in another fight today,' Anwen said as she poured her husband a tankard of tea from her overused and highly decorative Prince Albert teapot, a gift from her *Literary Society Ladies* several years ago *for always serving us and always encouraging us,* as they said at the time she stepped down as chairwoman of their meetings.

'Did you win?' Jacob asked Owen, when he came back from tending to Rosie.

'Yes.' Owen said, kicking off his boots.

'And was it worth it?'

'Yes,' he said, smiling at his father as he took off his jacket.

He thought of the caning, and the mocking boys, who now seemed more in number than the admiring ones—and were they admiring or sneering?

'I don't know.'

'Well when you do we can talk about it. I suppose you got a caning for your effort?'

'Yes.'

'Well I will talk to my old friend William tomorrow and then we will see where we all stand.'

'I think he may be getting something of a reputation,' Anwen whispered to her husband. 'We must channel this warrior instinct of his for the good, lest he begins to build his reputation on being good with his fists, like someone else we know,' she said.

'Headmaster hates you because you are a preacher that welcomes blacklegs,' Owen said, raiding the cake tin.

'I welcome anyone with legs—and without,' Jacob said.

'Hatred comes with the job, and if it was good enough for our Lord, it's good enough for me.' Jacob said.

'It's not good enough for me,' Owen said stuffing his mouth with round cake. He patted his legs and Meg came over. Owen began getting her to jump for the raisins he threw in the air.

'For goodness sake Owen, stop that,' Anwen said.

Meg responded to Jacob's timely whistling as he went outside and Owen, taking another cake from the tin on the dresser went and flopped down on the settle next to his mother. He sighed. Anwen hugged her son's head to her shoulder.

'It does not seem just Owen—'

'It is *not* just mother,' Owen said, placing one of his mother's embroidered cushions on his head. 'Obvious as this cushion mother,' he let the cushion slide off his head, tossed it in the air a few times, before plumping it up and arranging it with the other cushions; the words, *Love, Truth* and *Justice* were embroidered on the fronts of the cushions, framed by bold patterns of Anwen's own design. Owen blew imaginary dust off the 'Justice' cushion. Then he picked up the cushion marked 'Truth' and blew on that too.

'It is not just, Owen, but the Bible warns that we will be persecuted for our faith. Our troubles are momentary in the light of eternity, and we must be a witness to the world in what we say and do.'

'So we let them say and do what they like and just sit there smiling merrily like loons?'

'No, Owen, we ask God for wisdom and act accordingly.'

'So what I did was not wise? Would it have been wiser to put up with Aled Matthews' mockery, day in, day out?'

'Perhaps—perhaps not—did you ask for wisdom?'

'I was not going to say, hold on a minute fellows while I pray—'

'Well it might have diffused the situation. Perhaps you should pray for wisdom generally,' Anwen yawned and got up off the settle.

Owen puffed his cheeks as he exhaled. 'You do not know yourself, Mother. If I had not put an end to it, he would have started on someone else.'

'Off to bed now, my Owen,' Anwen said, taking his head in her hands and giving him a kiss.

As she walked away he called out, 'I put Aled Matthews straight about the prostitutes!'

Jacob gazed down the mountain towards the sea; a full moon hung above it, creating a path of light across its many black and blue surfaces. The cool air was sharp and crisp with the smell of peat fires.

'Your earth is a wonder and your sky speaks of your beauty and majesty Lord,' he said out loud. A ewe got up and ran further down the field.

'No need to be alarmed, lady ewe, I was merely giving God my appreciation.'

He picked up a stick and threw it in a wide arc towards the vegetable garden. Meg ran to get it, her back legs scrambling on the dirt of the track as she almost floored herself in her enthusiasm to retrieve it.

Jacob laughed and leaning over the back gate, took a sip of tea before cradling the mug in his hands. He thought of the men that he had seen that day. He saw both sides of the quarrymen's divide. The men that had decided to take up Lord Penhurst's offer and return to the quarry, had families that needed to eat, and slate quarrying was the only real work to be had in these parts. On the other side, the striking men had democratic principles that Jacob admired. They and their families would make the sacrifice in order to live with clear consciences. He only wished that men would respect other men's views. *We can only bear with one another in our convictions. Some of us are weaker than others.* He thought of how much Wales had changed since he had become a Christian. Men did not choose God as simply as they once did. The Nonconformist tradition born in the previous revivals had become a conformist irony. The lack of human intervention that the revivals had brought seemed like a thing long past. Jacob thought of how the publication of Origin of

Species had come out in the revival year of 1859; he considered it no coincidence but an act of the devil following hard on an act of God. Jacob understood that young people were hungry for an authentic experience of God and were unmoved by even the most fiery of ministers. He had heard it said that chapel sermons were becoming longer and more formulaic, though he hoped his were strong and to the point. Many were turning their attention to politics and to the prospect of a Wales free from English intervention. Jacob considered Christianity dead philosophy if it were not accompanied by the signs and wonders demonstrated by the book of Acts and Wales had seen those acts over and over again, he had experienced miracles in his chapel meetings too, but he longed for the trickle to become a stream, even a river. It pained Jacob that acts of faith were being replaced by human ideas and ways of doing things. Liberal theology and Higher Criticism had caused the life to be sucked out of the Bible and some people picked across its parts as if they were dry bones void of any life-transforming substance. There were the societies too: the humanists, the secularists, the agnostics and the atheists, the latter whose hatred for religion had become a religion in itself. There was talk of new political movements that were arising out of the unions that would support working men. Jacob was concerned that the unions and their politics were becoming the new religion; he understood why this was the case given the testimonies of workers complaining that Nonconformist ministers did not practise what they preached and thus they were turning elsewhere for practical help. The recent strike had helped this to become the case. Industrial unions from as far away as America and Australia sent money to help the families of striking men, many of whom had not worked for several years. Jacob acknowledged that the strike had brought a sense of brotherhood and solidarity that had been lacking in these lands for some time; but he felt this was solidarity based on agreement. It was conditional. Christian love was unconditional. It sprung from the agape love of the Father's heart. It was the love that sent Jesus to the cross and it was the only love, in Jacob's opinion, that could sort out the mess that North Wales was now in. *These lands need your touch again, Lord God. Just one touch from the*

King of heaven! Huw, who had dashed in from work only to freshen up and dash out again, came out looking dapper with his hair dampened down. He raised his hand to his father as he opened the gate for him.

'Too much ale makes you pale! His father called out to him.'

'Too much thought makes you gaunt!' Huw called back. 'Besides, I'm beyond the pale already being a preacher's son. I've learnt to embrace it!' Huw said as his father shut the yard gate behind him.

Jacob laughed. He felt sorrow that his eldest son was labouring for another man's gain, when he was sure his son was called to the ministry. He watched his son walk up the track towards the mountain. He would have to trust God for his son and for Wales as he always had. Jacob turned and caught Anwen's eye through the kitchen window as she set out his dinner, they smiled at one another; he looked forward to the food that he now saw steaming on the plate, and to lying next to her warm body in bed after that. Fixing his eyes on the sea, he got down on his knees and prayed earnestly about all the things that he had been meditating on. *Father God, make the church relevant again! Revitalise us Lord! Show me my role! What more shall I do?* He did not stop until he was sure his prayers had been heard and Anwen had heated his food a second time.

Chapter 8

Rosie's hooves rang sharply through the silent valley. Anwen sang as she held the reins, nodding at Owen to join in, but he declined. *If I wished for worldly wealth, it would swiftly go to seed...* Her voice echoed round the mountains. They were on their way to visit the prophet Anna, who being in her nineties, was past cooking for herself, so Anwen and some of the other women of the district, made sure that she had a hot meal once a day. The valley road led them through a sheer angular mountain that rose up thousands of feet on the one side; dressed with earth rivulets sculpted by rain that had cascaded heedlessly down; grass grew up a few thousand feet and then gave up, condemned by the forbidding rock, some of which had crumbled and fallen and lay in bits on the side of the track as a warning. This was a mountain that could change your life if you dared to scale its heights. The mountain on the other side was smoother, and more inviting, its steppes were rounded and gradual and covered with grassy jackets short as moss with smooth worn rock showing all over the place: this was a mountain to gambol over and mull on. The angular mountain was Huw's, Owen decided, and the rangy, rock cobbled one was his. Owen sometimes wondered whether he had been born to provide a contrast for Huw. Huw cut through life like a blade; his world was a simple one of geometric planes that he negotiated with ease, Owen's had knobbly bits that he tripped or slid over. His mood was constant and if other people fluctuated, Huw just smiled and got on with what he was doing, whatever the human weather; as far as Huw was concerned if other people had a problem, he might help them solve it, but it remained their problem. Owen was governed by a shifting inner landscape, *A thicker skin might benefit him*, an aunt of his once said; Owen had pictured the skin of the chameleon he had seen in one of his father's illustrated magazines. *Dark clouds on the* horizON! Huw would sometimes joke in the comedy voice of a general of the British Army if Owen became moody, *run for* CO-VAH! Or he would carry on as usual, or stay out of his way. *I know you want to engage in battle, Owen,* Huw once remarked, when Owen's anger had flared. *But I am sitting on a mountain, admiring the view.* Sometimes Owen wanted to hit Huw with a big stick; but he had also once drawn his brother as a solid and sturdy tree, with himself perched in the branches. Owen was still happy basking in Huw's shade, though he was increasingly being lured out of it into the gaping sunshine of the duality of life. The road swept around the lake that lay reflecting the mountain peaks, its blue depths cooling; scattered piles of ancient black rock surrounded the far side of the lake, a line of rock stretched into the lake, creating a ford that could be seen when the water was low; it was here that the children of the district came to swim in the heat of the summer, their trapped voices thrown up and batted about by the mountains; hours spent with Stephen and the other boys were happy etchings in his mind. Owen found himself imagining Stephen swimming in the depths, his bluish white body weaving fishlike through dark green weeds; his green eyes under water large; delicate gills flapping on the side of his neck. Confused by the images in his mind, and feeling faintly sick at the sight of them, Owen concentrated on his mother's singing instead, *The riches of a virtuous, pure heart, will bear eternal profit...* The side of her face was the colour of ivory; her reddish-brown hair had highlights of gold where it was parted in the middle and coiled and pinned at the back of her head. On the high collar of her shirt she wore a porcelain brooch with a profile of her great-grandmother carved white against beige. It was the fashion of the women to wear blouses with a row or two of lace ruffles beneath the neck area of the blouse, but Anwen preferred plain white blouses and said she would go in her husband's shirts, trousers and suspenders if it were not for offending the women of the district. Jacob's shirts and trousers were indeed worn by her when she worked in the garden or tended to her vegetables or to the livestock. Anwen stopped singing and began to talk to Owen about Anna. She had been orphaned after her father died of influenza and her mother died giving birth to her youngest brother. Anna had brought her two brothers and sister up herself, supporting them by selling some of the produce of the smallholding to the village shop; she taught them to know Jesus and the workings of the Holy Spirit, just as her mother had taught her, and the faith of her and her siblings was vital and real. Her sister had become a missionary to the coal miner's in the south and had seen many converted. Two of her brothers were missionaries to China following the end of the opium wars in 1860, and had seen many miracles of Biblical proportions, in Shanghai and Fuzhou.

'Why did Anna not go to China? I should like to go to China.'

'She felt called by God to Wales and for Wales.'

Owen wondered if he might be called and if so where to. He pictured a globe of the world in his mind, and as he did it began to spin. When it stopped he saw the bottom tip of Africa bathed in light; he also saw a mountain with a flat top. Owen listened to snatches of his mother's voice whilst mulling over the mountain in his mind: Anna's fiancé was killed at the slate mill when his sleeve got caught in one of the pulleys... Anna mourned him for three years... during this time she remained in her cottage, not even going out to chapel, even when the revival of 1839 began... the grocer's boy from town came up once a week, but apart from him hardly anyone ever caught sight of Anna, until one evening she appeared at chapel and went straight to the minister and told him that she had been praying for three years for the revival and that it would begin in three days. Which it did.

'Imagine being that prophetic Owen? From then on people sought Anna out, but she would only say what the Lord asked her to say, and when he asked her to say it. She told people to enquire of the Lord themselves, she said that the day would come when they would need the revelation of the word as well as the revelation of the Holy Spirit.'

'Is Anna a psychic?' Owen asked. 'Or a mind reader—is she

telepathic?'

'How do you know these things, my Owen? I shall have to monitor your magazines.'

'If I do not know the world mother, how will I know what to look out for?'

'True enough,' Anwen said laughing. 'Here, hold the reins while I re-pin my hair.'

'Anna is prophetic. Non-believers call this gift telepathy or second sight. When the gift of prophecy operates through the Holy Spirit, the gift is the gift of prophecy.'

'What's the difference?'

'The difference is the source. Prophecy comes from God through the Holy Spirit. Anything else comes from Satan through demonic spirits.'

Owen mulled on these things for a while and then asked:

'Why did God make Satan?'

'God did not make Satan. He made Lucifer. Lucifer made Satan,' Anwen pulled on Rosie's reins to get her to trot a little faster. She smiled as she took in her son's expression. 'God created us for relationship with Him, but he gives us the choice as to whether we enter into relationship with him or not. We can go our own way, but the alternative is a path that eventually leads to destruction, no matter how successfully we seem to navigate that journey. There is truth Owen, and there is non-truth, light and dark. It is simple but infinitely complicated at the same time. Satan's trickery is to keep the mind of man darkened in his understanding—for people to see the divine plan as ridiculous and the arrogance of his own mind as rational.'

'But He must have known what the devil was going to do? So why did He go ahead with it?' Owen asked.

'Out of love,' Anwen said. ' Love offers choice. Choice produces risk.'

They were arriving at Anna's cottage. Owen was running his hands through his hair in frustration. 'But did he know the outcome?'

'Ask God Owen. You hear from Him. He made the choice to give us choice and He is a God of His word.'

'Ha ha Mother, I see your plot, I will search the Bible, so far so maddening.' Owen jumped off the cart.

'God is a treasure who loves to be searched for. Keep asking the questions Owen—of God— and of those that are journeying through life with you. Never accept what you see around you as reality. The spiritual world is eternally real, but God has set eternity in your heart—keep you heart soft Owen,' Anwen said as she jumped off the cart to tether Rosie to the gatepost.

The cottage was built in the shadow of the mountain surrounded by grazing fields. A field of bluebells lay under the trees behind the cottage and foxgloves loomed over the low stone front wall and sheep frequently roamed in from the farmer's field across the track to graze freely in the garden. In the main room of the cottage, a kettle was suspended on a crane above an old fashioned hearth with an open fire; a fat bellied pot stood nearby; copper pans were displayed above the range, reflecting the light of the fire and a collection of jugs, fat and squat as pub landlords, stood on the mantelpiece ready for cream. Anwen set her basket of yellow primroses from her garden flowerbed down near the hearth, and bent to give Anna a kiss. Slim and straight as a girl, Anna sat in a rocking chair in front of a vast old-fashioned hearth in the main room, the clutter of basket weaving lay on the floor beside her, half of a round basket was on her lap; unweaved reeds saluted the ceiling. Anna reached out a hand riddled with blue veins towards Owen. Swathed in a heavy wool shawl, her white hair piled up on her head and held in place with painted enamel combs; her pale blue eyes that were not old looking, but neither young, blazed with light and life. Owen tried not to stare at her: a luminescence came off her. Due to this supernatural quality, it was impossible not to stare: so attractive was her presence. *It is the presence of the Holy Spirit in her. She is so much closer to God than most, and so there is so much more of Him in her*, Anwen had whispered to him once. Anwen was looking for a vase on the crowded mantelpiece.

'There now let me look at you. You are a fine looking boy to be sure, and your eyes are lake blue. A true deep, dark blue— put the primroses in that vase over there Anwen,' Anna said, pointing to a blue cut vase on the dresser across the room.

Why lake-blue? Does she know I saw all wrong by the lake?

'I have something for you Owen,' Anna leant over the side of her rocking chair and picked up a long tin box wrapped in brown paper and string. Inside were tin infantry soldiers with large bearskin hats and miniature weapons. *The Grenadier Guards.*

'Heroes of the Boer war,' Owen said. 'Thank you very much. I read all about it in the newspapers.'

'Highly trained and effective,' Anna said.

'*Honi soit qui mal y pense*,' Owen said examining an illustration of a soldier's button on the inside of the box.

'Dwell not on evil,' Anna said. 'Set your mind on things above, Owen, and evil will have a hard time pulling you back.'

Owen thought of the image he had seen by the lake and wondered whether it had come from dwelling on Stephen's death.

'Anna those are beautiful. Where did they come from?' Anwen asked, shaking tea into the teapot.

'They were my Jonathan's,' Anna said. 'I want Owen to have them and to remember that he is part of God's army—though he may be a little old to be playing with them—though in my view, playing should never cease—he is a defender of the King.'

'Will I take part in skirmishes?'

'Aye and you will be on lookout because God has given you eyes to see.'

'We all have eyes to see,' Owen said examining the box.

'Yes, but not all of us have our primary sight activated.'

'Why not?' Owen asked.

'It's a mystery,' Anna said. 'It takes one to know one. Now sit on the rug and contemplate the gift while I hear all your mother's news.'

Anna and Anwen were soon in deep discussion regarding chapel matters and the poor in the community, many of whom Anna only gave up visiting recently.

Anna leaned in towards Anwen. 'My present time is wonderful Anwen. I feel as though I truly inhabit two worlds now. Oh Anwen the things our Father has allowed me to see in these days. Glorious scenes from above, and scenes of agony to come.' She leaned forward in her chair. 'When the agony comes Anwen, you must remember the ecstasy to come, you see. Christ endured death for the joy that was set before him.'

Anwen had her hand resting on her throat. 'Oh Anna. My boys? I don't think I can hear it.'

'You are an overcomer by the blood of the lamb Anwen,' Anna said. 'Now tell me more. Is that Rhys Davies misbehaving now?'

Anwen updated her and Anna laughed. 'There is a shift coming for him,' she said raising her right hand. 'The Lord says that he has been on the night shift for too long and he is coming—yes, he is actually coming—oh the fortunate fellow,' Anna swept her hand upwards triumphantly, 'the Lord is coming to offer him a day shift. Oh He is merciful Anwen, you see,' Anna patted her hands on her lap. 'Let us have some tea.'

Sitting cross-legged on the rug, Owen examined the soldiers: they were beautifully detailed and ornate; the red paint of their jackets bright as blood; the gilt of their buttons shining, and the black of the bearskin hats and the glossy coat of the single trotting horse with its stately rider was as fresh as when it was first painted by expert hands. A grandfather clock ticked loudly in the corner of the room, and time slipped over the edge of the world as Owen regressed into earlier boyhood and lost himself in imagined battle scenes. Anwen sat on a stool near the hearth, drinking strong milky tea with Anna, whilst peeling vegetables into a basin on her lap, and all the while talking about how the women were coping since the troubles given they had so many troubles before the troubles as far as Owen could tell.

'Speak to me about your prayer life Anna,' Anwen said as she took the kettle off the crane and filled the cooking pot with water from the urn that stood on a slate mantel near the fireplace. 'I want to be inspired to pray more for revival,' she said as she heaved the pot over the flames. 'Get the bellows Owen,' she said.

Owen gave his mother a knowing glance; he knew that Anwen asked Anna these things so that he would learn from Anna's example. He took up the bellows and gave a few short puffs. The fire increased. Anwen placed pats of dry manure under the burning logs, Owen put heather from a basket on top. An earthy smell filled the room.

'Lavender in the basket behind the grate,' Anna said.

Owen pulled lavender from a smaller, lidded basket and placed it on top of the heather.

'Ah, that's better. Give me the odour of lavender over manure any day, though we must live with both for a time,' Anna
laughed.

Everyone was silent for a while, and then Anna began to
speak.

'My prayer life truly began when I was so angry with grief.
I said to the Lord that if He wanted Jonathan so badly then
why had he given him to me in the first place, you see? The
Lord replied that Jonathan was an impetus to me, and that I
would be with him in eternity anyway—this statement took time
to settle in me—it was so casual like you see—to God all things
are by the by, given His eternal eye, see? Why could He not
have used something else as an impetus? But the Lord has His
ways and they are higher than ours, so in time, with His grace,
I came to accept His divine will and began to ask what sort of
impetus Jonathan was. Now Jonathan was a praying man, you
see. When we decided to marry, he said to me, that I must learn
to spend long hours in prayer to be his equal. It was a funny
sort of courtship, but I was a particular sort of girl, particularly
about Jonathan Evans,' she laughed and took up her basket and
began to weave a reed, 'and so I learnt to pray long hours, so
when Jonathan died, you see, I had already learned to pray for
more than two or three hours a day. Once I had caught the
prayer fever, I found that I could not stop; often I was caught
up, lost in wonder between earth and heaven—now this must
be experienced to be understood, you see—I am speaking about
what St Paul experienced when he said that he knew not whether
he was still in his body or not, when he was caught up in the
spirit during his visions, you see. Most of the time, I did not
remember what I prayed for, often I prayed in other tongues,
heavenly tongues you see, in the gift of the Holy Spirit. I used
to be swept up into a sort of rapture. During my times of prayer
the Lord God Almighty would show me things, some of which I
could describe to you and some of which it would be impossible
to describe as I would not have the language fit for it, you see.
By the end of the second year, I knew I was praying for revival
and I knew that it was coming, you see, because I sensed the

change in the atmosphere, there was a tension in the air about to break—like a gathering of thunderclouds before the storm.'

Anna clenched her hands into fists and shook them either side of her head.

'During my times of prayer I saw visions of spiritual warfare in the heavenlies—angels warring with demons that belonged to the demonic principalities that Satan had put in charge over the earthly regions—I saw hideous winged creatures that spewed a substance that looked like blood and bile over the men and women of the community and surrounding districts; the blood was the life of the people—the demon spirits sucked the lifeblood out of the people every time they gave way to some sin or other, you see, when they gave in to temptation, they created an open airway for them to attack and sometimes even enter into the person. The blood turned to bile that was spewed out onto them by the demons that hated the people and wanted their deaths. The bile was so corrupting and evil—Owen it ruins peoples hearts and destroys their character.'

Owen was staring at Anna, he was beginning to feel unsettled, as he had that day with Catrin when he began to experience a sharpening of inner vision, that was transposed on the physical world. The surfaces of Anna's eyes seemed to project the words she spoke; her irises were like little wheels of slate blue, grey, green; he could not decide what colour they were. He became aware of a change in the atmosphere and to experience a sense of a presence in the room other than the three of them. The hair on the back of his neck prickled and with that sensation came the presence of a terrifying energy. Anwen, her eyes widening with excitement, swept her fingers over her forearm to indicate goose bumps.

'Oh yes, my boy. There is a war taking place and it is right here,' Anna held her hand a couple of inches from her face. 'This is how close the spiritual realm is, Owen,' she swept her hand like a wiper in front of her face. 'You can enter it in the spirit and you can see it with your spiritual eyes. There are only two kingdoms Owen: The Kingdom of Light and the Kingdom of Darkness. All belong to the Kingdom of Darkness whether they know this or believe it. There is only one way into the Kingdom of Light—

faith in the resurrected Christ, you see. It is imperative that you learn to discern between the two Owen. There is an awful lot of trickery and seduction from the dark side.'

'What's going on now then?' Owen said. 'Are you seeing something now?'

'No, Owen, it would be very distracting,' Anna said.

'So you can switch it on and off when you like?'

Anna laughed. 'Mostly, yes, I can.'

'Like opening and closing your eyes?'

'In a way,' Anna said. 'If people only knew what was going on in the spirit world, they would turn to Jesus with all of their hearts and sin no more!'

'Tell us more Anna,' Anwen said, cutting carrots into the pot with a paring knife.

'Other demons worked with the ones that sucked the lifeblood from the people. These ones, were also winged creatures, but with sharp faces.'

'What were the other faces like?' Owen asked.

'Close your eyes Owen,' Anna said.

Owen closed his eyes.

'Open your eyes Owen.'

Owen screamed and slid backwards on the mat. What he saw with his naked eye was a brown, skull-like head from which folds of greenish-brown skin hung; behind the demon was a shrivelled, grotesque body, with a long muscular tail, the tip of which was a snake-like creature with fangs that dripped the same blood and bile that dribbled from the mouth of the creature. The eyes of the demon were white; they locked eyes with Owen.

'Be gone in the name of Jesus,' Anna said, in a quiet voice.

Owen, his heart wreaking havoc in its chest cavity, stared at the empty space in the air that the demon had inhabited. His mother stood by the hearth, her hand on her throat.

'Peace Owen,' Anna said. 'You are able to see for yourself Owen. Authority will come.'

As she said this, Owen heard the words of Luke 9 verse 1 and 2. *When Jesus had called the twelve together, he gave them power and authority to drive out all demons and to cure diseases, and he sent them out to preach the kingdom of God and to heal the sick.'*

Anwen, who had experienced a sense of spiritual recognition despite having not witnessed the event with her physical eyes, put down her knife and came and sat on the mat next to Owen, her legs curled under her.

'We are all called to Christ, you see, Owen, though not all of us accept the gift, and when we truly come to be disciples, we are given this authority. Do not waver from this word,' Anna picked up her Bible from a table next to her, 'and make sure you are filled with the Holy Spirit daily, so that you are not seduced from the path of righteousness.'

Owen tried to digest what had just happened to him, but he could not swallow it all at once never mind begin to digest it. So he just sat there, trying to calm down, fiddling with the soldiers as he listened, and occasionally glancing at Anna. Anna continued calmly as if nothing had happened. Anwen listened to the penetrating sound of Anna's voice as she stared at the fire reflected in the polished tips of her boots.

'The job of the demons was to tempt the people into sin, you see. A particular aim was to tempt the person to drink in excess, or to be dependent on some substance or other, because then the pathway to other sins—sins of the flesh—was open you see—because of the weakness the substance causes in the mind. Or they would work with other demons that caused accidents and quarrels that led to death—theirs or another's, which is the ulti-mate aim of them all, to cause the person to die before accepting the gospel of salvation so that they enter into eternity without God, you see, a prospect too awful to dwell on, Owen.'

Owen asked what her role was in seeing all of this. 'Could you not have warned them?'

'Even if I ran around like a lunatic, I could not have accom-plished as much as I did with prayer. My role was to pray.'

'You could have sent wires,' Owen said. 'What did the prayer do?'

'Ah, my boy,' Anna laughed with Anwen, rocking backwards in her chair. 'If people only knew the power in their prayers they would never stop day and night, you see. Prayer is like that fire causing the pot to boil. God does nothing unless we pray. He has chosen us to be his co-workers on the earth. Prayer moves His divine hand. You need to remember to listen to what God is saying when you pray—he gets bored with lists. If you listen He will talk back.'

'Straight away—how?' Owen asked.

'Sometimes,' Anna said, putting down her basket. 'Through other people or remembered scripture, through nature, in your heart - in many other ways. You have to learn to hear, you see, and not just with these,' Anna tapped her earlobes. 'Owen his voice can be as clear as your own. Get to know Him.'

'I will pray more often,' Owen said. 'Father has been reading reports from the newspaper about revival starting in the south.'

'It will sweep up from the valleys of the south to the mountains of the north by Christmas,' Anna said. 'I always said the next one would come through the southern gates.

'What gates?' Owen asked.

'They are in the spiritual realm, but as in the natural, so in the spiritual. I will tell you another time. I am tired now and want breath to sing with your mother before you go. Pass me my harp Owen,' Anna said, indicating her lap harp that stood next to the dresser. 'Let us sing Anwen,' she said beginning to play. Owen contemplated that the harp, that was about the size of Anna's torso, looked roughly like a human heart, he wondered whether this was a coincidence or not, and whether it helped make the music so haunting and soulful. He decided that when he got to heaven he would ask God if he could hear King David play the harp as he did for Saul when he was having one of his mental turns; Anna's playing was transporting and brought peace in the wake of its melodies. Anwen began to sing. Owen watched his mother's slender hand stir the pot; the sweet smell of rosemary mingled with the aroma of the mutton and the turnips; the strange sounds of Anna's harp mingled with the sound of Anwen's voice that sounded to Owen like crisp, pure flowing water: *Evening and morning, my wish, rising to heaven on the wing of song, for God, for the sake of my Saviour, to give me a pure heart. . .*

'Tell Jacob to make sure the hearts of the people are ready Anwen,' Anna said as they were leaving. 'Revival starts here,'

66

Anna indicated her heart area with a fragile hand. Through her translucent skin, Anna's bones looked as though they were fashioned from wafer paper, on her ring finger was a gold ring with a large purple stone that looked far too heavy for her hand.

'Be prepared Owen. You will see further. God controls the tides but you are invited to captain the ship. There is purpose for the gift of seeing. It is crucial that you make sure you have the character to carry the gift—this is your choice. Engage fully with the Holy Spirit in the process of sanctification in order to unlock the gift completely. Obedience to the Master, who has gone ahead of you, is the key. The road leads from Him and to Him. He is the way and He is the destination.'

That night Owen lay in bed unable to sleep. He turned Anna's words over and over in his riddled mind; he wondered if he had really seen as he had or whether what he saw was a projection of his mind, as he considered the image of Stephen swimming underwater was, but Anna had seen the demon too, and plenty more, he was sure. *Why Father God? What is my purpose?* Owen prayed. *And who was the master?* He thought of what Anna had said about prayer and of how his mother always encouraged him to pray if he needed to know something. *Sometimes God answers straight away, in your thoughts, sometimes He shows you in other ways, through a conversation with someone or by some other means of discovery.* As Owen remembered these words he saw the osprey flying over the mountain again in his mind; he thought too of the small hand on the slate that he had hidden behind his oldest slates; he had not dared to look at it again since, preferring to forget about it, though he understood now, that God was reassuring him that life was continuing for Stephen in another dimension. In the darkness, Owen stared at the shafts of light coming through the cracks in the floorboards, before he drifted off to a peaceful sleep listening to his parent's murmuring voices like the sound of moving water coming from their bedroom beneath him. In Sunday School a few days later he heard the words from John 14, verse 6: *Jesus said unto him, I am the way, the truth, and the life: no man comes unto the Father, but by me.* Jesus was The Way; Jesus was the master that he needed to follow to understand why he had the gift.

May

Chapter 9

Owen was accompanying Huw to the quarry for the first time. On the lower slopes of the mountains yellow-headed gorse and mauve heather created a woven mountain garment the design of which would lend itself well to a carpet, Owen thought; a breeze swept over the shrubs causing the pattern to come alive; but the climb through sheep tracks would soon become craggy and desolate but for the lakes, trapped in prehistoric basins, the rocky pattern of which was more standing dead man's trousers, stacked sky high. As they made their way up to the quarry they could not feel the warmth of the sun so much up where the air was cool and the wind buffeted the mountains. Huw was already eating a hunk of bread from the lunch bag that Anwen had prepared for them, and swigging from his tea bottle. As they approached the quarry from the steep, slate strewn path, the dam in the valley could be seen below them from their rocky road. The quarried mountain loomed, casting its dark shadow over the dam and reaching out over the slate splitting sheds as if trying to pull them back into itself. The mountain's exposed innards were carved into vast terraces that rose up many hundreds of feet. To Owen, the scene was akin to photographs he had seen of the Wild West of America, except the higgledy-piggledy sheds arranged around single track railway lines, were made out of slate and there were no painted signs on the buildings. In the caban, men were sitting around a stove on benches, leaning against the slate walls, a long oblong table held their tin mugs, cloth bags of lunch and a newspaper. Gusts of tobacco smoke hung in the damp air; the men had hung their coats and rain sacks on the hooks by the door and some were still wet from the previous days rain and they gave a unique smell to the atmosphere: a blend of oniony sweat, grease, hessian and something tarry. The chairman of the caban was addressing the men; a man with a long bony face framed by silver side-whiskers that fanned out and flipped backwards to blend with hair that reached to his shoulders; a mauve bandana encircled his hat, that unlike the others he had not taken off; like the others, he was in his shirtsleeves, waistcoat and tie, but he had large brass buttons on his waist coat. Owen decided that he looked more like a circus man than a quarryman.

'The fellowship meeting last Wednesday was under attended men—ah here he is now—Huw, your father tells me the meeting this past Wednesday was under attended, not over attended as the case should be mun! Under attended! What shall you say to these men now mun?'

Huw took a bow and the men laughed and clapped and drummed their tin mugs on the table.

'Good men of... these mountain parts...' Huw said theatrically. 'Co-o-o-mmmmme tooo chape-a-a-al—to the many, many meetings—mooooore o-o-o-ften!' he sang. The men laughed and stamped their boots, building up to a crescendo that ended with them banging their mugs on the table as well as creating a mighty sound of percussion with their boots.

When the noise and the laughter died down, Huw said, 'Seriously men, I have it on authority that revival is imminent.'

'Did God tell you?' one said.

'Or your father?'

'We heard from Anna,' Owen said without thinking.

The men murmured respectfully, but Owen looked down embarrassed.

'I did not mean to say it, Huw, I am sorry,' he whispered to his brother, fiddling with the cap in his hand, his cheeks, slapped with embarrassment, burning. Huw pulled his brother's cap down in playful reassurance and a man joked that Owen would need to make sure the fountain never ran dry, given the men were fuelled by tea. Owen said he would be sure to keep the tea flowing like a river and all the men laughed and held up

71

their mugs to him. During the making of the tea he agonised as he did not know whether he had leave to repeat what Anna had said about revival coming or not. Since he had been to Anna's he had experienced a quickening of conscience. *The proximity of holiness*, as his mother had described being around Anna. He had wanted to show himself as knowledgeable to the men and now he felt foolish. A lad called Mal, who sat nearest the door, as befitting his status, was looking at him sideways and he could not make out his expression, but Owen was sure he found him stupid. When he gave him his tea, Mal said. 'I cart the waste away like, from the bargain after all the splittings, with the big mallet—there's hills of waste—the bargain rock is that big.'

The men joked that Owen would need to bring the tea several times at least before getting it right. *Revival will come before the year is out.* Owen heard these words so clearly in his own heart and mind that they made him jump. He coughed and shuffled his feet in case anyone had noticed but the men were engaged in debate. He watched their faces; some of them had large moustaches in otherwise clean-shaven faces. Huw's friend, Bryn, a driller had the expression of a bulldog; he was stout with a head that leaned in, and narrow dark eyes that turned downwards giving them a kindness that they might not have had; his arms hung rounded by his sides and he constantly pressed his thumbs into his forefingers. *Watchful.* That was the word; they looked ready for anything, Owen decided. And many of them had had surprises thrown at them. He knew that Bryn's brother had been killed by falling rock the year before. He discovered too, that the lad, Mal's, father, and his uncle, both quarrymen, had died of lung disease. The talk that morning was of the battle to get the steward to raise the price of the bargain that the men had struck to thirty-five shillings. Two of the men had recently joined the union and one of them was passing union literature to the other, when the steward walked in looking very impressive in a three-piece wool suit and a fancy bowler; but he was as stiff as an undertaker.

'Did I hear talk of a union? And so soon after Lord Penhurst allowed you back from the goodness of his own heart?'

One of the men exploded with laughter. Another said that

Lord Penhurst's heart was as hard as the rock they had been given to work.

Furnaced in the face, the steward took his bowler hat off and flung it on the table.

'The door is right there,' he said, jabbing his finger at the door. 'I will have no more talk of unions here and you will work out the bargain we agreed till you are paid at the end of the month.'

'We struck the bargain for decent slate. We cannot produce thousands of good quality slates a day out of the farewell rock you have given us,' a man said.

'If you split and dress the slate properly you will produce what we agreed,' the steward shouted.

Huw stood up. 'The men are speaking the truth,' he said. 'The slate is of poor quality and when we discussed the bargain the rock you showed us was good.'

'Are you calling me a liar?' The steward yelled at Huw.

Owen was shocked to see that Huw and the men had to put up with the kind of treatment he received from his schoolmaster, though they were grown men.

'No,' Huw said. 'I am calling the stone a lie. Nevertheless, we will work out the bargain, will we not?' Huw looked at each of the men.

'The stone does not lie,' Llywelyn said, standing up and looking the steward directly in the eye. He was known throughout the district as an expert slate splitter.

The men were silent; the steward stared at Llywelyn; Llywelyn stared back and then sat down. The steward stood there for a moment, his cheeks red in the areas above his trim beard, as if unsure of what to say and then he turned and rapidly left the shed, slamming the wooden door behind him. Huw had explained to Owen that quarrying was the only work to be had, even if it meant them being had; conditions were slacker than ever now due to cheap slate being imported from abroad, since the strike.

'Fatherless bastard!' A man said as they put their jackets on.

'Lying toe rag,' said another.

'Do you think he and Penfirst sleep in the same bed at night?'

'Plotting in their nightcaps!'

The door swung open again. 'If the boy is spending the day here I expect him to make himself useful,' the steward said.

'He will be helping to dress the slate,' Huw said smiling at the steward.

The steward nodded and left the shed again.

'Lying rock,' Bryn laughed at Huw, who laughed back. 'Bastard liars—they have our hands tied—their agents will be round for the rent in a few days and then we'll be deciding whether to give them their money back or eat leeks till the end of the month.'

'Bastard damp in the house too,' another said. 'The sheep have better pens, little wonder we share our fevers.'

'It's slave labour. They own us and they own the cottages we live in.'

'Speak for yourselves, I live in the barracks,' a young man said.

'They own those too,' the men laughed as they went outside.

'But they don't own this,' Huw clapped his hand over his heart. 'This is where freedom lies. They are bound by money.'

'So are we!' the men chorused.

'But not in the same way—let us agree not to be bound. Maybe God will melt their hard hearts.'

'It'd take an act of God,' a man said.

Owen stared up at the mountain, where men began to appear on the galleries; three men stood with what looked to Owen like spears of different sizes. Huw explained that they were for packing gunpowder into the rock and for prying the loosened blocks of rock following the blasting; a man stood with a drill at least six feet long, the back of which came up to his shoulder. At ground level, a man with a murderously massive mallet was breaking into a block of stone that was longer than him and about half his width. Inside one of the open-fronted sheds, Owen watched Llywelyn splitting slate from a block of tombstone-shaped rock with mallet and cold chisel; sitting on his short, high backed chair, legs outstretched, and crossed at the ankles, the block of slate balanced between his knees, he split the slate into impossibly delicate sheets; he knew exactly where to tap and exactly how much pressure to exert given the grain of the slab. Twins, Morys and Lloyd Jones both knelt on one knee with their other feet flat on the ground, splitting slate in unison; their moustaches, like the wings of ascending birds, flying on either sides of their faces; their facial muscles twitched with each blow of their mallets and their bowlers perched stiff as blackbirds on their heads. Slate was piled up on trolleys, ready to be taken down the incline to the narrow-gauge railway further down the mountain where the steam train would carry them to port and the ships that would take them to the roofs of Europe, America and Australia. Taryn, the slate dresser, sat on a traval like a rider at a rodeo, had his horse been a long oblong block. His cap was cocked at a jaunty angle and his striped shirtsleeves were rolled up above his elbows; he trimmed the edge of the slate into a right angle on the iron edge of the traval before dressing it with a guillotine knife to the required size. The men had English ladies names for the different sized slates. Owen noticed that three of the men, though they worked continuously, spent most of the time laughing and the rest of the time coughing.

After a lunch of bread and cheese, during which Anwen's apples were carved up and passed around, Owen was taken up to the gallery to watch the drilling and explosive packing. He was most interested in how the drill worked but when Bryn explained it to him, the noise in the quarry and the wind whistling and Owen's scarf muffling his ears made it difficult to hear; after a while he stopped pulling down his scarf and shouting 'Please explain that again,' and just nodded, watching Bryn's motor-driven mouth and body working, and trying to look interested, despite having only caught snatches of what he said. After Bryn had pointed out all the parts of the drill, he stood up, and facing the mountain, swept his hands, and his whole body too, upwards, as if he was cleaning the mountain face, in an effort to show Owen how extensive the pipe workings were, an act which was fascinating in itself. All Owen really caught was that the pipes, that were attached to the mountains, forced air into the drill that drove the motor, and that all by watching Bryn's body miming. He hoped he would not be quizzed about it afterwards. Besides, he was past caring, the wind was howling and it had begun to rain, and the ringing noise of the chisels and mallets were grinding his nerves; he had already decided you would need to be cracked to work up here, or without choice, as Huw had pointed out. The gallery where Huw and Bryn were working had recently been named the Boer gallery; all the galleries on the terraces had names. Bryn was now preparing to light the gunpowder fuse following the drilling; he pushed the gunpowder into the hole with a long rod, then he tipped his cap. A long call sounded a warning to the men in the galleries to move to the safety of the blasting shelter. Huw grabbed Owen by the arm and they ran with Bryn to a grassy area of the mountain where the blast shelter was located. Like almost everything else, the shelter was made of slate and shaped like a squat cylinder with a narrow open doorway; it smelt of moss and damp. Bryn and Huw crouched on the ground and Owen sat near the far wall, facing the doorway, his arms cradling his lower legs; he could see mountains on either side of the valley stretching into a distant haze. A few seconds later the blasts began; Owen felt them travel through the ground towards him and then move through his whole body. He drew his scarf up over his ears and placed his hands either side of his head. The mountain trembled; the noise died down and then there was another blast. As the second blast came, Owen began to feel as he had done when talking to Catrin at the cellar house and at Anna's, and he knew that something other than the blasting was about to happen. There was so much smoke from the blasting that for a moment or two, Owen could see nothing at all through the doorway. When the smoke cleared, to Owen's eye, the mountains had disappeared and the day darkened completely. Instead, he could see an expanse of flat and desolate terrain; burnt trees rose up here and there across the landscape, outlined sharply against a coal-dark sky. Across this terrain, Owen saw that the earth had opened up in a jagged split as if lightening had struck it and left its imprint there. There was a shout and out of this gash in the ground, that now resembled a long ditch, a man appeared on the top of a ladder, followed swiftly by many others, all wearing uniforms, they had helmets on their heads like tin basins and they were carrying long guns. A sharp explosion turned the sky white; the noise was deafening. Owen clutched his ears with his hands. The soldiers began walking towards the other side of the field, firing their guns as they went. Across the burnt field he saw other soldiers behind a wall of hessian sacks; some were lying on their fronts firing at the men that came towards them. A gigantic gun on wheels, similar to a cannon and not unlike the drill he had recently been examining, was aimed across the landscape at the soldiers that had come out of the ditch; four or five men were loading and firing, they aimed at the men that walked towards it, who were in turn firing their guns. Owen wanted to scream out to them to look ahead, but they seemed aware of its being there but walked resolutely towards it nonetheless. A booming noise caused the entire scene to shudder; Owen's ears were screaming with sound. He saw arms and legs spinning in the air, some unattached to bodies. A head, still strapped into its helmet was flung into the sky like a football. Through the chaos of deafening sound, Owen could just make out the peripheral sound of men screaming against the deafening thuds and sounds of the explosions. He saw the upper part of a man come down to earth and plant itself limbless on the land as the noise died down. He thrust his head down between his knees, before becoming aware of the sound of the call and of Huw shouting in his ear.

'Get up Owen! We are finished blasting and it is time for me to be lowered.'

Owen stared at his brother's face. 'Are you alright?' Huw asked. 'You're trembling. Are you going to turn?' Huw shoved Owen's head playfully. 'No you're not.'

Owen followed his brother to an area safely away from loosened rock, but where he would be able to see Huw being lowered. His ears were ringing and his heart pounding. He felt sick and wondered whether he would collapse, immediately another thought came: *Do not fear*, the angel's remembered words began to calm him down and he was able to focus on watching Bryn help his brother rope up before he was lowered slowly over the top of the terrace; the rope was tied around his upper thigh and waist; he swayed slightly away from the rock face like a spider on a web. From his perspective, Owen saw him swing up over the mountains in the far distance and into the sky. As Huw met the sky, Owen felt the fear again, but also a dreadful sense of premonition. He forced himself to focus on the angel's words, *Do not fear*, which again had the effect of calming him down. Huw waved at Owen as he swung gently back and forth, kicking away from the rock with his boot as he swung too close to it; all the while being lowered with the help of Bryn who crouched with the rope workings on the terrace above Huw. Owen wondered whether what he had seen was the end of the world. There appeared to be no sun or stars or light of any kind in the vision that he saw, with little differentiation between the darkness of the sky and the blackness of the earth. Huw was reaching the area of blasting; he stood on a tiny rock ledge and drove his chisel into the rock with a mallet. Sections of blast-loosened mountain came away and fell to the ground hundreds of yards below. As Huw was being pulled up, two men appeared, who began preparing the chunk of rock into several pillars with their chisel and mallets; Mal and another lad began picking up the waste and flinging it into rubble trolleys. Huw waved his cap at Owen and whistled.

Later that afternoon, Owen was asked to make the tea as the men smoked and joked. Feeling disconnected from his body, he went through the motions, wondering whether he was out of his mind as well as his body, but were it not for the sense of dislocation, he might be battling the fear, so he welcomed it, smiling and laughing on cue. Worried that the men might see his shaking hands as he poured tea into the mugs, he turned his back to them to block their view, though they were not likely to notice. They were happy with the rock that Bryn and Huw had freed and that a new bargain was to be struck with the steward the following Monday, and rowdy with talk. Owen carried each mug with two hands so as not to spill it, praying that the men would not see his hands shaking and draw attention to them. Mal, who did not join in with the conversation, winked at Owen as he set his tea down on the table rather than putting it in Mal's outstretched hands. Owen did not know why he had winked, but wondered whether Mal wanted him to sit with him and be friendly, but though he felt bad for it, Owen could not face it; he sat on the bench next to Huw, his own carefully placed tea growing cold in the mug on the table, for fear of lifting it up and shaking it all over the place. He felt awe as he went over the events in his mind, awe that was soon muddied with resentment as he wondered why he had seen the vision; he wanted to be left alone to enjoy his boyhood, the parts where he did not think about Stephen or the world to come; where he simply lived in brightly lit moments: skimming stones on the diamond peaked surfaces of the lake on a sunny day, or sitting on the mountain with Huw, discussing the merits of the peaks that lay spread out beneath the cloud. He glanced at the weathered faces of the men who worked from early morning to evening in this place, with only Sundays and Easter and Christmas days to spend with their families, apart from chapel in the evenings. Owen felt depressed on their behalf; he thought their lives mechanical; they were no different from plough horses working for men, though Huw said that some of these men had fine minds and may have become university men had the wheel of life turned differently. Surely God intended something more? As he thought this, Owen became aware of life taking place on a vaster scale elsewhere; he had a feeling that he was taking part in a rehearsal; he watched his still slightly shaky hands lift the tin mug to his lips and took in, with the tea, a sense that elsewhere was as close as his own skin.

Chapter 10

Using Meg, who was curled on the mat in front of the range, as a footrest, Owen was sitting on the settle near his father, drinking tea and poking bits of heather into the fire. Rain drenched the cottage and, thrown there by the buckets of wind, washed the windows. From his armchair, that he had pulled closer to the fire so that he could place his stockinged feet on the fender, Jacob was reading aloud from the newspaper, while Anwen wrote letters at his desk.

'This journalist here,' Jacob said, poking the newspaper audibly in his excitement, 'has been attending all the meetings in the Rhondda Valley my love. He says there is a fervour of feeling in the meetings there, with many of the colliers giving their lives over to Jesus as the strange workings of the Holy Spirit—as he puts it—become more and more tangible.'

Anwen gave Owen a knowing glance. It was as Anna said. *It will sweep up from the valleys of the south to the mountains of the north by Christmas.*

A musical rap at the door announced Seth Williams and Martyn Rees. Anwen, who had spent the day boiling all the household whites as well as Huw's corduroy work trousers in the washing-pot on the range, cried out in a jokey manner against the rain and her floor as she snatched up the drying trousers and other sundry items of clothing from the range and flung them on her bed, closing the bedroom door behind her. Seth Williams engulfed the width of the door. He paused and stamped his feet on the cloth that Anwen had gestured to Owen to fling in their path.

'The weather is inclement, but the news is good my brother,' Seth stretched his arms wide before clapping them on his friend's shoulders.

'Pull up to the fire, Seth my boy—and Owen my boy—fill the kettle,' Jacob said as Anwen came in from the bedroom patting the sides of her new hairstyle, that was, as Owen had remarked earlier, 'like two crabs, stretched out, clinging sideways to either side of her face—in the manner of crabs.' Martyn took off his hat as he stooped to come in, before dramatically bowing on the threshold; he winked at Owen who began to get out of his chair, but the men said in unison, 'Sit boy, sit, sit, we don't need tea.'

Owen picked up the bellows to get the fire burning higher, but with a strategic movement of her eyes, Anwen sent him off to the scullery to fill the kettle anyway. The men wore black suits and waistcoats with white starched shirts and collars, though Seth's collar was quite formal and fancy in keeping with his moustache; that looked to Owen like a blackened hearth brush; ruddy faced and wide of fleshy-mouth, Owen had once drawn a cartoon of Seth as a Toby Jug. By contrast, Martyn Rees was tall and lean, with a large curved nose between cheekbones that served as shelves holding his bright blue eyes up; he wore his pale hair tied back with a black ribbon. Owen brought back the kettle and paid no further attention to the men, nor to his mother, as she made the tea, and buttered the extra loaf of bread that she was now glad she had baked yesterday; she placed slices artfully on her grandmother's ornate handled display plate that, as if to suggest the kind of bounty to serve, was decorated with peacocks and piles of fruit rather than the bread and bara brith, that Anwen was now taking from its tin on the kitchen table. Out of the dresser drawer came a starched white cloth that snapped to attention as Anwen let it fly before spreading it over the hastily cleared dining table. Martyn began to protest at the trouble Anwen was going to but she batted his words away with her hands. Owen was used to men and women in need of advice, appearing at all hours to speak to his father or mother about chapel matters. Lately, with all the news of a revival building up in the south, these meetings were becoming even more frequent. Owen settled back into the chair and stared at the flames behind the grate as he munched on cake, challenging himself to flick the crumbs that landed on the crocheted blanket further and further into the fire burning in the range in front of him. The pictures that the flames gave up were like the shrieking figures of Breughel's hell. He contemplated the mechanics of his mind working within the hinges of his skull, picturing it tipping forwards and balancing delicately on the top of his vertebrae. For Owen, the skull and bones lurking beneath his flesh, were the dead parts of him that were capable of exposing themselves whitely at any given time. He had read that in Mexico, people had a festival of the dead where they decorated their towns with skulls and left food out for dead spirits. Owen imagined the dead as skeletons, rampaging around the colourful streets of Mexico, dressed in patterned shawls and black hats; pipes clamped between their unhinged jaws; barging into people's square houses and seating themselves at the supper table amongst the diners, smiling their forever gaping smiles. They had the right idea in Mexico, Owen thought, welcoming and entertaining the death that shadowed them. Perhaps it was less of a shock when the Grim Reaper actually arrived, scything aside years of life, given they were used to making merry with the dead. He was so engrossed in these thoughts, that it took him a while to come to and respond to his mother's face asking him if he would like a cup of tea and it took him a moment or two to come to himself and give her the nod that he knew was expected of him. 'Revival is coming, Jacob,' Martyn was saying, as he sat down in the chair that Anwen offered him at the table. 'On my way up here from town I noticed that the public house was so full, that it had spilled some of its contents on the street!'

Anwen, who was pouring tea, smiled outwardly at the vividness of Martyn's poetry, but grimaced inwardly at the thought of men and women under the influence; she had seen the effects of drinking in the community and in the town. During the last revival, many had forsaken the public houses for the chapels, but in the last few years since the strike, people had turned again to drink in their despair. She was concerned too, for the families of the quarrymen whose father's had turned to drink. The Women's

Temperance Movement had been a powerful influence in Wales. It had succeeded in helping put drink money back on the backs of children and food returned to the table in some of the poorer districts, but now Anwen had noticed the children of drinking fathers coming to Sunday School less and less and looking more and more ragged. Poverty was a disease that was a magnet for other diseases. *How quickly they forget you, Lord, when the crossing is rough!* Anwen thought. *Like the Hebrews led to the desert out of Egypt, they begin to long again for their comfortable slavery.* The three men that were now continuing their discussion at the dining table were members of three Nonconformist denominations that had worked together in unity during the previous revival. Seth and Martyn's tiny lungs had sucked up revival air from the moment they took their first breaths, they grew up attending Sunday School and all the chapel meetings as well as the annual denominational field events, where thousands came to hear fiery preachers preach from their wagons. Jacob was a Baptist, Martyn was a Methodist and Seth was Presbyterian: they indulged in much good-natured banter regarding their differing theology; but they all believed in the same fundamental truth: the faith of Christ crucified and risen from the dead, as being the only way to relationship with the triune God and eternal life thereafter. As Seth was fond of saying: *When the spirit of God comes there is no denomination, class or creed!* Anwen's parents had spent many years passionately praying for continued revival too. One of the leading lights of the revival of 1859, her father was one of the well known 'fiery' travelling preachers. Knee high to him, Anwen began travelling the country with her father; she was known as 'Sweet Singing Annie.' Her voice was said to have an 'anointing' on it given so many people gave their lives to Jesus when Annie was singing and her father was preaching at meetings. Anwen joked that she was so steeped in revival prayer that it oozed out of her when she was hugged. As a teenager, she continued to travel the country with other revival singers, one of which, Eilwen, she still sung and occasionally travelled with. *"Stoking the revival embers till the breath of God blew them to life again,"* as their banners announced them. Anwen and Jacob had prayed all their marriage for God to visit Wales again and pour out his power as he had done in the many revivals that Wales had experienced since the third century, *only in greater measure, please, Father God.* In the evenings they often spoke long into the night of the many ways that God had manifested in Wales, *Lest we forget*, reminding themselves that the revivals had greatly aided the spreading of the gospel around the world as inspiration to continue to pray with fervour.

'There is a wind of change coming,' Seth was saying, he pushed his dainty plate away with a plump finger and put on his spectacles, he rubbed the tips of his fingers together, 'I can feel it. I have received a letter from my brother that I would like to read to you.' He took a letter from his top pocket, and began to read. '"Something is afoot Seth, there is a strange feeling in the air, like the suggestion of a storm coming."' Seth swirled his hand in the air above his head theatrically. '"We truly believe that revival is coming soon. *Many* of us are feeling this way. Only last week one of the children got up in Sunday School to say, *Jesus you must bring revival so that Father will come home after work and Mother will be happy again.* When the child said this, a spirit of prayer came upon the assembly, and *all* the children prayed in unison. Seth, we have not seen that spirit of unity before. It was as if a divine hand came in and led the prayer. From one to the other, voices were raised in supplication, until finally the prayer led to spontaneous singing of such purity, it was as if the angels were with us in the room."' Seth looked up at the others. Anwen had her hand clasped to her throat and tears in her eyes.

'I can just see it—those children singing—I can feel it,' she turned and put her hand on her husbands arm. 'Jacob, can it be coming?'

'Well Anna did say revival would come from the south by Christmas,' Owen said. This time he had no compunction in saying so.

'There you are then. Well done my boy, well done,' Seth said.

'Thanks said Owen, pumping the bellows. 'I'll borrow the credit and take it back to her when I can.'

'Yes, clever boy, well done indeed,' Martyn said, which made Owen laugh; he patted himself jokily on the head.

'The vessels *must* be prepared to hold the water of the Holy Spirit,' Martyn said. 'Our proposal is to begin regular meetings. What do you say Jacob? Can we have access to your chapel?'

'I'd be glad. We will need to have day meetings—apart from Friday night, there are no meetings that night.' he glanced at his wife. Anwen nodded. 'And we can open the chapel further— later—as God leads. Though how many of yours will walk up the mountain?' Jacob said, crossing his legs and rubbing his hands together in glee.

'Our congregations would walk up Tryfan to meet with God,' Seth said with a slap on the table, in response to his friend's cheek.

'Oh that's nothing,' said Jacob. 'Our Huw skips up Tryfan in a jiffy, you will have to raise the stakes.'

'You may have to lead a party up Tryfan like Moses,' Seth said to Owen. 'Gird your loins boy, we need all the Gideon's we can get.'

'You're muddling your prophets and your warriors together all in one sentence there I see,' Jacob joked.

'Will I roast my face, like Moses did too?' Owen said, continuing to pump the bellows.

'Prophets release the fire of God first—before warriors are released.' Seth said.

Anwen, her elbows propped on the table and her hands under her chin, laughed. 'Well Huw can be Moses then and Owen can be Gideon.'

'There you have it,' Seth said. 'You'll be seeing angels before long in the manner of Gideon.'

Owen smiled, he fancied his angel winking at him, as he pumped the bellows again. The fire rose so high it threatened to burst the grate. Owen glanced at his mother, but she was still engaged in banter with Seth. The fire died down a little so he pumped some more. *The Holy Spirit is the breath of life that creates the fire in men to will and to act according to My good purpose. It is the wind in your sails. You will not travel with purpose without it.* Owen thought of the clipper that he had recently drawn, and of the speed that the design of the sails enabled while he found himself agreeing with the words that had popped into his mind before the realisation came that God had spoken to him again. He poked the fire again.

'That is the point, my friend,' Jacob said. 'Who will walk up the mountain? For revival to come we must desire to seek his face. Revival begins in the heart and is birthed in relationship with the living God. We must desire relationship more than the signs, though the signs of that relationship inevitably follow. Who will be Moses this time?'

'He will raise us up if we humble ourselves in prayer,' Seth said. 'If my people who are called by my name, will humble themselves and seek my face, then I will hear from heaven and come and heal their land,' he quoted 2 Chronicles 7 verse 14.

Anwen stood, her hands clasped under her chin. 'Let's begin crying out afresh for God to visit our land. It has been so wounded by the strike and so shamed by the lockout, and so swayed by the politics of anger that rose up out of its deathbed. We must pray with one heart for forgiveness and reconciliation for our divided communities—to invite God's blessing.'

Jacob put his arm around his wife, while Martyn and Seth stood opposite them.

'Will you join us in prayer Owen?' Anwen asked.

Owen went and stood with his parents, each put an arm on either side of his shoulders. Seth waved his fist in the air passionately as he walked back and forth, crying out his prayers in a loud voice; Jacob raised his fists on either side of his head and punctuated the air with them as he prayed. His mother had her hands raised in supplication. Martyn prayed seated at the table, head tipped back, one hand across his heart. Though he had recently heard the Holy Spirit speaking to him in his thoughts, Owen did not really feel like praying and his mind began to wander after a few minutes. He had heard his family speak of and pray for revival all his life. During one of his father's services a few years ago, his father threw his hands up. *They're red hot!* He had shouted out. *Does anyone need healing? The spirit is here!* He clamped his hands around Gwyndaf's head. Gwyndaf, who had been sitting in the front pew as usual had stood up and began uttering sounds despite the fact that he had been born deaf and dumb. The congregation had clapped and praised God as they watched Gwyndaf's father dance round and round in circles as his son uttered sounds for the first time. Word of the healing spread around the district and people streamed to the chapel eager for healing, but they came in vain; there were no more healings. Owen had asked his father why God only healed once. They had been out trapping rabbits near the river.

'Do you love me Owen?' his father had asked, leading his son away from the water's edge and over a ford formed by smooth rocks, some of which were submerged in the water; others had become their stepping stones.

'Yes,' Owen had said, slightly embarrassed. He jumped onto the rock behind his father. When he crouched down, he saw a shoal of tiny fish like slivers of blue jewels.

'How would I know that? Jacob had asked, adjusting the sack that held the recently deceased hare over his shoulder.

'Because I live with you and don't run away.'

'Exactly,' Jacob said. 'You live with me and don't run away. God wants us to live with him and not run off to do our own thing all the time. If he kept performing, would we grow weary of the miraculous? Would we take him for granted?'

'But couldn't He do other stuff? Different stuff over and over?'

On the other side of the river, Jacob had crouched down and gripped Owen by the shoulders. 'God lives in you and me by His Holy Spirit. He wants us to spend time with Him, to have a relationship with him through prayer. Prayer is just talking to Him. He wants to talk back so we have to be quiet and listen.'

'I can't hear him,' Owen said.

'Sssh,' Jacob said. 'Close your eyes and listen with your heart. You will hear his voice in your mind. If it is encouraging it is the right voice. You need only respond and continue the conversation. He wants to guide us. And if we let Him, Owen, if we truly let Him, life can be an amazing adventure that will lead us to the life to come—and the more we pursue that life the closer heaven comes to earth. But it is our choice to follow Him or go our own way.'

'Now listen to that,' Jacob said, drawing Owen's attention to the river. The sound of the water resounded through the valley.

'That is living water. When I say it is living I mean it speaks to us of the creator who made it. The Bible says that streams of living water will flow through us if we believe. The water is a metaphor for the Holy Spirit. When you believe in God the Holy Spirit comes to live in you and transforms you and then the power of God works through you.'

'How?' Owen watched the water cascade over the dark rocks, the moss covering them was a rich green: they looked like the mint crunch covered chocolates that Derwyn Gwilt sold at in his shop in the village.

'It turns you in to a good person and it brings with it gifts.'

'Like the gift of healing?' Owen said, thinking that the water going over the chocolate rocks was like lemonade.

'Yes. There are other gifts too. Do you see how He speaks?'

Owen was not sure that he did. They walked on and Owen asked how else God spoke.

'Sometimes he gives you a sign that only you can understand. Owen, the more time you spend with Him the more you understand, though there are mysteries upon mysteries, the journey becomes deeper and deeper and more fascinating if you will be a true disciple.'

Owen looked up at his praying parents. He felt a surge of joy inside himself. Now he did know how God spoke.

June

Chapter 11

Nerves shivered at the back of Anwen's legs as she woke; she could hear the clock ticking loudly from the mantel in the otherwise silent cottage. Outside the window of her bedroom, thin clouds skittered across a small tight moon. In the grate of the fireplace, near the foot of their bed, ash-pink coals gleamed slightly. She knew it had to do with Owen, and that it had something to do with war, but she could not remember any detail at all. Wrestling with her fear for Owen, she woke Jacob up to pray as she often did. Jacob rolled over and muttered.

'Dear God release my beloved from this fear so that we can sleep peacefully.

Anwen became quite angry. 'Jacob! Be serious. I am terrified for our boy.'

'I'm not' he said, rolling over and embracing his pillow.' If God gave you a dream that was frightening it is to warn you to pray, so pray and be released, my love.'

Anwen stared up at the oak beams above her and at the chest of drawers opposite, on top of which stood the oval dressing mirror that her mother had given her when she married Jacob along with the photo of her parents, her mother dressed traditionally for market day in her best shawl, rimmed with patterned fabric; high hat, the frills of her cap *jugging her head like ears* as Huw once put it to his brother. *Grandfather has side whiskers and beard that compete with her frills*, Owen had replied. Anwen had heard them, and was not unamused, but said nothing. She always afforded her boys their privacy, even if she caught snatches of 'up to no good,' rather, she encouraged them to lay their hearts bare before the Lord. Troubled, Anwen prayed for some time for Owen, then for Huw, followed by a number of other people while Jacob grunted in agreement here and there but mostly carried on sleeping.

'And dear Lord, release her from fear and anger and any other emotion or plague of the wee hours that may hinder her,' Jacob said, rolling over.

Anwen heard him wheezing with laughter into the pillow and hit him with her own, but as she did so she knew she was released from the fear. *I will not fear for Owen at school or for the future that I sense will take him away from me, or for Huw at the quarry. The Lord gave them to me. He can keep them for me. But oh God keep them safe.* Anwen stroked her husband's head and thought about their love and thanked God for it. Jacob's long curly hair that she was so fond of was splayed on the pillow; the fine tendrils at his temple were delicate as a child's. Jacob had been converted to Christ as a young man thanks to an encounter with *a passionate lover of Jesus* as Anwen called herself back then. Anwen smiled as she remembered her youthful passion for Christ. The day they met, Jacob had been part of a jeering crowd of young men who had watched Anwen ride into his town on her way to chapel for a revival meeting with a troupe of young lady revival singers. Amused by the way she stood up in the cart, with her hands on her hips—she had met his playful stare with her own steady gaze. He had followed her to the chapel, 'for sport.' Bold as Bernie, he walked in looking for her as she rehearsed for that evening's service. Jacob laughed when she said that he would not get through this life or the next without the living God. He had said that he was 'fine and dandy and fit for a brandy without God.' She had responded that he might proceed with ignorance in this life, but he would most certainly need him in the next life unless he wanted eternal separation from him. Jacob had replied that he would not know any better because he would be dead, and anyway he was separated from him now, and that was fine. Anwen had told him that 'he would not be dead in the spirit as the spirit once created cannot die and goes on to eternity in heaven or hell conscious of what is happening, and that in hell, he would rather not know what was happening given the inconceivable hell of it, but he won't have the choice that was now being presented to him.' Jacob had guffawed at her words. Across the empty chapel, Anwen had called out to him from the stage as he left: 'Goodbye my heathen friend, I will see you again and you will be changed!' Jacob had laughed, but next day, as he made his way to the quarry where he had begun work the previous summer, her words rang in his spirit and he found himself at the chapel that night. As the women began to sing that evening, he felt the power of God for the first time and he was terrified. As he said: 'In his terror he became acutely aware of his own sin and of his desperate need for a saviour.' He went to the altar, knowing, with his *heart* and mind that he needed salvation. As he did so, he felt the power of God enter his body with such force that he fell to the floor and landed on his back on the floor unhurt. That night, the minister prophesied over him that he would be a torch in the hand of God to light revival fires in the next century. He took this to heart, or *spirit*, as he liked to say, and prayed that it would come to pass; alert in his spirit for guidance concerning when and how to play his role.

For the rest of the night Anwen lay there communing with God, now in the heavenly language, and again in Welsh, as the night drained away and with it what needed to leave her. The sky welcomed the sun and Anwen welcomed her emotional healing. *It feels like there is more room in my heart for you now Dear Holy Spirit of God. Please make me ready for revival and visit me—and all of us in greater measure.* Two brown ducks sailed past her window and across the pale-orange sky; the sight made her laugh with happiness. *You have healed me Father God and helped me understand that the fear I have been carrying for them is due to my loss that I have carried for too long. I lay the burden down now, Lord. I know I will see him again—Samuel—there. I said his name Lord. I know I will see him again. Oh my God, can you heal the heart of Wales too? What would that look like?* In the first wake of freedom from fear, she was joyous, and thrilled too, that one did not need to pray like the clappers for God to hear.

Chapter 12

Anwen left it until they had walked halfway down the track before telling Owen that the prayer meeting that evening was going to take place at Heledd Jones house.

'Thank you indeed Mother—the sun is out, butterflies flutter above the hedgerows and all seems pleasant in the world - and now this. I do not want to have my head kicked around like a football at school, Mother, though you might not mind.'

'You will not be seen, don't worry,' Anwen swept a gust of gnats from her face. It was the hottest day of the year so far and the hedgerows were abuzz with insects.

'Are you going to drape me in your shawl and usher me in like a foundling?'

He did not want to be seen going to Heledd Jones' house, especially by the boys whose fathers were working in the south and particularly not by Edryd, who had gone to the school in town that Owen might also attend if he received the scholarship that was being extended to boys his age; Edryd was captaining a new district football team and worse, his father was Gryff Thomas, the union man who was recruiting for the new labour party, who only associated with the quarrymen that attended his father's chapel to recruit them.

'Why did you not tell me, Mother? I don't want to see her. She makes me think of him.'

'You can say Stephen's name Owen. He hasn't vanished into the ether.'

'Yes he has.'

'Well if he has, he is alive and well in heaven, ethereal or not.'

At school, Owen carefully avoided Stephen's two brothers, who reciprocated the care; neither parties wanted to confront their mutual memories and so engaged in a curious dance where they side-stepped each other if any one of them hoved into view.

'I thought it would be good for you to face your fear Owen. It will make Heledd happy to see you now that she has moved on a little.'

Owen said nothing; he could hardly run away and hide amongst the mountain boulders until his mother had returned. He veered off the track to pick a grass stem from the side of the road.

'How can you be sure about heaven?' he said, chewing on the sweet green of the bottom of the stem.

'I'm not sure. The flip side of faith is doubt, but I believe it,' Anwen turned to face her son. She tucked her Bible under her arm and straightened her hat.

'You mean you choose to believe?' Owen ran the fingers of his right hand through his hair.

'Yes. But the evidence is overwhelming,' Anwen flapped her hand at a gust of midges that suspended in the heat. She adjusted her hat. 'Too much at an angle?'

'Yes. Why bother with it? What evidence?' Owen pulled another stem.

'You don't understand hats Owen—' Anwen laughed, '— the evidence of heart and head. I first believed with my heart,' she said, her hand on her chest, 'but I devoured the Bible,' Anwen said, raising the Bible she held. 'It is a history book, a love letter to us, *and* a book of prophecy. The new confirms the old and the old confirms the new.'

'Explain,' Owen said, chewing at the same time.

'It is a *prophetic* book—each section proving the next—all the historical evidence for the birth, death and resurrection, as well as the works of Jesus are prophesied in the Old Testament. Isaiah and the Psalms prophesy Jesus and his crucifixion and works again and again, which is why I have struggled to understand why most of the Jews have rejected Jesus being the Messiah.' Anwen tapped her temple. 'Study it for yourself Owen, don't just take it as gospel from us, many are led astray by accepting things they haven't studied for themselves, or they have received revelation in and of themselves, though even revelation should be reflected in the Bible.'

They were approaching the cottages. 'I don't,' Owen said. He looked around him quickly and then bolted for the door of the new Jones' place.

'Hurry up Mother!' he said from the doorstep.

Anwen laughed and quickened her step, but only slightly.

'Coward,' she laughed. 'I had a spiritual revelation that it was true, I just knew, in my heart. But then I set about proving what I already knew in my heart, with my head,' she said.

'Yes, thank you Mother, now can we go inside please?'

Anwen's gospel singers, Eilwen and Bethan, were already there, sitting on stools as they tuned up in front of the fire. Bethan had a hand drum and Eilwen, her violin. Bethan, who had been gently banging on her drum with little flourishes, raised the little hammer in Owen's direction in greeting. Owen tapped his fingers to his brow in salute and Bethan formed a comedic facial reply, momentarily transforming from a pretty blonde woman with piled up curls into a pantomime dame. Eilwen raised her chin in mock judgement. Anwen, who was already humming and singing the occasional phrase, took her large black hat and cape off, smiling at her friends by way of greeting as she swayed to the music. Owen glanced around the room. *All the usual villains are about* he thought, avoiding the glances of ten or so chapel women and their daughters. Stephen's bed had been removed from the sitting room where he had been laid out after the fall; a new fancy sofa, a gift from Lord Penhurst's family, had been placed beneath the window. He went and sat on it; but feeling like he was sitting on a pony he soon sprung up and went and looked out of the window. Heledd, came over and Owen braced himself for her lilac-scented embrace; he was cross with his mother for not telling him that the meeting was taking place here. Taking his lower face in her hands, she kissed him hard on both cheeks.

'You are a handsome lad now, to be sure,' Mrs Jones said. 'Stephen was so handsome, that black hair, those green eyes,' she said, her free hand on Owen's shoulder. She began to weep, her

95

hands worrying a lace handkerchief.

Owen shot his mother a desperate glance.

'He was a beautiful boy, Heledd,' Anwen said, coming over and putting her arm around her.

'Why my beautiful boy?' Heledd said, reaching out for Anwen, her hand still on Owen's shoulder. 'And why before time?' she gripped Anwen's forearm. 'He can't have died in vain,' Heledd said, dabbing at her eyes. 'We will pray for revival—I can cope with it if many other souls are saved, Annie. I have said to our Father, that I want souls in return—' Heledd gulped down her sob. 'In return for my boy—otherwise, I told him I *cannot* live.'

Anwen kissed her.

'I mean it Annie. And I believe he heard me,' Heledd said, standing up. 'We will have revival by and by ladies!' she said to the assembled women.

Owen studied the pattern on the carpet. Bethan cheered and beating on her drum, began to sing, *We will have revival by and by.* She repeated this several times until Eilwen took up the tune on her violin, and Anwen echoed the refrain and then added to it, singing, *This is our heartfelt cry: We will have revival by and by. We declare it to the mountains and we declare it to the sea. We declare it over you and we declare it over me. We will have revival by and by. We will have revival by and by.*

Anwen sang 'we declare it over you,' directly to Heledd and urged everyone to do the same, Bethan beat a staccato beat on her drum and echoed *we will have revival,* every time Anwen sang the phrase, and soon she began to lead the women in a line to dance around the room, as the women in the room clapped and sang the little song based on Heledd's phrase. Owen was accustomed to the women making up songs like these, many of them found their way into chapel; he glanced up reluctantly and caught Eilwen's eye; her chin firmly gripping her violin, she wrinkled her brow as she looked up and jiggled her eyebrows to make him laugh. Owen was shaking his head in amused embarrassment. Owen noticed that Heledd sung the loudest and that her eyes were shining. At the end of the song she swung round to Owen who was sitting cross-legged on the floor.

'I'll bring you some milk and biscuits by and by.' Heledd said laughing. 'Hasn't your mother got an angel's voice?'

Heledd, went out of the room to make tea and fetch the milk and biscuits she had promised and soon returned, wheeling a wooden trolley with teacups and pot on the top part and cake and jam and sliced bread and butter on the bottom.

The women had begun singing again, Anwen smiled at Heledd.

'It only takes a spark to get a fire going!' Heledd shouted out.

'Words of encouragement from heaven!' Anwen shouted above the sound of Eilwen's violin and the rhythmic beats of Bethan's drum.

'Use us as sparks to get the revival fires going!' a young girl stood up and called out from the back of the room. As she spoke, the atmosphere in the room shifted and they were aware of a supernatural presence in the room with them. The women began to confess as the Holy Spirit moved them. Owen, his former discomfort having vanished given this new and exciting state of affairs, was amazed that the girl was not ashamed to make a show of herself; she did not seem much younger than he, with her long hair tied in the front with a ribbon but trailing down her back. The girl's mother smiled encouragingly at her and began to pray out loud herself, at which point, Owen realised it was Catrin and Mary Davies. Catrin looked different, as did Mary, they appeared radiant. Catrin caught his eye and cupped her hands as she had the day he poured water into them at her house. Embarrassed, and somewhat taken aback at her boldness, Owen looked down, but then he felt bad and looked up again. Catrin smiled again, and he was able to smile back. Soon all the women began crying out in prayer and as each prayer came, the atmosphere, and the sense of supernatural presence in the room increased. Swept up by the presence of the invisible God of heaven, that brought joy in its wake, the corporate prayer died down and the women began to start up worship songs in turn, some of them began praising God, waving their hands up to the heavens. This went on for an hour or more, until, spiritually high, the praise and worship gave way to excited chatter from the women. Heledd Jones came and sat back down next to Owen on the sofa. Owen noticed a slight tremble in her right hand, and thought she looked tired.

'It is a wonder indeed to feel the presence of God,' she said. Quite *intoxicating.*'

She stared into the middle distance. After a while, she seemed to come back to herself, smiled around the room and patted her hair as she went to the trolley and began pouring tea. After she and some of the other ladies had served everyone, Heledd began to speak again.

'What we have experienced today ladies, was a taste of things to come. I would like to thank Catrin for bravely crying out and so ushering in the presence of the Holy Spirit—'

'Hear hear!' The women clapped and cheered.

'It is the hungry heart that God feeds!' Anwen said. 'Let us be vigilant in our prayers!'

'May he give us soft hearts!' one said.

'Give us a care for the lost!' another called out.

'Remind us that there are only two gates. The narrow and the wide!' said another. As these words were spoken, Owen, who had been taking a large bite out of his cake, began to go into an internal vision. What he saw was throngs of people going about their daily business, unaware that the ground beneath their feet was moving inexorably towards a vast cavern of swirling darkness, the substance of which was so evil that it made Owen feel physically sick. At the entrance to the chasm were vast black wrought iron gates; Owen's internal eye focussed on a parallel group of people, a little way across from the people that were heading into darkness—a mere stream of people, who seemed to be lit up from within. These people were also being propelled forward, but also upward, towards an ornate, narrow gate of gold. They gave off a strange kind of translucence, not unlike Anna's presence. These people were also going about their daily business, but they seemed more engaged with others along their way. Every now and again, one of these bright ones would seek out one from the vast throng that was moving towards the dark chasm; on occasion, a person from the dark throng would come over to the glowing stream and a person there would engage them in conversation or offer them a cup of water from the substance beneath their feet which seemed to be water so clear that it was almost bluish; though the water also seemed to be the ground beneath their feet as they were walking on it and did not sink into it. Owen thought of Jesus walking on the water. When they drank, they too became lit up and joined the narrow stream. Most of those in the vast throng ignored the ones in the life-giving stream. As the vision cleared, Owen heard the words of Jesus from the gospel of Matthew 7 verse 13 *Enter through the narrow gate. For wide is the gate and broad is the road that leads to destruction, and many enter through it.* Owen was left staring at his half eaten cake; his hand was trembling on the plate. The vision was terrifying. He began to hear the words from Luke 14:23: *And the lord said unto the servant, Go out into the highways and hedges, and compel them to come in, that my house may be filled.* He understood that if people were not reached with the living water of the gospel, if they rejected the gospel they would plunge into eternal darkness and suffering. He did not wonder at the right or the wrong of it, as he often did, he simply saw it with his spiritual eyes and accepted that it was true. Owen realised that every believer was called to share the gospel, and he felt a sense of urgency within himself to prevent people from going into the chasm. His mother's voice had risen and began to soar again. *Be thou my vision oh Lord of my heart, naught be all else to me save that Thou art.* Owen looked at Heledd crouching over the trolley in her long black dress and shawl as she placed slices of sugar dusted cake on her best fancy plates; he felt himself being filled with compassion for her; a surge of warmth that travelled up through his body, he was aware of a tingling feeling at the tips of his fingers and at the same time he felt a rush of joy as he felt the compassion physically as well as emotionally and spiritually. He felt an intense desire to communicate what he was feeling to Heledd, even though his usual embarrassment was simultaneously there. Heledd was coming towards him with the promised milk and more cake. The feeling in Owen began to build until he was filled with such compassion for Heledd that he knew he had to communicate something of it.

'I have something to say to you, Mrs Jones,' Owen said, surprised at the words that came from his mouth before he had properly formed them in his mind; he had no idea as to what he was going to say. Mrs Jones set the plate and glass on the little table next to the sofa and sat down next to him, her hands in her lap. The compulsive feeling was still there, so much so, that it felt like his heart was going to burst through his chest if he did not give utterance immediately. He glanced up at the side of Mrs Jones' face. She wore a half-smile, part sadness, part expectancy.

'Are you going to tell me something about Stephen?' she said, her eyes fixed on Anwen who was still singing.

'I think so.'

Owen began telling her about the angelic dream he had had; as he did so, he felt a little of the awe he had experienced in the dream return to him; simultaneously, he was aware of a prickling energy in his body. Mrs Jones showed no sign of feeling anything out of the ordinary. As he began to describe the fire and the green shoots coming up from the earth, Owen began to understand their meaning for the first time.

'After a fire—after death—there is new grass—new birth— and—the new birth gives life—I do not fully understand it, but I think the dream was so that I would not fear about Stephen, about where he was and how he was,' he finished quickly, concerned that the look on Heledd's face was disapproval, and that he had spoken out of turn about so delicate and painful a matter. 'Also I think there is some kind of reason for his death. It's just that I do not understand it, but I think just as Jesus had to die for the Holy Spirit to come, maybe Stephen's death will bring new life—perhaps through revival. Even as I say this it seems wrong, but I just have this understanding that it will all be right somehow.'

Heledd continued to stare across the room. She did not say anything, which made Owen wonder whether he had offended her in some way.

'Except a corn of wheat fall into the ground and die, it abideth alone: but if it die, it bringeth forth much fruit.' Heledd said, looking at her hands in her lap as she quoted John 12 verse 24. 'There is a real sense of God's presence in here tonight, isn't it Owen?' she said. 'Thank you for telling me that, Stephen—I mean Owen—about Stephen.'

Tears had begun to slide down her face as she continued to look at the opposite wall. 'You see, I have been so afraid since he went, and so—but now, since today really, I have a determination to pray, to ensure that people go the right way.'

Owen looked down at the little calluses on the palms of his right hand. He had an urge to touch Heledd's hand but again he was embarrassed.

'Through the narrow gate?' Owen said.

'Exactly that,' Heledd said, putting her hand on his. As she did so, she jumped. 'Did you feel that electricity? Oh—' she said. 'Owen, I think the electricity is in you—oh my—Owen the power of God works very powerfully in you. I am sure you will see the dead raised one day.'

Owen felt her words land in his heart and realised that she too had the gift of knowing. They were silent for some time and Owen wondered if he had said enough, but he felt empty of words. He was aware that the presence in the room was increasing again, bringing a sense of awe. Bethan had put down her drum and had taken up her harp and begun to play. The music, with the hymn that was being sung, was almost unbearably exquisite; his mother's voice had never sounded more beautiful to him; he watched her face, lit up as it was by the evening sun that still streamed; her auburn hair was tinged with gold and the pupils in her hazel eyes were dilated, giving her the appearance of a young girl, her face was flushed as she sang, *Be Thou my breastplate, my sword for the fight, be thou my whole armour, be thou my true might; be thou my soul's shelter, be thou my strong tower:* with power and passion. His mother had always been beautiful to him, but as he looked at her he saw a purity that was made known by her clear voice and he understood that there was an inner beauty in her that was unusual. Her voice washed over him as Bethan began to play some higher notes; rather than his mother, she seemed a person set apart: a creature transformed in her deepest self. Owen felt a mixture of pride and fascination; he was sure she had never sounded so well, the sound of her voice: *O raise thou me heavenward, great Power of my power...* mingling with the chords of Eilwen's violin, was almost intoxicatingly beautiful. The presence of the Holy Spirit in the room increased still more and with it came the most extraordinary perfume; its notes impossible to describe, the fragrance drenched the room. Owen shifted on the sofa, afraid that he might emit some uncontrollable sound and make a show of himself as he drank the aroma in; he tentatively stretched his hand out, sure that there must be something tangibly thick in the air in front of him; as he did so, he sensed a presence so loving, that it seemed to Owen that it was about to envelop him. Mrs Jones continued to stare at the wall.

'Such a sense of His glorious presence,' she said. 'Oh He is so good to come like this. He is the comforter.'

Bethan had gathered what was happening and was walking towards them with her violin. She stopped next to the sofa where Heledd was sitting and began to improvise a musical piece of extraordinary simplicity and beauty. Anwen, who had been about to start on the fifth verse of the hymn paused and began to sing in the heavenly language of the spirit. The words sounded like Hebrew and so married with the sound of Eilwen's violin that all in the room were mesmerised by the sound. Heledd continued to weep, but now her tears were of joy as well as pain. Eilwen who had stopped playing herself, widened her eyes at Owen as if to say 'extraordinary,' a word she used a lot. *I found it quite extraordinary. Isn't it extraordinary to be alive? An extraordinary thing happened today while I was playing. Isn't life a series of extraordinary events?* And then, as though she had read Owen's mind, she mouthed the word 'extraordinary.' Eilwen was not in the least bit religious, and thought it *perfectly acceptable to intrude on ceremony* as she put it, *as long as it was a heart-motivated intrusion.* She was fond of saying that God could be as *down to earth, as Jesus, who, having literally come down to earth, was homespun in the image of the Father, as well being the miracle worker who parted the seas.* The atmosphere in the room had now become so peaceful, that Owen found himself in something of a trance that was only broken when Mrs Jones stood up to kiss some of the ladies that were leaving, causing Anwen to bring her singing to a close and Eilwen to lower her violin and bless Mrs Jones with a beautiful smile. The captivating perfume was receding and Owen breathed in as deeply as he could in an effort to subsume what was left of it. Heledd raised a hand to Bethan and the other to Anwen.

'You ladies are vessels of beauty,' she said.

Then she turned to Owen. 'You unlocked something in me Owen, by bringing those words. I felt a *release* of something, as if all these bats that had been going around in my head just flew away,' she swept her hands outwards from her temples.

'And I will be holding our heavenly father to account she said. I want to see many hundreds of thousands of souls saved.'

She hugged Owen who did not mind, he almost hugged her back. 'And we know that all things work together for good to them that love God, to them who are the called according to *his* purpose,' she said.

'John eight verse twenty-eight,' Owen said.

'Though it has been like swallowing winter,' Heledd said. 'I can see the summer now.'

Anwen and Owen walked home in shared silence. Every now and again Anwen would look down at her son and their eyes would share what had happened in the room that was impossible to speak of. *How could you describe it?* Owen thought. *The presence of God has to be felt*, as his father said. Owen began to think of how lit up Catrin had looked; he wondered whether she had received more than just the water he gave her that day; had she drunk of the spiritual words that he had given her, that he thought were just by the by; and in so doing become one of the bright ones?

Chapter 13

Like a swat-worthy fly, Owen had buzzed around Huw, nagging to be taken to one of the evening union meetings because of Edryd Thomas. Owen often saw Edryd and some of the lads playing in the fields near the village, and he hoped to be asked to join them; but so far all his loitering near the fields affecting disinterest had resulted in what seemed like disinterest. All the local boys wanted to play for the district team and because Edryd was the captain of the team he held some influence. Owen was pleased when Huw announced one Friday evening that he was going to take him to the labour meeting that night. He hoped to meet Edryd and ask about the football and the town school.

In the cottage, Jacob threw the newspaper down with impatience and went to stoke the fire.

'Theyre attacking the revival already and its hardly even begun!'

'Who father?' Huw asked, popping his head round his bedroom door where he was combing his hair above the basin that was afloat with soap scum; his shaving brush bobbing and drowning amongst it.

'So called medical men. They are warning against social hysteria—creating it more like, with their unfounded gossip,' Jacob shouted out. 'They should be lanced!' He laughed at his own pun. 'A lot,' he added, laughing some more. But the punning was between him and God. 'Lancelot was probably Welsh anyway,' Jacob continued his dialogue with himself. 'I thought The Lancet was supposed to be an arched window to let in the light,' Jacob said, quoting The Lancet's founder, Thomas Wakley, 'Well they are not letting in the light, who is Jesus Christ. They are obstructing the light!' Jacob warmed to his theme. 'And the members of The Lancet are self satisfied sprigs of—of Thyme—and in thyme they will be submerged in the great stew of history.' Having defused himself in this way, Jacob read on contentedly, an amused grin on his face.

Huw was stripped to the waist, his braces hanging down in leather loops on either side of his thighs. The physical evidence of abseiling the quarry ropes was plain to see and Owen hoped that one day he might be the proud possessor of a physique like his brother's. Owen was sitting on Huw's bed wearing a foamy moustache and beard that was sliding chestward. He was too young to shave, but Huw had lathered him up for the kick of it. Owen sucked his stomach in and tried in vain to feel the notches of muscle over his belly that his brother displayed. Owen was reading dramatic headlines from the North Wales Quarrymen's Union literature out loud in a dramatic voice.

'A red mist is descending... the men have had enou-ou-ough...' Owen sang.

'They will take up arms...' Huw sang in a high pitched tone.

'For they are not armless...' Owen lowered his voice to as deep a baritone as he could muster.

'No they are not aaaarmless...' Huw sang in an even higher pitch.

Owen collapsed on the bed laughing.

'Don't fill his head with politics,' Jacob said, picking up the bellows. 'Most of it is just hot air,' he blasted each word with a blast of the bellows.

'Yes, but look at the great fire that has just been set going.' Huw leaned around the door in the direction of his father who was opposite him at the far end of the room. 'Why should he not learn about politics father?' This was said in his usual, reasonable tones. And then, moving back to his position in front of the mirror he sang,

'Particularly if he is to go to the school in town?' Huw raised an arm to the ceiling in the manner of an opera singer. 'Go to school in tooown!' he sang in a high pitch to Owen. 'He must go to school in town, yes he must go to school in town, no pray do not frown, he must know the ways of the English gentlemen.' Huw was dancing around the room waving and lifting his imaginary skirts. 'Yes gentlemen. He must know the ways of English gentle-meeen.' Huw pitched his voice higher and higher until he ended with a screech.

Owen was curled up on Huw's bed laughing uncontrollably.

'To be independent, to preserve our language, these issues should be at the heart of any Welshman,' Huw said to his father, popping his head out of the room again.

'He will not be taught to be an independent Welshman at school in town,' Jacob said, sitting back down in his armchair and snapping his newspaper open again. 'He will be taught to be an Englishman with Tory leanings,' Jacob winked at Owen.

'I will never be taught to be an Englishman,' Owen said. 'I am Welsh mun!' Owen mimicked Llywelyn.

'It is our Nonconformist traditions that have saved our language, Huw. If it weren't for our Sunday Schools and our chapels, our Eisteddfods and our learning the scripture by rote, the English may have swallowed up our language,' he mimed a gulping sound at Owen. 'As Gladstone was glad to say, The Nonconformists of Wales are the people of Wales.'

'All good things Father, but there is talk of a youth labour party being formed. The young are tired of Liberalism father,' Huw said, combing his hair in the mirror. 'It has brought them wind off the mountains—they want something done about the Capitalists, the Tory landowners to whom they feel they are slaves. They need a party who will look after their own interests.'

'High drama indeed! They also need to respect the authority over them,' Jacob said.

'Those in authority need to respect and protect those under them,' Huw said. 'The battle will be between the working man and the capitalist,' Huw said popping his head around the door.

Jacob pursed his lips but nodded in agreement. 'True enough son, on both counts.'

'Provision must continue to be made for the widows and the orphans,' Anwen said, coming into the room with a basket full of dry washing that she had taken from the line outside. 'Lloyd

George is the man who cares about these matters,' Liberalism seems to be the only political movement that reflects the religion that Jesus gave us, to look after the widows and the orphans. 'I saw Mrs Ellis and her children this afternoon, Jacob, and she looked so old, but not yet thirty—and the children so ragged. And her poor husband—the coughing and the blood coming up in great spurts on the handkerchief. I have taken her washing in for this week and have asked Bethan and Eilwen to do the same next week and the one after. Heledd is going to take supper round tonight and the ladies from Band of Hope have formed a rota and are going to do the same for the foreseeable weeks,' Anwen put the basket on the table, then hands on hips, she arched her back and tipped her head back, emitting a great, loud yawn. 'A woman's work is never done,' she said with humour. She began lifting the sheets to fold. Owen got off the bed to help her.

'It's a great life, if you do not ail,' Jacob said with mischief. 'Do not slacken dear.'

Anwen threw one of his own freshly laundered singlets from the tub at him. Jacob caught it in his newspaper. 'A singular riposte,' Jacob said, in a silly foreign accent, throwing the singlet back. It landed in the basket, where Anwen snatched it up and folded it with a smile.

'Seriously, though, we must make sure to supply Mrs Ellis with fuel for the winter,' Jacob said.

'Huw, tell your labour party that provision should be made for the widows and the orphans. This was the work that the Lord gave us, but we are straining underneath it and it is worse in the valleys.'

'Keir Hardie cares about women's rights mother, and Robert Blanchford has a Women's Letter section in The Clarion.'

'Make sure you do not fall into the path of atheism by venerating man and his ideas over God's,' Jacob said. 'Ideology can very quickly become idolatry, my sons. It can be as *dangerous* for the man who is raised up as for the *followers*. We must pray for men like Gryff, who lead men in these new movements. If they lead men away from God, sooner or later they will fall on their own swords as Saul did.'

'As you have so often said yourself my love, Jesus was a great socialist,' Anwen said. 'He was so *moved* by the poor. Any great move of God will transform the very *fabric* of society for the better, as individuals themselves are transformed to be more like their creator—and this is what we know must come.'

'I agree with you my love,' Jacob said. 'I am asking Huw not to be unduly swerved by the politics of the mind. The mind has a way of building itself up and leaving the heart behind,' He got up and went to his desk to prepare himself for that evening's chapel meeting. Huw stood up and put on his cap and bent down to kiss his mother. 'You look after Owen and cover his ears if you need to,' she said, patting his cheek.

'And cover your own as well, should you need to,' Jacob said, picking up his notes.

Anwen stood on the doorstep watching her sons walk up the track. Meg stood in front of her, wagging her tail in anticipation of being fed.

'Don't get carried away now! Remember that Owen has chores in the morning—and you have work!' Anwen called after them.

Huw turned slightly from the track above the backfield and lifted his hand; the gesture caused in Anwen a momentary sorrow, perhaps for some future parting. Anwen dismissed the feeling by appreciating all that she had around her. The air was cooling and shadows lengthened across the yard; she loved the atmosphere on the smallholding when day surrendered to night. The three geese, 'The Watchmen,' as they were affectionately known, walked past and barked at Meg, who barked back. Anwen laughed and sat down with her tea on the step; she could hear the hens fussing in the henhouse. She thought of the conversation that had just taken place. Anwen sympathised with what lay behind recent politics, the church did need to be relevant to society, as Huw had warned; some of the younger women who attended Chapel meetings had said that they no longer felt church was the solution to today's social injustices. Anwen tried not to be hurt by these thoughtless comments, given she and Jacob were doing all they could to help the poor in their community; she was concerned that the new politics were becoming the new religion; in her mind, there was a battle between the spiritual world and the physical world that manifested in man-made ideas and movements. Anwen's mother had been a great admirer of Abraham Lincoln; she considered that the success of America was due to it having been founded on Christian principles and had used American history to illustrate the ways of justice and freedom to Anwen, teaching Anwen about the abolition of slavery and about the many ways that men and women could be enslaved; so it was that Anwen grew up understanding that freedom took place in the heart and that only Christianity made manifest in the individual and thence society brought true and lasting freedom. Clear as a bell, Anwen could hear her mother's voice, *Man-made ideas brought control in one form or another, and control eventually leads to death in one form or another. Christianity is freedom from start to finish.* In turn, Anwen taught her sons that man's highest ideals needed to come from the perfect law of the heart that Christ had preached; to her, the intellectual organisations that had been springing up more and more since the middle of the last century, often negated God and to Anwen's mind, were propelled by a satanic oppositional force intent on scuppering the force of God, though the men that strived for these high ideals were often good men. She was not against politics, believing as she did in a creative God of order who had given man the capacity to reason and order his world both rationally and creatively in turn; she applauded liberal thinking for the advancement of a just society, and admired politicians such as Lloyd George, and all that he was doing for Wales, particularly in arguing for disestablishment, but it disturbed her when politics raised the man above God. To her, the earth should mirror the heaven that it was birthed out of, with room for creative reflection and expression within that reflection. Anwen had found that some, though by no means all, of the men and women that scorned 'narrow' Christianity in favour of the religion of the intellect, were in fact, narrow-minded themselves, though they, from their exclusive viewpoint, did not seem to grasp this irony. She felt that God had given man the ability to reason, but man's reasoning needed to be sought in the courts of God, or the insidious logic of satanic reason would bring about the death of all things in keeping with its destructive desire masquerading as a truth more palatable to men than the true freedom of the gospel. Anwen got up to fill her cup. *History will prove that where God is taken out of the equation, chaos and disorder will be the end result*, she thought as she went inside.

The wind was howling as Owen and Huw made their way up steeper and steeper rocky paths to the cabanod, the smaller caban that was situated up in the galleries of the quarry, like a man made cave. Huw whistled as he went, his boots crunching on the slate-strewn path. Below them, the mountains lay before them like sleeping giants. Not many years ago, Owen used to imagine the mountains springing up during the night to trample over the cottages, crushing the bones of the district and burying them in the dust. Abandoned in the yard of the quarry below them, the railway and trolleys reminded Owen of a ghost train that he had seen illustrated in his book of American Stories. His short jacket rode up when he bent down and picked up bits of rock from the winding path and hurled them, watching them bounce and scatter down the mountainside. Huddled around a stove; the urn above steaming away for the tea, men in caps sat in a 'u' shape around the cabanod wall. Owen recognised Llywelyn and Bryn who were swigging out of a hip flask. Llywelyn was smoking a pipe, his legs crossed, one ankle bobbing up and down as he laughed at something Bryn was saying. Bryn was practically weeping with laughter as he held the flask out to the man next to him, who refused it.

'You willow branches! Will none of you drink like a man?' he said, still laughing.

The men gave Huw a rousing welcome and a few of them ruffled Owen's hair, which he found distinctly annoying given he was growing up and would probably soon be getting a scholarship to the school in town. He felt like telling the men that this was to be the case, but then reconsidered, as he thought it might come across as boastful and Huw hated boasters. The men made space on the bench for Huw; Owen sat on the floor and looked around at the men; even the young ones looked as crumpled in their faces as they did in their jackets. *They work too hard and die too soon*, people said of the quarrymen. Owen eyed a man who had one eye closed to the smoke curling upwards from his pipe like a toxic genie; he looked as ancient as father time, his cheeks so sunken they seemed to meet in the middle of his mouth. He stopped smoking and knocked the contents of the pipe on the floor, before filling his pipe again with tobacco from a tin that remained balanced on his knee, but for a slight wobble, as he hacked away on his cough. A man wearing a soft pale hat with a wavy brim asked Huw whether he thought revival would come and whether it would last.

'If revival brings one man to heaven's door it has served its purpose,' Huw said. 'And there have been many thousands of conversions on Welsh mountains and in the valleys due to the revivals.'

'Temperance!' A man said as he passed the flask on.

'A little drink never harmed anyone,' another said, taking a sip.

'And a stream leads to a river, mun!' the man next to Owen also refrained to drink and passed the flask on.

'My father says many travelled over the sea to Africa and India to be missionaries after the last revival.' Owen said.

'Well what good is that?' the man with the funny hat said. 'We need all the good Welshmen we can muster. Look at that lot drinking. It won't spare their wages and it's no example to set to this young fellow here, is it now? My brother left to become a missionary in Southern Rhodesia. We never heard from him again and wondered if he had been eaten by lions.'

'Perhaps he didn't like you,' Bryn said laughing with Llywelyn. 'For being dry,' Bryn guffawed, slapping his thigh with one hand and swigging with the flask from the other, he wiped his mouth and laughed some more as he handed the flask to Llewelyn who said 'Or on account of your wearing women's hats.' Bryn spluttered his drink with laughter and Llywelyn wheezed as he stuffed his pipe.

'You're a fine one to talk with your fancy Nancy ribbon on your hat,' the man said. 'You'd scare the crows in that.'

Llwelyn and Bryn laughed a little less, but the men around them laughed more.

Owen said, 'If he had the courage of David he would have slayed the lions with a slingshot.'

'And will you be a missionary? Perhaps you will slay some lions of your own?' The man in the funny hat said.

Owen began forming a reply, but the door opened and the men stood and cheered; all six feet and five inches of Gryff Thomas stood on the threshold, Edryd by his side. Owen later reflected that his words were smart-mouthed, and so he was glad he did not have a chance to utter them. Since his visionary experiences had become more frequent he found that he checked what he said more and more. Anwen had noticed this and had remarked that *God was changing him 'from glory to glory' and pride was always the thing that was crushed first. There is no power and no glory, not ever, in a man who is proud, my Owen. Humility and a teachable spirit will drive you to the heart of God like that drill you were so impressed with at the quarry.* He was left feeling relieved that he had been rescued from his own self-important musings.

'Men!' Gryff shouted. 'What would we do for an independent Wales! How do we feel about this land of ours? This spir-it-ual land of ours?' All this was said as he strode to the centre of the cabanod, with a swoop upwards of his fisted arm.

The men rose to their feet and cheered. 'Why is it that God pours out his spirit on Wales again and again? Could it be that there is something spe-cial about this land? Is this land saturated with God's pre-sence? Do these mountains and these valleys speak of his pre-sence more than the mountains and valleys of o-ther places? Does he feel an affin-ity with us as a people? Are we like the Israelites with their promised land?' Gryff said.

The men cheered and some stood up and waved their caps in the air.

'Men! The Lord wants to clear our land of heathen hands! We must have an independent Wales! We must protect this spir-it-ual land of ours. We must defend our language! We must defend the rights of our workers! Who is with me? Who will support me in my campaign? Let me have your names and the names of your families, so that we can make sure our lands are protected.' The men began to vocalise their support. 'Or would you have Englishmen ruling you from their castles? Mincing round on their horses, surveying their lands while we risk our lives to bring the slate that buys their fancy plates?' Gryff mimed a mincing lord. 'Creaming all the wealth wrung from the sweat of your brow?' The men were in an uproar; some waved their hats in the air. Huw wondered what his father would say to Gryff using spiritual language for political gain given Gryff had likely honed his rhetoric at the chapel meetings that he no longer attended. Owen was also being reminded of the great orators that he had seen speak in similar style at chapel meetings. Huw had noticed this happening more and more at union meetings and particularly when in discussion with the university students that he sometimes debated with in the public house in town. He had heard Christ's beatitudes had become platitudes on social justice, the life-transforming power sucked out of them; he had listened to his mother's young friend, Bethan, who often spoke about women being allowed the vote, speak of how radical it was of Jesus to approach the Samarian woman at the well; and of how much Jesus had done for women. Huw was moved by the injustices that he saw in his community and by the plight of some of the working men, not all of whom managed to join a bargain gang and had to make do with scrappy rock begged from the gangs that they tagged, and truthfully, Huw enjoyed being a rockman, he enjoyed the company of the men, and he stood in solidarity with them. He was comfortable at home too; he did not have a family yet, and the large proportion of his wages, combined with his father's, saw the Evans' living a reasonably comfortable life; he had money to buy the current affairs journals and magazines that he liked to read and he read about socialism with interest; agreeing with the philosophy in principle, but deep down his spirit agreed with his mother: without the supernatural power of the Holy Spirit acting in the heart, Christianity was a philosophy of the mind. It wasn't that the wisdom of the Proverbs or the benefit of God's teachings was completely nullified to the casual reader, but he felt that the power to fully live them out would never be there without the experiential Pentecostal power. Huw knew this because he had tasted that power when he had made the decision to be baptised on his thirteenth birthday. As he had come up out of the river, he had felt the power surge through him and he discovered that evening that he could speak in the heavenly language of tongues, as his mother did. He had practised this language, and during the time that he did, he found that he had a powerful influence in converting people to Christ. He spoke to quarrymen, shopkeepers, friends and associates and for a period of three years, he saw many hearts turned by the power generated through his words. In time however, Huw had stopped spending time praying in tongues and the distractions of life crowded his quiet times in communion with God in his bedroom or when out in the fields helping with the livestock. Huw was popular with his peers, and with the young ladies with whom he spoke at chapel or at the Eisteddfod's. He had been for walks with one or two and lately he had noticed that Bethan paid him particular attention despite the fact that she was older than him by at least ten years; and though he had a healthy attitude towards women, trying as he usually succeeded in doing, to see them as friends and equals, he noticed that when he prayed less, he dwelt on the fineness of their outward features more and then suffered guilt on their behalf. He realised that he was distracted by many things these days, and less and less so by God, unless he was provoked to think of him. The talk was still there and it came from inside him somewhere, but he felt as though his engine was idling and he lacked the inclination to get going again; but now, as he watched Gryff preach socialism, he felt a gentle stirring within him to preach the truth that he had always known. Perhaps if he began to preach he would reconvert himself in the process. He remembered the fire that had once burnt through him, ruining him but for the things of God; how powerfully the word of God spoke to him when he read it during the time when he first felt the Holy Spirit flowing through him. He glanced at his brother who was sitting on the floor, his arms wrapped around his raised legs, listening intently. His smooth, ivory-skinned face and prominent cheekbones were just like their mother's; his well-spaced, yet deep-set dark blue eyes were like Jacob's, as was his wide mouth. Owen was cut to the quick by Gryff's story of a woman in the valleys whose husband had been killed in a collapse. The mine owners had refused to pay her anything though they had paid her husband 'pittance,' as Gryff said. It was the union that helped pay for the funeral expenses of her husband and of her baby who died soon after. Huw recalled his brother coming to him a few months ago with a visual image that he had had concerning him. Owen had said that he had seen a mountain eroding in the rain and had told his brother that the mountain that was eroding was Huw's faith and that the rain was the emotion of God at the loss of his presence. Huw had been astonished, this wasn't the first time Owen had given him these visual statements, but this one did cause Huw to start reading the Bible again; he found he was stirring up the spirit within him more often in prayer and chapel debate too. Owen had begun relating these parabolic internal visions to the family as a small child, there were dreams too that came to pass; they were always accurate and contained information that only the recipient could know. Huw was protective over Owen because of his singular strangeness. Huw noticed that Owen spoke less about visions these days and wondered whether he had become self-conscious about them; he did not know about the strengthening effect that the angelic encounter had had on Owen and that Owen had learnt that he should not share everything that he saw, until or unless called upon to do so. The boys were very close despite their age gap. Huw knew that it was this closeness that had strengthened Owen in recent years; he had not noticed a shaking episode since Huw had left him on the mountain following Stephen's death, but Owen had also not had another close friendship since the death of Stephen and this concerned him. Huw thought that it would be good for Owen to do less drawing at home and have more scrapes with boys of his age and hoped that a friendship with Edryd might develop, though he was not sure his parents would want Owen to be friends with a boy from a political family, who did not attend chapel and was keen on football, a sport that the women of the temperance movement, did not approve of, given the drinking and ensuing violence that often went with club football. His mother still supported the temperance movement, though she went to many other women's meetings now, lobbying and writing letters as she did on behalf of many of the poorer women in support of their rights, despite the amount of work she did at home and in supporting the ministry. Huw knew she went to bed exhausted most nights, but she never complained. Gryff had finished his speech and was being clapped on the back by some of the men. Edryd was standing up and handing a notebook and pencil round. Huw noticed that The Independent Labour Party and the name of the district had been scrawled on the cover of the notebook in pencil. The word 'independent' had been underlined. All the men wrote their names in the book and paid their union fees as well. The book carried the complaints of the men regarding justice in the quarries: *Why should the English speaking, Anglican church going, quarry owners and their lackey stewards, get fat on the backs of men that died before they had reached the end of their fourth decade and not pay them properly or not at all if the conditions for quarrying were too wet on any given day? Why did they not ensure their conditions were safe? Or pay their widows when they were stone dead?* Huw was the last man to write his name, and as he reached up to hand the book back to Edryd, Owen asked if he could write his name in the book too. Gryff noticed and came over to express his thanks. Huw shook his hand and then Gryff offered his hand to Owen. As Owen took it, he pulled him to his feet.

'I like a man that knows his own mind,' he said to Owen. 'Well done my boy, write down your name.'

Edryd held out the book to him. He looked a smaller version of his father, straight black hair all over his skull like paintbrush bristles and deep furrowed brows made for contemplating Wales.

'One day your name will be written in Welsh history books. I can always tell a man marked for greatness, and you are one of those men,' Gryff said.

So the man is a prophet too, Huw thought. Owen felt his face heating up; he did not know the strange ways of his own mind and heart and was not sure whether he liked the attention of this big man or not; though he felt it might help his cause with Edryd, so he doffed his cap, which made everyone laugh though that was not his intention.

July

Chapter 14

On a night that was crisp and clear, the Evan's family were having a quarryman's supper of five minute potatoes and discussing the good news of Owen's scholarship, when Martyn arrived early to meet Jacob for their usual prayer walk.

'Forgive me for being early Jacob, Anwen—'

Your sins are forgiven my friend,' said Jacob.

Martyn laughed at his friend's joke. 'John Parry and Dafydd Baines from our denomination in South Wales have agreed to come to North Wales to speak on the revival. Jacob, let us act in faith and send all over the district. They can come next week.'

'Where will we seat them all Martyn?' Jacob said.

'God will make a way! Martyn said. What do you say Jacob? Shall I send the wires?'

'Father,' Owen said. 'Anna told Mother and I that revival would come through the southern gateways and spread to the north by Christmas.'

Jacob looked at Anwen, who nodded.

'Send them, Martyn. We will trust God to fill the chapels, seated or not.'

After supper Bethan dropped in on her way back from the Woman's Suffrage Meeting at chapel. Her eyes were red from crying.

At the dining table, Owen concentrated on his illustrated magazine. He was reading about Christopher Columbus and his first landing in the pacific. In the margins of the magazine, he sketched the aboriginal pacific islanders that Columbus described, given the magazine only had an illustration of the ship out at sea with the islands in the distance.

Bethan grabbed Anwen's upper arm. 'It's coming isn't it Anwen? On my way here, I was full of feeling for the injustices of this world, for why should poorer men and women be discriminated against? Then I looked up at the sky and the stars and the moon and I thought of that night in Bethlehem with the three men following the stars. It was as if the stars spoke to me of something coming—as if the sky was about to break open, and I could feel creation willing Him to come!'

'Have you seen the moon?' She led Anwen to the window. 'Look at that. I'm sure it's a sign. It looks as though it's about to explode and shower us with the gold of heaven.'

Anwen moved her blue jug and oil lamp to the side of the window ledge. The rich yellow moon was fat with promise in a sky bursting with stars.

'It is unusually beautiful,' Anwen said, peering out of the window. 'Most unusual indeed.'

'Come Holy Spirit!' Bethan said.

Huw opened the door at that moment and came in to the room. 'Oh! You're not the Holy Spirit!' Bethan laughed.

'Well no, and yes.' Huw said. 'Clearly I am me and not the Holy Ghost personified, but I carry him within me.'

Owen rolled his eyes and Anwen laughed. 'Bethan was just calling for the Holy Spirit to come.'

'And look what she got instead,' Owen said, shading the waves on his beach. 'A circus clown.'

'Well then,' Huw said. 'It seems your prayers have been answered. He has come,' he sat down at the table.

'What are you saying Huw?' Anwen asked, gripping Bethan's arm as they too went to sit down.

Jacob and Martyn returned from their prayer walk.

'Father,' Huw said. 'Send the wires. It has begun. I have just come from town. Some of us from the Sunday School, decided to go and speak to the university students that were in the public house.'

'Drinking with the thinking men Huw?' his father said as he hung his hat and coat up.

119

'There were a few of them. I was with Margaret and Florence as well—they did not drink in case you are wondering father, but I tell you it does not matter. God is not concerned whether I had a pint of ale or not. He is concerned about people's soul's father—'

Martyn and Jacob sat down at the dining table. Anwen put her hand on her husband's arm and urged Huw to go on.

'When we arrived, some of them were having a heated debate about the revival reports coming in from the south,' Huw said. 'One of them said that the news disturbed him and that he did not know what to make of it. The other two were mocking and scornful. One of them denied the existence of God and the other said it was not possible to prove the existence of God. I introduced myself to them, and the lads and ladies sat down.'

'And rightly so,' said Bethan referring to the fact that the ladies sat down in a place where they did not usually go.

Huw smiled at Bethan. 'Yes indeed, but these are missionary ladies, imbibing nothing more than the Holy Spirit.'

Huw leaned his forearms across the table to where his father and Martyn were sitting. 'A boldness came upon me father and I asked them whether they thought it possible that the existence of God could be proved. They laughed and asked whether I was the man to prove it. The publican was eyeing me like I was a fox after his hens so I suggested we step outside. The man who had denied that God existed joked that perhaps I was preparing to beat the truth into them. I replied that I was going to show them.'

'Did you have something in mind?' Bethan asked, gripping the back of Owen's chair.

'To be honest with you Bethan, I did not,' Huw smiled at Bethan.

'He was moving in faith Jacob,' Martyn said.

'Go on son,' Jacob said, putting his arm around Anwen.

'We stood outside on the forecourt—and I looked up at the sky to pray inwardly. As I did so, I noticed that the stars were particularly sharp and the moon seemed full of promise—'

'I felt that tonight myself,' Bethan said. She placed her hand on the back of Huw's chair. Then, as if realising her gesture was inappropriate, she took her hand back quickly.

Owen watched Bethan's face as she watched his brother. If he were drawing, his brother's outstretched arms would fill the page like spread wings with Bethan's profile appearing from the wings; the rest of his family would be partly hidden by Huw's arms.

'Outside, they were still laughing and joking,' Huw said. 'I had no idea how I was going to prove God to them, so as I was inwardly praying, I asked them to look up. They did. I asked them who put the stars in the sky. One of them said nothing, the atheist continued to mock saying, *Isn't beauty random? And sometimes cruelly so?* The agnostic joked that beauty was cruel mockery to the ugly, and said that if there were a divine hand we would never see it until we are dead. The one who was saying nothing continued to stare at the heavens. When I asked him what it was that he saw, he claimed that the stars had gone from white to blue as he looked at them. The others laughed with astonishment because apparently this young man was the most philosophical amongst them. He seemed quite jittery and asked the others if they sensed something in the air. I said that I did — that there was indeed a sense that something was gathering in the atmosphere. I felt it right to ask the Holy Spirit to make himself known to the young man, whose name was Robert. I suggested he held his hands out, palms up. As he did his hands began to tremble. It came to the point that his hands were flapping rapidly, and then his arms too. His friend joked that he looked as though he was about to take off. Robert began to shout that there were currents going through his hands and travelling up his arms. He said that he could see the currents and they were like blue flame. The atheist was still joking that his friend had had too much to drink, but the other believed in what was happening to his friend. I sensed that the Holy Spirit was saying that this man had a healing anointing and told him so.

'Yes, quite so,' Martyn said. 'Well done lad,' Martyn tapped his fingers on the table in his enthusiasm.

'He was dumbfounded by what was happening to him. People were coming out of the public house now, so I suggested to Robert that we test this power that was coursing through him on the infirm.

'Rightly so!' Martyn said, slapping the table.

I jumped up on the low wall and called out to the sick, explaining that Robert had just received power from God to heal, and if anyone wanted a touch of it in turn they should gather round. Well, Mother,' Huw said to Anwen, reaching for her hand. 'No less than twenty gathered round for healing and this is what happened. Gwynfor Bevan was thrown to the floor under the power when Robert laid hands on him. He was literally blown across the yard like a leaf. When he got up he said his leg had straightened and the hip pain that had plagued him from birth was gone. Mother, his hunched shoulders sort of unrolled before our eyes—it was phenomenal—I still can't take it in.'

Anwen began to laugh. 'Oh Bethan,' she said to her friend, her head tipped back on Jacob's shoulder.

'Mother, Bethan, when Aron Hughes got up he was stone cold sober and so full of the awe of God that he said he would *never* drink again.'

Bethan clapped her hands. 'And there will at last be a smile on Gwyneth Hughes' face,' the women laughed.

'And love rekindled,' Anwen said. 'All that woman needs is some due care and attention.'

Owen groaned and ran his fingers through his hair.

'Put the kettle on my love,' Anwen said.

Owen got up from the table. 'Tea, always tea,' he said.

'The same thing happened to Branwen Lewis,' Huw said. 'She stood there with her arms raised for some time after Robert prayed for her, her face changed completely, she was like a young girl again. The years of drinking and pipe-smoking just melted off her face. She ran off to find her Bible.'

Anwen had her hand clasped to her throat. 'Oh Jacob, we are seeing our prayers come to pass. Praise God.'

'Mother,' Huw said. 'The best case was Dai Bevans. As you know he has been completely deaf since childhood.'

'Father, he began uttering sounds—and then he copied the words I spoke. Father you must go and see him for yourself tomorrow.'

Anwen and Bethan became tearful. 'He is here in greater

measure.' Anwen said, her eyes shining.

'As Dafyd's leg testifies,' Owen said.

Everyone laughed, but none more so than Martyn who found it difficult to stop and had to cough to do so.

'See now you have made the ladies weep, Huw,' Jacob said. He was struggling with his emotions, thinking of the many times he had prayed for Dai to be healed.

Anwen knew what he was thinking and hugged him to herself.

'Robert has asked me to join him at the university tomorrow. He would like me to preach the gospel and then he intends to give his testimony.'

'The power is unbelievable—and transferable—you know Mother!' Huw said.

'I know my son, I know!'

Jacob loosened his grip from his wife's shoulder and looked down at her face. 'How do you know my dear? In what sense do you *know*?'

'It was in the cowshed—'Anwen laughed some more and Bethan joined in.

'What was in the cowshed?' Jacob asked his wife.

Bethan, who had come to stand with her friend too, was also gripped with laughter.

'See?' Anwen said. 'It's ca—ca—catching,' she clutched Bethan's arm in her hilarity.

Jacob pushed his chair away from his wife's and arms folded observed her now bending over laughing, clutching her knees. Huw's eyes were shining with amusement. Jacob began to get a little impatient, which seemed to make his wife laugh even more, and then so much so that she could not speak. Every time she touched Bethan, she too would become convulsed with laughter. Owen, who had returned from setting the kettle on, stared at his mother with amusement.

'The—the—the,' Anwen was crying with laughter.'

'The what my dear wife?' Jacob asked becoming impatient.

'The cow pats?' Owen offered, taking up a pencil from a jar on the table. 'They're always in the cowshed and too many of them too.'

Anwen was clutching her sides now and Bethan, gripping her

friends arm was bent double with laughter too. 'It's catching isn't it?' Anwen looked at her friend and practically howled with laughter.

Bethan nodded and wheezed with laughter. Owen caught his brother's eye.

'Yes Father. It is catching and it is transferrable.'

'It's the joy of the Lord,' Martyn said, standing up and moving over to Jacob. 'I've not seen it like this before. A merry sight indeed is it not my friend?'

'I have work to do,' Jacob said, beginning to walk away.

Huw stood up. The women continued to laugh.

'Father for goodness sake. No for God's sake and for ours, please sit down.'

'Let us hear the end of the story, please Jacob,' Martyn said.

Jacob sat back down. Anwen was still laughing.

'I met the Holy Spirit in the cowshed when I was milking. He asked me if I was—' she collapsed again in a fit of giggles. 'He asked me if I was ready for something stronger than milk.' Anwen dried her eyes.

'What audibly?' Jacob looked confused.

'I don't know' Anwen said, stopping her laughter for a moment. 'Loud enough for me to hear—in my spirit—my heart—my thoughts—I caught it—I know that—'

Bethan shrieked with laughter as Anwen uttered the words 'caught it,' grabbing her friend's arm at the same time.

'I felt the power go through me. It was so strong I had to ask the Spirit to—' Anwen started to laugh again, 'to turn it down a little, so that I could live,' she laughed. Martyn and Huw were laughing too.

'Oh my beloved Jacob, forgive, me, it's just that I am so, I became so, I am so, filled with joy, I cannot describe it—and what has been with me since the death of—' Anwen held the gaze of her disapproving husband.

Jacob raised his hand to indicate that he had heard enough. Anwen reached out to her husband.

'Beloved, I am sorry, I will try not to laugh -'

But even as she said the words, Anwen laughed all the harder.

Jacob began to walk away, 'I will be at the chapel. I need to pray. I think my wife may have gone mad.'

At this, Anwen stopped laughing and dried her eyes. 'Forgive me beloved. I don't want to offend you, nor anyone.'

'I will join you shortly Father. I hope to get involved with the prayer meetings,' Huw said.

Jacob raised his arm in agreement and walked out into the night.

Martyn put his hat and coat on before returning and patting Anwen's arm. 'I am delighted for you. I can see it is God. And if there is anyone who deserves joy it is you Anwen.'

Anwen put her hand momentarily on Martyn's. 'Thank you dear Martyn—and thank you for the friend you are to him.'

Martyn placed his hands on Anwen's shoulders and looking over at Huw for a moment too, he said: 'The fire has begun to take hold. I pray it will consume us all for the Lord Jesus Christ, and spread like wildfire!'

'Well did you get something stronger than milk?' Owen asked as Martyn went out of the door.

Anwen got up and went and put her arms around her son.'

'Yes I did. I had to say 'yes' though. You have to ask to receive.'

'Well you didn't ask. He just came into the cowshed. Uninvited.'

'This is true, my dear one, but I had to say yes when He,' she began to giggle again, 'when He, when he asked if I would like something stronger.'

'Well you do look as though you have had something stronger, Mother.'

Everyone laughed at this.

'What happened after you said yes?' Huw asked.

'My whole body was filled with what felt like fire. And I was shuddering so much that I scared Bessie,' she began to laugh until she cried and could hardly get her next words out. 'Who produced—who produced a—a—a cowpat. But since then,' she hugged Owen. 'I have been filled with unspeakable joy.'

'Jesus was born in a cowshed,' Owen said. 'He obviously likes them.' And they all fell about laughing again.

After Bethan had left, Anwen took the slop bucket and went outside to throw the contents to the pigs. The mountains were shrouded in a heavy mist that crept over the stone wall and hung over the front yard like an ethereal blanket waiting to drop. The pigs rushed at the potato and turnip peelings, their snouts fossicking over the food like separate beasts. She was concerned by Jacob's reaction to her admittedly unusual encounter with the Holy Spirit and began to pray that they would be of one mind. *Please bring harmony to us Lord. Discord will only hinder your work, please keep us alert to the enemy's subtle work at this time. It is the little foxes that spoil the vine.* She recalled watching Jacob preach for the first time; she had been ashamed of the feelings he aroused in her. Alarmed by the potency of her feelings, she had decided to give him up before he had even indicated to her that he was going to propose anything other than friendship. During his training for the ministry, her father had become his mentor and in the evenings, during his visits to the family home, he had given Anwen no indication of feeling for her, even though it had obviously been attraction to her that had brought him to the chapel the first time they met. They would sit at dinner, discussing church matters; passing the potatoes, or the butter, just as if he was any other ministry friend. Anwen, tried not to notice the way his hair curled against his temple, or the way that his dark eyes lit up when he discussed the state of the nation and how the church was not reaching the people as it needed to. This went on for weeks, until one day she met him on the road on her way to the quarry hospital to visit a family friend. Jacob had jumped down from the cart and insisted on giving her a lift to the hospital even though she protested that she would rather walk. On the way to the hospital, he told her that he had made up his mind to marry her and would she spend some time praying and considering whether she felt the same? Anwen was taken by surprise. Jacob spoke about marriage as if he was commenting on the stooks of corn that were gathered in the field that they were passing. He said he would give her twenty-one days to pray and then he would ask her again. Anwen went to the hospital, where she had sat praying with Mrs Barry who was ill with pneumonia, whilst she tried to keep her mind from wandering; she remembered staring at the starched cap of the nurse as she came in to take the bedpans and knowing then that she would marry Jacob. She spent the next twenty-one days praying for signs that she should not marry him, but none came. They were married in the community chapel where her father was minister. Jacob worked in the quarry until he had finished his ministerial studies, and they were able to buy the smallholding with a small inheritance that he received from his father. It was Jacob that gave her the news that her brother had died at the age of thirty-seven during a rockslide following a detonation on the mountain. And it was Jacob too, that gently told her that her father had died in his sleep. Her father had been a big man in stature as well as in society; and as a teenager, she had wondered whether she would ever find a man that could fill his boots. She sat on the step, her eyes full of tears at the knowledge that she had and also for inadvertently hurting him.

Chapter 15

Early on a Saturday afternoon, Huw had recently returned from his half day at the quarry and the family were at table about to partake of Anwen's pork and leeks when there was an urgent knock at the door. Lloyd Morgan, Evan Morgan's son stood on the threshold trembling.

'Come inside boy and warm yourself,' Jacob said, putting down his fork.

'There has been word that the men are going to kill my father for being a blackleg. And not just him—the others too—they want to remove the cottages.' Lloyd was panting with the exertion of running. 'Rhys Davies is baying for blood—you must stop them Minister Evans, you are the man of God.'

'When will this nonsense end!' Anwen said.

Jacob stood, and asked Huw to hitch the cart.

'We will find them on the road and warn them,' Jacob said. 'We will need to have words with Rhys too or he will only plot again.'

'Would it not be better to go and intercept them all? We cannot guarantee some of the men having split up before they pass the pub?' Huw said.

Owen got up and Jacob told him to sit down again. 'I will stay in the cart and pray, I promise father!' Owen walked towards the door and his parents did not stop him. After they had gone, Anwen stared at the flecks of thyme in the gravy on her plate, and prayed for their return. The wind howled around the cottage, but the silence pressed in on her. She picked up her fork again, but found she did not have the heart to eat; instead she sat in the gathering darkness thinking of Rhys Davies' gigantic misshapen knuckles, spread by contact on men's faces. *Rhys Davies Fighter! He will fell you in one blow!* So the posters for his fights gaily announced. On the mantelpiece above the range, the double dial clock ticked away the minutes, the calendar beneath it pointing to a day in the month that arrived naked and unashamed. Anwen prayed until she grew cold enough to stoke the fire and the evening chores could be put off no longer.

When Jacob, Huw and Owen arrived at the public house the scene was normal. They pulled up under an ash tree near the outer wall, so that they were obscured from the buildings. Beyond the front yard, men and women could be seen through the windows of the Railway Tavern. Rowdy, but not angry sounds came from the packed interior that could be seen through the open door as people jostled with tankards of beer and ale, joking as they pushed through the crowds, merry that it was the end of the working week and that Saturday afternoon had come at last.

'Run along son,' Jacob said to Lloyd as he got down from the cart. 'You can tell your mother we are here, but it is better she waits at home for your father to return.'

Lloyd stared up at him hesitating. Owen could see that he wanted to say something and felt sorry for him; he watched him turn to go and then Owen saw him hesitate again before walking off. Owen jumped off the back of the cart and ran after him.

'Was there something you wanted to ask my father?' Owen asked, raking his hair with both hands.

'No.' Lloyd said and continued to walk away.

'Are you sure?' Owen said. 'I could ask him for you.'

Lloyd did not turn round. 'I was going to ask him to pray. I know that's what my mother would have asked him.'

'I will ask my father to pray,' Owen said. He watched Lloyd walk away, thinking with shame how he had not defended him the day at school when Lloyd was verbally attacked by some of the other boys for his father's stance; but Owen had felt weary of fighting his own fights; he had felt even worse when he remembered how Lloyd's little brother had died of tuberculosis because his parents could not afford to send for the doctor and his father had been banned from the quarry hospital during the lockout.

Owen bolted off the wall and ran to his father who was deep in conversation with Huw. 'Lloyd asked that you pray Father,' Owen said.

Jacob nodded at his son, said that he would and told him to hop back up in the cart with Huw.

'Don't hesitate to leave if you need to,' Jacob said to Huw. 'Owen, run inside if you need to.'

'I will not need to leave without you father,' Huw said, putting his arm around his brother and leading him back to the cart.

Jacob said nothing, though he was proud of his son. He glanced at his pocket clock and then up the mountain road. The quarrymen would have clocked off over an hour ago, to begin the walk of several miles around the mountains, making their way on foot to the new settlement of houses just below the public house where they now stood. The sky that Jacob scanned as he prayed was slate-grey, white with swirling cloud, lit pale yellow beneath. As Jacob prayed, his face raised, mist descended, obscuring the road completely. Rhys Davies came out of the public house chewing tobacco. He spotted them from half way across the courtyard.

'You are a long way from home Jacob.'

'My home is where God's work is.'

Rhys rolled his eyes to the heavens he did not believe in. The mist was on the road now, curling and dispersing amongst the rocky mounds buried in the short grass lying either side of the road.

'It will be an act of God that prevents what's coming here today, Jacob,' Rhys picked tobacco from his teeth.

'I pray that will be the case.'

'If you warn them, Jacob, I cannot answer for what may happen,' Rhys spat on the ground. Jacob did not show his disgust for the spitting habit that Rhys employed.

'I understand the cause of the working man, Rhys, but what you are working for is finite. You must also consider what is infinite. I do, however, apologise for the failures of the church—'

'What do you understand? Apologising on behalf of the

church are you? Who—do—you—think—you—are?' Rhys jabbed his finger in Jacob's face as he said each word.

On the cart, Owen felt a bristling in his body. He found it hard to put Catrin and Rhys together in his mind as father and daughter; he decided that he hated Rhys and would have liked it if his father planted him one there and then, but he knew there was as much chance of that as Rhys Davies curtseying while whistling the English anthem.

'The men have had all they can take of living alongside traitors,' Rhys said, bringing his face close to Jacobs as he slammed his right fist into the palms of his left hand.

Owen jumped off the cart to look for stones.

'Get up here Owen' Huw said. 'You won't be throwing stones. You will be staying here to drive the cart if necessary.'

Owen got back onto the cart, stuffing a couple of stones into his pocket as he did so, he would drive like a merry clipper if he had to.

'I am not threatened by you Rhys,' Jacob said, not moving. 'You seem to forget that I was a quarryman once.'

'And did you fight for the rights of the common mun?' Rhys swiped a strand of long black hair from his cheek.

'Perhaps not in the way that you fight Rhys.'

'Ah, you make me sick mun!—with your lofty ways and your high talk.' Rhys spun on his heel. Get out of it!' he flicked the back of his hand upwards, an incongruously effeminate gesture in Owen's eyes, given he was a bare knuckle fighter.

'Think of the consequences for you and your family,' Jacob called to Rhys as he walked towards the road.

Rhys spat more tobacco on the ground and Huw jumped down from the cart where he was sitting holding Rosie's reins. 'Easy son,' Jacob said.

'Yes, jump back up on the cart where you belong, boy,' Rhys said. 'A rockman now are you? Could you not find yourself an honest job like your father?'

Huw said nothing as he got back into the cart; he was not easily provoked, though he would always step in to defend someone. Huw found something lacking in Rhys' character; he hated dishonesty and provocation, preferring men who said what they meant; he felt Rhys was using the situation to his advantage, to further his position in the union; it was power that held meaning for Rhys Davies and he sucked power from fear whilst neglecting his family; his cause might be just, but his motives and his means, were impure. The sound of whistling could be heard, this was followed by the faint sound of many boots on the road that was still swirling with mist. Rhys gave a low whistle and ten or fifteen men came out of the public house and began to congregate in the front yard near the road. Some of the men began to joke.

'Come to preach a sermon Jacob?'

'Collecting alms for the poor?'

There was laughter, but the atmosphere was tense. The whistling grew louder and the sound of quarrymen's boots became stronger as their percussion flooded the valley road above.

'Men!' Jacob addressed the strikers.

The steady march of the boots became louder, ringing out through the valley.

'This is no place for a minister.' Rhys shouted, turning to engage the men who were with him.

The boots became louder still.

'Go home quietly now, Jacob,' Rhys said, he was swaying as if about to face a boxing opponent.

As he watched, Owen pictured a swaying cobra preparing to strike. He checked the position of the reins and the way that Huw had looped Rosie's knot to the lower branch of the tree they were under; his hands were sweating and he kept running them through his hair creating waves that he did not see. Huw sat, his elbows on his knees, perfectly calm. The men's boots announced their imminent arrival. Jacob went and stood in the middle of the road facing the pub so that he had a good view of the road in both directions. The men looked to Rhys.

'Don't be foolish Jacob,' Rhys said.

The first men to come down the road caught sight of Jacob but did not recognise him at first.

'Hello there, are you lost traveller?'

'The public house is behind you!' Another joked.

The strikers came up behind Jacob and stood in the road; the quarrymen became aware of what was going on and began to shout at those behind them. 'It's a trap! Go back!'

But the men continued to come, stepping through the mist like ghostly figures.

'Black legs!' Rhys shouted. 'Traitors! Call yourselves Welsh-men? Why do you not go and work in England?

The men took up the chorus.

'Or emigrate?'

'You are not wanted here!'

'How can you show your faces?'

This last was said with a shove to the chest by a striker to a quarryman; the man fell to the ground and soon strikers were kicking him, over and over again, as if he were the quarry, the steward and Lord Penhurst all rolled into one man. Owen prayed that it was not Lloyd's father that was being kicked; he searched in vain for Stephen's father too. Huw stood up to see what was happening. Both sides were tearing into each other. Men were kicking and punching. Owen saw Rhys smash his forehead into the nose of another and heard a crack. The centre of the man's face resembled smashed strawberries. Owen felt nausea swell within him. Rhys wiped at his head and looked round; spotting another victim, he ran and jumped on his shoulders from behind, wrestling him to the ground. This time he was not so fortunate. The man who had been attacked managed to straddle him and in so doing, Rhys hit his head on a low rock on the side of the road. The quarryman began punching him over and over, shouting as he did so. Rhys' head began to swell and change colour as it was battered this way and that. The man above began to lessen the impact of his blows as he tipped his head back and screamed at the sky. Owen realised that the man was crying. Now he pummelled the fleshy parts of his fists into Rhys' chest, but now not in fury, but in something like exasperation. Huw came over and gently pulled the man off Rhys. Then he took hold of Rhys under his arms and pulled him towards the low wall that ran around the yard of the public house, and ran inside to get help. Owen recognised Evan Morgan. Evan, who was well into his forties but fit and strong from his work at the quarry, got up slowly and went and sat down on the low stone wall, not far from Rhys who lay against the wall like a wounded soldier; Evan ignored Rhys, but looked at the men who were still fighting; shirts were being ripped and hats pulled from heads, a man was red in the face from his tie being pulled by another man. Evan put his head in his hands and began to weep; huge sobs racked his shoulders. Jacob was trying in vain to pull men apart. Huw, who had run over to help Jacob, shouted over to Owen to untie Rosie and get under the sacks in the back of the cart and to hold on to the front rim. Owen did as he was told and as soon as he had, he saw Huw run back to him and shouting at Rosie, he jerked on her reins. The cart sprang forward and Huw jumped into the seat. Huw drove the cart straight through the fighting men who scattered. Huw pulled up near his father and told Jacob to get in. After looking around for a moment, Jacob got in. Some of the men had been knocked over by the cart or flung to the side of the road. The fighting had stopped. Jacob stood up in the cart.

'You should be ashamed of yourselves! Ambushing men in the road. It is cowardly.' He looked down at Rhys. 'This is an act of the small-minded. You may not agree with these men going back to work, and that is your right. But if the Lord God gave us all the right to choose whether we accept him or go our own way, you too should give these men the right to go their own way if they choose to,' he turned to sit down, but then turned back. 'I will pray that both sides find the freedom of forgiveness, so that this bitter virus will cease. I hope you will all do the same.'

Owen thought that some of the men looked ashamed, but many of them just looked shocked and confused about what had just happened with the cart; some had faces and shirts dark with blood. Rhys glared at Jacob with hatred; the features of his face, already softened by years of bare-knuckle fighting, had lost their definition to the swelling that was increasing. Jacob met his stare. Owen did not see him return hatred; he saw reflected there, sadness but also the fire of conviction. Huw jumped to the ground to tend to Rhys who had tried to get up, but had fallen back down.

'Father!' Huw shouted. 'We must take Rhys to the hospital.'

'Get in the cart,' Jacob said, sitting down.

'Over my dead body,' Rhys said, his words slurring in his

bloodied mouth.

'The choice is yours Rhys,' Jacob said

Two men came to help Rhys up. They began walking him into the pub; John Isaacs, the publican, came out and made his way over to Rhys; he was a friend of Rhys' who had invested money in his fights; Huw speculated that he and his wife would no doubt tend to him, given the commodity that he was.

'You haven't heard the last of this,' Rhys shouted at Jacob as he walked away with John and the two men. At the door to the pub, Rhys looked back at them. Owen thought that Rhys might have spat in the dirt at that point, were he able to without looking lame. A quarryman with an injured leg was grimacing with pain as his friends helped him to stand on his good leg. Jacob helped Huw to get the injured man onto the cart where Owen was making a bed out of bran sacks. Most of the men were walking away; some were doubled over slightly from the blows that they had received. Others seemed dazed but appeared to have no injuries. Owen pointed out another man who was bleeding heavily from a cut above his eye. After helping his father, Huw held out his hand to the man who was bleeding. The man hesitated when he saw the quarryman in the cart.

'I'll not ride with him,' he said, glancing in Rhys' direction.

'Don't be foolish man—you're bleeding. That wound needs tending to,' Jacob said.

'Throw him off then. He is a blackleg.'

'He is a man with an injured leg who is going to be taken to the hospital,' Jacob said. 'Get in and sit down man.'

'I will not sit with that man,' the bleeding striker said.

'Suit yourself,' Jacob said, moving to the front of the cart and sitting down on the seat, 'I have had enough foolishness for one night and for one day.'

Huw sprang up beside him, Owen sat on the toolbox at the back of the cart. Jacob pulled gently on the reins and Rosie walked slowly away. They broke into a trot as they made their way back up the road, leaving the man with the blood rivering down his face standing in the yard of the public house staring after them. Owen watched the figure of the man slowly recede in to the distance; he continued to gaze at the yard and at the man, until the road began to curl around the solemnly dark mountains and he could see the scene no more. It seemed to Owen that it was the mountains that were shifting and moving around the cart, inspecting the foolishness of men, rather than being observed by the people far beneath them. The man did not move, despite the large gash in his thigh that Owen tried not to look at. Owen wondered where his friends were and why they did not wait for him; he remembered a man helping him to his feet, but he had not come with him to the cart.

As Jacob drove home, he was relieved that events had not become worse, but his main emotion was sorrow. Rhys' words echoed in his mind *What do you understand? Apologising on behalf of the church are you? Who—do—you—think—you—are?* He felt genuine grief that Rhys seemed to feel that there was no understanding between the chapel and the working man—what had he called him?—*lofty.* Did he speak down to men? *Forgive me if I have—if I do Lord. I don't want to have the sin of pride—if I am Lord—please forgive me.* Jacob let his tears flow, but he prayed that these were not tears of pity for himself; he thought of how he might come across to his fellow man and felt shame; but the shame brought with it a resolve to try to come to a new place of understanding with these men that he often visited to resolve disputes; and the men generally responded, at least with their words, but did he come alongside them—even with the solidarity of brotherhood? He was aware that there was indeed a chasm between them. He heard Huw's words in his mind: *The church has to be relevant Father.* These men were raised in the chapels, but they were turning to new philosophies and responding with the dead ways of the world, that led to the continuous bitterness that wrecked lives. *Oh God, give them a revelation of their slavery, followed hard by the true freedom of the cross!* He remembered the many times he had asked the Lord for a teachable spirit; and now that he had experienced what that looked like, he laughed respectfully at the ways of God: so not like the ways of man. *I came to resolve a battle and one was resolved within me.* He recalled the words of 2 Corinthians 5 verse 17, *Therefore if any man be in Christ, he is a new creature: old things are passed away; behold, all things are become new.*

'It's always darkest before the dawn, Father,' Huw said. 'In the face of opposition, let us believe the dawn of revival has truly come.'

Jacob smiled at Huw and urged Rosie on.

Chapter 16

Owen woke at dawn. He heard his mother get out of bed and walk from her bedroom to put more peat on the fire, before the clang of the milk pail signalled she was going outside to do the milking. An hour later when she returned to start that morning's baking, he was still lying there going over the previous evening's events in his mind. His father and his brother had become heroic characters in a book; he had seen them in a familiar, yet unrecognisable light; when the men had approached on either side he had been afraid but also excited: with beating heart, he had been caught up in a strange suspension; wanting to run and help his father, but compelled to watch and see what would happen. There was a moment when his fear had dissipated and he knew that his father, who was standing in the middle of the road, with men coming at him from either side, was capable of parting the red sea. His father was the one who carried something that the men on both sides recognised; his father, as he stood there, waiting as the quarrymen's boots became louder on the road, was immovable. Owen knew that it was his father's faith that kept him rooted there, but he wondered whether he had been afraid; had he been, it did not show. Rhys and the men did not want him there, but they were unable to move him. Perhaps his father was the act of God that the Rhys had mentioned. Rhys was known as a powerful fighter; a man that instilled fear in even his closest friends, yet it was Evan Morgan that felled him, not the other way round. If Rhys was vengeful before, Owen imagined he would want to tear Evan's throat out now. Owen wondered whether his father was displeased with Huw for engaging Rosie in the battle, and about what might have happened if Huw had not charged into the crowd. They had dropped the man off at the quarry hospital late that night; a stretcher had been brought and he was put on it and then taken into the quarry hospital. Owen thought of the man's leg as he had seen it lying on the ground, his trousers soaked and the flesh livery and exposed.

At school that morning, the children rushed him, wanting details. During the drill as the children moved the wooden hand weights above their heads, Owen noticed that the children of the men that had moved to the south and the ones who had stayed, divided themselves on either side of him. The former kept away and the latter were friendlier to him. The girls too, were behaving in the same way; little gifts of cake, marbles and feathers appeared in his desk. Lloyd came and spoke to Owen after the drill. Owen asked how Lloyd's father was; he saw that Lloyd was hoping for friendship with him, but Owen did not know how to make that happen; he felt no natural affinity with this boy apart from the fact that they were connected by the previous night's events; he wondered whether Lloyd was hoping that Owen would protect him, but Owen was not prepared to shelter him; he would have to face this and walk through it, because even if Owen chose to shelter him, he could not shelter him at all times.

In the classroom that day, Owen wrote his essay on the Welsh migration to Patagonia in 1886, in a quick, creative burst. Afterwards, without thinking, he began drawing in the margins of his copybook; he drew the ship carrying the Welsh migrants over the sea in rough waters; he imagined the fear of the people on board ship, some of whom had never been off dry land; he drew the waves threatening to come over the ship and in the waves, horses leaping out of the surf.

'What are you doing boy?'

Owen looked up at the face of his schoolmaster and found he could not speak.

'I said what are you doing? Are you deaf as well as dumb?'

'I am not dumb sir.' Owen replied.

Owen was given a blow to the side of the head.

'You will be now,' said one of the boys, a striker's son.

'You be quiet Edwards,' the schoolmaster said. Gripping his jacket, he pulled Owen out of his seat. 'Stand up boy!'

'Tell the class what you were doing.'

'I was drawing.'

Seated in rows behind their little wooden desks, the class murmured. Some of them giggled. Owen, keeping his gaze above their heads, tried not to smile.

'Drawing? Why were you not writing your essay on PAT-A-GO-NIA?' This last word was yelled in Owen's ear so that it began to ring.

'I had finished my essay?'

'What?' The word was yelled at him again. 'Do you think you are cleverer than these other children? You think yourself so much quicker than them? Do you?'

'I am not saying anything,' Owen said.

'Not saying anything? So you do think you are cleverer than these children — children you should be keeping company with — keeping pace with? Or do you pride yourself on having your own way of doing things?'

Owen did not look at his schoolmaster though in his peripheral vision he was aware of his red face, its irregular moustache and of his hair that had flopped over his furious face that Schoolmaster kept pushing roughly away. Owen did not respond. He knew that the schoolmaster, whose brother, had gone to work in the coalmines was likely to be one of the men who spoke badly about his father. Owen wondered whether to remain silent. He was damned if he did and damned if he did not; he knew from experience that his words would be interpreted in the way that the schoolmaster decided; it occurred to him that he could say anything he wanted; the reaction of his schoolmaster would be the same. Owen kept his gaze on the yellowed map on the back wall of the classroom; a fly, like a black blot, was crawling over South America. Some of the boys in the back row a few steps in front of him were sneering. In his mind's eye he saw his father walk to the centre of the road. Owen looked directly at the boys, who stopped sneering and glancing at each other and sniggered instead. The schoolmaster hit him across the side of the head and one of the girls started crying.

'Do you pride yourself in doing things differently?' The schoolmaster asked.

'No. I try to do what is right,' Owen said, his ear ringing from the cuff and the side of his head stinging. He was thinking of Huw driving the cart into the angry crowd. His leg began to shake and he felt fury jump on his back like a demon, demanding a physical outlet.

'And is it right to draw in your book and to pride yourself on being different?' The schoolmaster shouted. 'Do you like making a show of yourself?'

'I do not think it is wrong to draw. I do not think myself proud. I am not making a show of myself.'

Owen felt himself being pulled upwards by the shoulders and flung to the floor, where he received a kick in the seat area that was so painful that for a time he did not feel it following the initial shock.

'How dare you answer to me like that? Are you too good for us now that you have a scholarship? You only got it because of your father's deviousness isn't it boy?'

Owen stared at the ink from the pot that had been on his desk darkening the wood floor that stank of Jeyes fluid.

'Blot that immediately!' The schoolmaster said, bits of his spittle settling with the dust on the floor of the classroom. Owen blotted the floor with blotting paper that he groped for on his desk, in a daze. Chalk marks on the blackboard wormed before his eyes; he sat through the rest of the day's lessons gritting his teeth and clenching and unclenching his fists when steel-edged waves of pain came, and with them, the slicing fury. He glared defiantly at his desk, his school master's back and at the boys that had sneered at him, one of whom looked down at his desk as he did so; he wondered whether the boy felt shame at his behaviour, given the extreme nature of Schoolmaster's treatment of him; he was glad he was leaving this hated school soon. The children kept their distance, though he could tell some of the girls wanted to speak to him; one of the girls came and offered him a biscuit during the break. The only time the tears threatened to come was when Owen thought of Stephen, whose solidarity he particularly missed that day; miserable at the loss of his friend, he wondered at the nature of grief, that could recede like the tide, for days, weeks, months at a time and then came again in sudden waves of attack. He was sure Stephen would have won a scholarship too. The day dragged slowly and painfully on with Owen seated at a right angle, unable to move his back beyond ninety degrees, observing the lesson from a painful distance.

When it was time to leave, Owen was walking slowly through the gate when he heard a low whistle and saw Huw standing across the road from the school. Sunshine lit up an ash tree from behind him, its gold tipped leaves contrasting brightly against the bronzy heather that swept up the dark slopes of the mountain behind it. He waved and Owen made his way over to him, trying his best to walk without sticking his tailbone out.

'Why are you not at the quarry?' Owen asked.

Huw held up his wrist that was bandaged tightly. Only his fingers were exposed.

'The rope slipped as I was lowered from the top and I fell on to a ledge. My hand saved me,' Huw smiled. 'It acted as the hand of God.'

'You could have been killed.'

'The rope just went. And so did I.'

'But for your dear hand!' Owen said. 'Was mother worried?'

'I asked them not to say.'

'Good choice,' Owen said, slapping his brother on the shoulder.

Huw noticed his brother leaning forward as he walked.

'What happened to you?' Huw said as they began to walk up the road. Owen told Huw what had happened. After a while, Huw stopped in the road. 'So he kicked you, in your rear, on the classroom floor in front of all the others? He did not take you to the other room to give you the stripe after class, as is usual?'

Owen shook his head.

'Wait here Owen,' Huw said.

Owen went and stood near an exposed rock a little way off the road, facing the schoolhouse: a small stone building with white

142

doors, surrounded by a slope of lawn in the front and fields at the back. He had no idea what Huw intended to do, but a large part of him wanted Huw to punch his schoolmaster between the eyes and fell him; he had felt his schoolmaster's hatred in his hot breath that smelt of peeled eggs. Owen knew he was hated because he was Jacob's son or Huw's brother or both. You were always someone's son or grandson or brother in this district: their choices became your choices. Owen was gripped with a desire to flee up the mountain. He decided he would leave when he was old enough to; but as soon as this thought had formed in his mind he felt sorrow, how could he leave this beautiful land that God had visited over and over again? He had heard his father preach that the Welsh were like the Israelites. God kept visiting these mountains, just like he visited Moses on Mount Sinai. Perhaps it was the singing that attracted Him. But why did God not make everyone sing like the Welsh? That way he could visit everyone and not just prefer the Israelites and the Welsh. The Welsh had the music, but why were they so poor? It was a mystery, though he knew that Jesus had said *Blessed are the poor in spirit for theirs is the Kingdom of Heaven.* Perhaps you needed to actually *be* poor to grasp this; his father often said that the wealthy were not aware of their lack, until it was taken from them in some way, through loss of some kind; it was often only when Jacob leaned over their deathbeds that he was able to help them *slip into heaven*, as he put it. But as Jacob often warned, he had known many die before this point and there was no way in but for the acceptance of the blood of Jesus. He thought of his schoolmaster's lack of control: it was this that made Owen fearful; he wondered whether schoolmaster might kill him by mistake one day, he could not understand why these things were allowed to happen. *Why do you allow people like that anywhere near children God?* Owen asked internally; Owen did not detect a reply. Huw came out in front of the schoolhouse.

'What did he say?' Owen asked, pulling at a grass stem.

'Nothing. He refused to answer to me as he put it,' Huw swung his jacket over his shoulder with his good hand.

'What did you say?'

'I asked him questions.'

'Such as?' Owen chewed the grass .

'I asked him how he might have felt had he been in your boots.'

'And?' Owen looked behind him, fearful that one of the schoolmasters, or sharp-tongued Miss Roberts might be lurking.

'I replayed the scene with him.'

Owen imagined Huw acting out his degraded part in that morning's proceedings and laughed, but He wanted to forget all about school.

'Huw? Can we go to the cliffs?'

Huw looked up at the sky. 'You will be late back to do your chores, but due to the suffering you endured having to focus on that meathead in there,' Huw jerked his head in the direction of the schoolhouse, 'I will help you.'

They made their way to the cliffs overlooking the bay; Stephen and Owen often used to go up there after school, to sit on the headland and throw stones into the ocean, or to stand, arms thrust out like wings, to be held up by the winds that warred with the edges of the cliffs. On a clear day they could see the edge of Ireland. Owen sat down next to his brother on a grassy mound facing the sea and then immediately stood up again.

'You cannot sit can you? Lie down on your side. Mother is going to be livid.'

'What about Father?'

'Father too will be livid. But he will go out to the fields and pray, or maybe he will go a little way up the mountain and shout in to the wind. When he returns he will have forgiven schoolmaster and be checking to see if Mother has forgiven too. Then, just to check, he will have us all pray for the man's salvation—'

'I thought my schoolmaster was a Christian?' Owen was playful now. He did not care about anything at all except for this moment, with Huw, energised by land and sea. He stood up and pointing his rear in the direction of the sea and with arms outstretched he waggled it back and forth. 'Rearly I say unto you, Schoolmaster. Find yourself a more useful occupation than messing with young minds—and their behinds,' he said laughing.

'I am sure he is, in here,' Huw tapped at his head. 'But is he a Christian *anything* in here?' Huw tapped at his chest.

144

'The more I read the word of God Owen, the more I realise that Christianity without works is a dead religion as Father says. The book of Acts was not called the Acts of the Apostles for nothing. We need more of the power I saw with Robert flowing through us. I am contending for more.'

'But we are not all apostles Huw,' Owen said.

'Are we not? Why not?' Huw jumped up and began making his way down the almost sheer rock of the cliff. 'I think we should all be apostles,' he shouted back up at his brother.

'Mother too?' Owen moved sideways to the cliff edge. He felt like a crippled crab.

Mother too and Eilwen,' Huw said, coming back up to the cliff edge with a large white shell. 'This should placate Mother,' he said, hauling himself up to sit next to Owen.

'And Bethan?' said Owen, examining the smooth white shell and then putting it to his ear. 'I can hear the sea,' he said.

Huw laughed at his brother's joke. 'No Bethan is too pretty to be an apostle.'

Owen glanced at his brother's face, he had noticed a potency to Huw's friendliness with Bethan lately, which, to him, was odd, and unpalatable to him in some way, Bethan was his mother's friend, though she was a lot younger than her. Anwen referred to Bethan as her *little sister*. He did not realise that jealousy might be a factor in his distaste, though he liked Bethan well enough. But Huw gave nothing further away. He watched the seagulls on the slick rocks below them.

'She could travel the seven seas disguised as a pirate in a false beard,' Owen said. 'We'll fashion one from one of the ewe's coat next time they are shorn. It will give her a learned appearance.'

'Good idea—I will suggest it next time I see her.' Huw tipped his cap to the shepherd that was passing with his dog a little way away from them.

I see her. 'But there were no women apostles,' Owen said standing up.

'Actually, that is not true. There was the apostle Junia mentioned by Paul in his greeting in the letter of Romans. Mary Magdalene, worked closely with Jesus. It is ridiculous that women do not have equal status to men in the church. Or anywhere else

145

for that matter.'

'Well they couldn't go to war,' Owen said.

'Why not?' said Huw. 'They could be trained.'

Owen laughed. 'They are not strong enough.'

'In some ways they are stronger. Look at our mother. Women have endurance. How else could they give birth?'

'Or do all the cooking, baking and cleaning?' Owen joked.

Huw laughed. 'Mother could lead Wales in to battle. What about Old Testament Deborah, who led Israel in to battle? In the New Testament, women led house churches—women were prophets.'

Owen lay down on his side and watched the sea churning in the bay below him.

'Wales,' Huw said. 'God's own country,' he handed Owen an apple from his pocket and began chewing on one he produced from the other. He too lay down on his side. Owen chewed on his apple and contemplated the beauty of the land and sea. 'Huw?' he said. 'Do you think God really made the earth in seven days?'

'What does it matter?

'Is it not a fundament of belief?'

'To some, but not to me—why should it matter whether He made the earth in seven days or seven million years? Either He did or he didn't make it, that's the point—for me anyway.'

'Because the Bible says so.'

'What if a day to us is a thousand years to him? St Paul said words to that effect, it's in the Bible somewhere.'

'He is outside time anyway,' Owen said. 'Do you think that means we can time travel after we die? I would like to try out different lives, in other times.'

'I would like to be a lighthouse keeper,' Huw said, looking out to the headland at the end of which was a white lighthouse.

'You might get lonely,' Owen flung his apple core over the cliff.

'I would have a wife to keep me warm. And you could come and help me light the lamp.'

Waves crashed high up the cliffs and Owen felt the spray like millions of miniscule pinpricks on his face. He found it so invigorating that it gave him a surge of joy

'Come on,' Huw said, laughing as he got up. 'We must get back or we will be paying our dues.' He pulled his brother up. When they reached the road, Huw carried Owen like a sack over his shoulder for a good way while they took turns making up lines to silly songs set to chapel melodies.

Unsettled, Anwen left off the milking, and wrapping her shawl around her, she walked across the backfield to scan the road above the smallholding to see if Owen was coming from the direction of the schoolhouse; Meg scuttled along beside her, stopping every now and again to sniff the ground for rabbits. Owen was not usually late and she had a feeling that something might have happened as he had been coming to her mind since that morning, but she had been so busy meeting with the quarrymen's wives that morning, before taking Rosie to the blacksmith to be shod and then mucking out the barn and sty, before spreading the manure on the vegetable fields, that afternoon, that she had kept her thoughts for Owen in check, apart from her usual daily prayer with Jacob early that morning when she had prayed for the safety of her children as usual; but apart from this, she had not dwelt on him further. Finding the road void of travellers, she walked back to the cowshed to resume the evening's milking, but as she settled back onto the milking stool and laid her cheek on Bess's warm flank, it occurred to her that Owen may have gone down to the village for some reason or another, so she set the pail and stool out of the reach of the cow's back legs and walked to the front garden to scan the lower road that ran past the front stone wall and wound down the mountain to the town. The big sky was flaunting pink and blue hues as the late afternoon made way for the evening, but not a soul textured the road that curled itself around the mountains and down to the sea, like grey silk ribbon. She returned and resumed her milking, her prayers coming out in quick bursts like the milk hitting the sides of the tin pail. When she had finished milking, she came out of the cowshed, stretching her back and twisting her neck this way and that to rid it of the stiffness of having been pressed against Bess for another half hour, as she looked at the red eye of the sun preparing to merge with the sea. She turned back to the cottage and heard the click of the sheep gate and both her sons appeared on the road above the smallholding. She stood with her hands on her hips, watching her sons walk towards her, the fronds of her shawl fluttering in the wind.

'Why must you do this to me Huw?' She shouted as they came nearer.

'Mother, there was no need to be concerned. You knew he was with me.'

The sound of Rosie's freshly shod hooves rang out from the lower road. They could hear Jacob whistling.

'You will need to do your chores Owen,' Anwen said. She went back to the barn to fetch the milk, but then came straight out again.

'What happened to your hand? Come here.'

'It has been dealt with Mother. Don't worry,' Huw said. 'It is not serious.'

Anwen went back to the barn. She was annoyed with Huw, but did not want to speak to him further until she had settled her emotions. She realised that she was struggling with his new friendship with Bethan, who had been spending more time at the cottage lingering in conversation with Huw. She was struggling too, with the distance that had sprung up between her and her husband since her encounter with the Holy Spirit recently. She understood she was experiencing an attack from the enemy of God in her emotions to rob her of her joy and to cause her to doubt what had happened to her, but she was nevertheless struggling to give them to God in faith that He would work them out. Anwen loved Bethan, who was in many ways like a younger sister, but she struggled not to be annoyed at her attraction to her son, partly, she knew, because she felt possessive for him, but also because she did not sense that they were meant for each other. She had had Huw when she was twenty years old, as he almost was now, and as he had grown into the handsome man that he now was, she had noticed the girls his own age struggling to contain their feelings at chapel as they glanced at him, their flushed faces aroused by deep spiritual feeling, but also, as Anwen could not fail to notice, by the sight of Huw. Anwen understood these feelings very well. Jacob, who Huw was so like, shared the same charismatic presence.

'Owen, go and do your chores,' Anwen said from the back doorstep.

'Mother that will not be possible,' Huw said.

Owen related what had happened.

'Father forgive that man,' Anwen said. 'I am struggling to right now, but forgive Him and I will try to myself. For now, I need a cup of tea. Inside Owen.'

'I can do the shed mother,' Owen said. I would like to—to take my mind off things.'

'To delay Mother's ministrations you mean,' Huw said after Anwen had gone inside.

In the cowshed, Owen began forking Bess's dung into a pail. Through the grille in Bess's shed, he could hear his recently returned father and Huw talking in the back garden.

'He came straight round to the chapel after you had left Huw—he was red with fury.'

'Hypocrite,' Huw said. 'Father I am sure he has broken Owen's tailbone. He is a violent man who should not be in charge of children. He kicked him because he could not kick *you* father.'

Owen imagined the look on Huw's face.

'That may be Huw, and if so, there is an injustice, as I knew there would be many when I made the sacrifice for this ministry.'

Huw was unrepentant about having seen Owen's schoolmaster. 'I wanted to make him think father. I simply asked him questions. He seemed guilty and uncomfortable and rightly so.'

'It was not your place to judge him, Huw, leave it to God to correct his conscience.'

'Did you do nothing father?' Huw asked in an exasperated tone. 'Why should Owen be made an Isaac? He is still a boy. He is caught in a vicious war that is not of his own making.'

'I made my feelings on the matter clear to him Huw. It will not happen again,' Jacob said. There was a pause and then: 'Owen is my son Huw. I must be the judge of what is right and wrong.'

'I think that may be the role of God.'

'Don't be childish Huw.'

149

'Just because we are Christians Father, does not mean we should lie down in the dirt for people to walk over us.'

'Does it not?'

'Not in my view Father—so you will not take it further?'

'No. I will not.'

Owen resumed his work. He was glad his brother had stood up for him, but he was concerned that Schoolmaster would make Huw pay for it one way or another. Huw stopped in the doorway of the cowshed with an armful of hay.

'I'll do the pigs for you Owen. And as I do so I will keep your teacher in mind.'

The boys laughed as the sun sank and the manure-scented air began to cool.

Inside, Jacob led Anwen into the bedroom and took his wife in his arms. 'I have had the most wonderful time this afternoon with Dai Bevans, my love. He is already beginning to speak. His mother is like a young girl—suffice to say I am full of love and wonder at the Lord, but I have an apology to make. The Lord showed me that I had allowed resentment to creep into my heart over Dai Bevans.'

Anwen's eyes filled with tears as she placed her hand on her husband's thigh. 'But you prayed so long and hard for his healing—'

'I know, but I have resented God for not healing him—I expected Him to use me as He had with Gwyndaf.'

'Oh but He did—and he will again—' Anwen placed her hands on her husband's upper arms.

'Yes, but hear me out my love,' Jacob said, taking her face in his hands. 'The enemy offered me pride and I consumed it. I wanted him to be healed through me.'

Anwen pulled away from her husband and sat down on the edge of the bed.

'I too took the enemy's pill,' her fingers worried at the lace border of her apron.

Jacob sat down next to her, his hand over hers. 'Wait beloved—I allowed resentment to grow and it spilled over to you—I resented the Holy Spirit visiting you in the way that He did

150

recently. Forgive me my love.'

Anwen looked up at her husband through her tears. 'I am no different, I have allowed resentment against my own son and dear friend to grow—and now—' she sobbed as she felt in the pocket of her apron for a cotton handkerchief. 'I should like to pummel that man who hurt our son.'

'Come,' Jacob smiled as he took his wife's hand. 'We cannot allow unforgiveness to impede the work of the Spirit. We have confessed to one another and so we shall be healed. Let us offer prayers of forgiveness and healing for William—he has wounds that only the Lord can heal—he had a brutal father. There may not be excuse, but there is always understanding.'

Their arms around each other, Jacob and Anwen remained on the bed cloaked intimacy, until the room grew dark, and Anwen rose, her heart lighter, to attend to her sons.

August

Chapter 17

From the back of the chapel, Owen watched the quarrymen's choir. The men stood on a slightly raised dais facing the pews. Owen could sit down but only by pushing his rear out and arching his back, which he was not keen to do on a pew. Owen marvelled that such a sound could come from men, *O Jesus, let Thy spirit bless, this frail one in the wilderness, to guide him through the snares of life, on Canaan's way to Thee on high...* the sound the men made seemed to sweep the whole world up into its suspension; the music caused him to recall being in Penrhyn Bay the year of the storms when the waves broke free of the buttresses and curved over the road causing the horses to fall over and the carts to slide on their sides. He and Huw and their grandparents, Anwen's mother and father, had watched from the hill as the waves came over the road and gave the doors and windows of the houses a good cleaning. The scene was repeated in Rhos, where some of the boats that were pulled up on the beach found themselves floating unexpectedly out to sea again. It seemed to Owen that the sound of the men's voices were a thing apart from them, like the waves that he had seen rising over the roads and crashing against the houses, and that they too were capable of knocking over anything in their path, causing the spirits of all to merge themselves with the power and the purity of the sound: *All grace that through Thy Church doth flow, in heaven above and here below, all shall I have, all shall be mine, If I but have Thy grace divine...* the men sang. Owen became aware of the words, where a moment before he was only aware of them as part of the sound that the men were making. Anwen said that true singing came from the spirit, though it relied on the mechanics of a man's body to issue forth, and that spiritual men and women were the ones that truly knew how to sing. These men sang with the full force of their being, as if they were involved in an act of creation. A swell of emotion rose in Owen. He was proud to be there and he was proud to be Welsh. He had nothing with which to compare his Welshness, but he felt he knew that there was something sacred about the land of Wales, and he could feel it flowing in the song of the men; he felt that the spirit of Wales was present in the notes that were exhaled by their breath and that the breath of God was in their song and he saw that their song was creative, in that the song was creating images in his mind and feelings in his spirit that he could not explain, though he was aware of tiny changes going on in his heart like the minute mechanics of a clock. *To Thy most holy feet I'll cling, the virtues of Thy blood I'll sing, the cross I'll bear, the wave I'll ride, If Thou but with me now abide...* as the men sang, Owen had a vivid picture in his mind of the raw and bloody Christ on the cross. As the tide of the song began to diminish, the picture shifted and he saw the tomb where Jesus had been laid; the resurrected Jesus materialised through the rock that sealed the tomb as these words from the gospel of Matthew came to him: *He has risen from the dead and is going ahead of you.* Owen wondered for a moment why he did not see the rock rolled away but rather Jesus materialising through the rock, similarly, he did not hear 'into Galilee,' but only 'ahead of you.' He understood it was significant but did not have time to contemplate the picture in his mind any further. Jacob stood and gave Huw a signal to alert him that it was time for him to give his testimony, and his son leapt to his feet and ran up to the podium, holding up the newspaper that he had carried from home in his back pocket.

'Men! There is revival in the South and it has begun sweeping up to the north and there is more to come if we will have it!'

The men stirred. 'But will it feed us? Will it make our families warm this winter?'

'Revival warms the hearts of men! Revival warms hearts of stone!'

'If we have tropical sun this winter,' a man cried out.

'Yes, David,' Huw said. 'Revival is like tropical sun in winter. Revival changes people's hearts and minds. It moves cold men to action. Does it not? We saw this happen, in 1829, 39, 49, 59, 79...'

Huw told them about what had happened with Robert outside the pub. 'The trickle has begun but the Holy Spirit must come like a river, 'He that believes on me, as the scripture has said, out of his heart shall flow rivers of living water.' Huw quoted John 7 verse 38.

Owen felt again the strange trickling sensation that he felt in his chest, like water trickling through his heart and he understood what it was: the presence of the Holy Spirit inside him: *Streams of living water.*

It is time!' Huw crouched before the congregation,' his fingers gripping an imaginary Wales, like Hamlet holding the skull. 'Wales is the *land* of revival. No other *country* has been blessed so by God. It *heals* people. Perhaps we Welsh are like the *Israelites* to him.'

Owen began to count the beats in the pentameter of his brother's voice. Again, it was like the sea, it was part of the sea, part of the spiritual fabric of this current life that he was becoming more and more aware of; of the current that Owen was being swept up in. Now he saw the sea with all its teeming fish and weed and then he felt the current of the sea, almost physically, like wind; and he saw that the physical and the spiritual could be entwined and he understood these things somehow, but didn't know how he would explain them were he ever asked. He felt the current again, like wind on his face. The congregation began to respond.

'Does He have a special *love* for us? When he was *flinging* gifts to earth and we caught *singing*, did we catch His heart? Why *question*?' Huw said.

Several men in the congregation threw up their hats and one shouted out, 'Yes! Come Lord, we are all in for you!'

One of the quarrymen struck up a prayer and soon others joined in. 'Lord bring us revival, and make us ready!

'We must be ready. Can we confess all sin?' Huw said. 'Will

155

we scour our hearts so that we can hold more of the Holy Spirit?'
The atmosphere shifted. Owen felt the hair on his body begin to
prickle with such a primal fear that he sensed it might be better
to be dead, truly dead, spiritually dead than to cross the presence
that had come into the room. As he contemplated these things,
he heard a voice in his thoughts say: *Do not fear*. The thickening
presence brought such a motivating change to the room, and such
an immediate reaction from the men that Owen almost laughed.
He worried about his thoughts causing offense to what he now
realised was the presence of God within him; and so he began
concentrating on keeping his face straight. *Don't worry. I'm
not religious.* Owen almost jumped at the next thought that
came. *Men are. I'm not.* Owen almost laughed but he did not
want to make a show of himself so he tried to control himself,
but when he did, he felt the presence lift and felt disappointed.
Fear God, not man. Owen took this instruction to heart and
began laughing. As he did so, he felt a deep sense of relief as
something emotionally heavy was lifted from him. He found he
could not stop laughing; he bent forwards with the weight of it
all, until he was on his knees, crying with laughter. *Laugh until
you cry, better than crying until you eventually laugh.* Owen
laughed so hard that he was sure he was going to explode. He
heard the laughter of Stephen too, but this was now, inexplicably,
a delightful thing, and he laughed all the harder for it. Owen
dared not look around him in case anyone saw him, but as he
was on his own back there, with no deacons guarding the big
doors behind him, he need not have worried.

'Bless that university man Robert. Thank you that you are
no respecter of persons!' a man called out.

'Lord change my heart to make me want it!' another said.

'Forgive me for wanting the pleasures of this world more than
you!'

For some time the quarrymen, motivated by the purifying
power of the presence, called out to God in prayer in this way,
asking God for forgiveness for a plethora of astonishing things,
many of which would not normally be uttered in the light of day.
After a while some of the men began to tremble with the realisation that the presence that had come into the room seemed to

be increasing further. Owen's hands trembled on his knees, as the presence in the room became heavier and he almost found it difficult to breathe. *Bear with me, the more weight you can stand the more weight you will bear.* He thought of Anna's words. It was as if there was going to be a lightning storm, at any moment, there had to be. Owen expected to hear a charge, something to break the atmosphere; he glanced at Huw who was staring ahead in awe as if he could see something on the opposite side of the wall. Many of the men were on their knees, crying out to God as the sense of the supernatural presence increased. And then the atmosphere did break, and in the breaking came such a sense of peace; it felt as if they were suspended in thick, golden light and were being drawn into heavenly places at the same time. Owen felt transposed into warm butter and honey melting onto toast. He felt deliciously alive and more fully present than he had ever felt in his life; he also felt fully connected to the men in the room; as though his heart was being connected with theirs by golden threads; he became aware of a pulse that resounded in his ears, it became louder and louder until his whole body resonated with it and he felt that he had become part of the heartbeat of God. As this pulse continued he heard one of the men in the congregation begin to sing; his brother was still staring directly ahead of himself; his face transformed, beatific even. Owen looked around at the faces of the quarrymen as they began to sing again; they looked like innocent children, their faces unmarked by what they had seen and what they had done. One by one the men joined in the song as if conducted by the unseen hand that was now guiding events in the room. The men began to take their parts in a harmony that was so divine that Owen felt that he might not be able to bear it, but he was aware of a kind of expansion taking place within him; with his inner eye he saw his inner walls contracting and expanding: each of his cells contracting and glowing with light, his whole body seemed to buzz with electricity. He knew that he should be alarmed as there was a sense that what was happening could cause some kind of explosion or unwanted act of the body, but Owen was not alarmed, because he had never felt such extraordinary peace, he wanted the feeling to last forever, and he wanted forever to mean forever, and he had never been able to contemplate that word before without untold agony of the mind. Still on his knees, but with his head tipped back, he laughed out loud. When Owen finally stood up, he realised he was completely healed. He jumped up and down to be sure. Huw spotted him and came running over to him, and then, in the back of the chapel, he danced a jig with his brother as he shared his healing. Some of the men in the back row began to dance with them. Owen realised that they had caught the laughing bug too. The men spilled out from the chapel and into the night. Their laughter echoing through the mountains as the snow began to fall like lace on the shoulders and the hats of the men.

When they arrived home, Huw swept his mother into the air by her waist. 'God filled Owen with the Holy Spirit and healed his backside!'

Anwen laughed as Huw set her down again, then she threw her arms around her husband.

Later, Owen lay in bed listening to his family talk in the main room below. Every detail of the evening was discussed and the family was high on the wonder of it all.

'Oh, we have prayed for so many years for The Spirit to come again,' Anwen said.

'It is only the beginning, ' Huw said.

'The beginning of the beginning!' Jacob said.

Jacob paused for a moment and then said. 'I went to see William this evening, Huw. I told him never to lay a hand on my son again or I would not answer to what may happen.'

'And how did he respond?'

He did not. I invited him to chapel.

'And how did he respond to that?' Huw asked.

'He said nothing.'

There was another pause and then Owen heard the three of them laughing.

'And there is more news. Rhys Davies has gone south to work in the coalmines.'

'I don't know whether to feel happy or sad for Mary,' Anwen said. 'Oh Lord, may he come back a changed man.'

Owen threw his pillow into the air. Then he began to punch it until it burst and the feathers swirled; he threw the feathers up in the air. Owen had such a lightness of being he felt like one of the floating feathers. Eventually, he fell exhausted onto his mattress and slept immediately.

Chapter 18

On his way home from town, where he had been fitted out for new school clothes, Owen veered off the road from school in the direction of the lake. He imagined its liquid eye gazing on the living and the dead for millennia, secrets stored in its prehistoric depths; the edges of the lake quivered like mercury on the curve of a silt shore. Blown sideways by the fierce wind coming off the mountain, rain was coming down from an iron sky in vast sheets; tiny bullet-like shards of rain, were penetrating Owen's left cheek. He heard a group of town lads coming up behind him.

'Going to do the crawl with your black legs?' Garreth Ellis called out.

'I suppose you would float with all that pie girth of yours but I doubt you could swim,' Owen said.

Garreth went for him, but Edryd tripped him up. Garreth cried out, but got up and dusted himself off, when he caught Edryd's look.

'I am going to the lake to throw stones,' Edryd said, the rain streaming over his cheeks. 'Do you have stones to throw?' he asked Owen.

'No,' Owen said, wondering whether to wander off home with the others or stay to find out what fun he was to be made of.

'I am speaking metaphorically. Do you know what that means?' He ran a hand through his hair, before ineffectually shaking the rain off his hand.

'Yes. I am not stupid,' Owen said. 'But it's raining buckets,' he said, continuing to walk.

'Raining buckets? A cliché if ever there was one—one pilfered from the English too. Not as stupid as you sound you mean?' Edryd said sideways, blinking rain droplets, which, to Owen, made him look vulnerable despite the tough talk.

'Is it? I'll be careful to use Welsh clichs next time,' Owen shouted into the wind.

'Touche,' Edryd said.

The wind took the unfamiliar word before Owen could grasp it.

'What?'

Edryd stopped and repeated the word.

'Why use French?' Owen asked, thinking what a pretentious ass Edryd was. 'To make a show of yourself?'

'At least the French are revolutionary, as we should be. Read Viktor Hugo,' Edryd said hurrying on, his hands in his pockets, in the way of men even though he was still a boy. Owen thought he was making a show of himself. The lake drew closer.

'Who says I haven't?' Owen said, immediately wishing he hadn't. He came to a halt, annoyed that he had been caught in an argument, and was not now eating his mother's cake by the fire, and enjoying the fact that it was Friday and there was no school the next day. Once drawn into an argument, Owen would pick at a bone until finally jabbing to draw blood. *Why must an argument be won Owen?* Anwen would say. *Can you not be content to have your mind broadened by another point of view? Must you always drown a point with your own?*

Ignoring the comment, Edryd stopped and turned to face Owen, 'I have discovered, after a morning in the company of Miss Roberts and co—'

'Miss Roberts and cow?'

'Yes, Miss Roberts the cow and other animals.' Edryd laughed and so did Owen. 'Little wonder she is a spinster.'

'Yes, other animals, such as the walrus,' said Owen referring to his schoolmaster and feeling relieved that he understood that Edryd had been talking about his former teachers at the village school. Edryd had been making him feel inadequate and he had been hoping to appear to be on equal ground with him.

'The walrus is an ugly beast,' said Edryd. 'I hear he left his mark on your backside? A stone must be thrown. For old times sake in my case, he left his marks on me too. See that rock over there—on the other side of the beach? That is the walrus and he must be bombarded. Six stones each—find the ammunition on the way. The loser must forfeit something.'

He set off running, stooping every now and again to pick up stones. 'I'll draw the start line in the sand,' he shouted.

'No. I will,' Owen yelled at Edryd through the wind and the rain as he passed him.

Edryd ran harder but Owen was faster. He stooped to pick up three smooth pebbles from the beach and continued to run until he was approximately four yards from the newly Christened Walrus; Owen carved a line in the sand, then, hands on hip, in a victory stance, he turned to look for Edryd. Edryd was peering into the rushes on the edge of the lake where swampy ground met water, not far from where Owen had passed him.

'Come and see!' he shouted. 'There are two rams that have locked horns in the water. I think it is a fight to the death!'

Owen stood for a moment, wondering whether Edryd had some kind of ploy. He decided that if he were bluffing he would box him one in the middle and knock the cleverness out of him for that day at least. Owen ran up to the marshy area. Two rams had indeed tangled horns; only their heads appeared above the waterline. They butted then stopped, their yellowy eyes fixed, horns coiled together like snakes. Then they repeated the process.

'They seem to be having a good time,' Edryd said.

'And they will be taking it. They will fight to the death now. Come on, what about the walrus,' Owen said.

Edryd stood for a moment and then without replying ran off, stupidly as far as Owen was concerned. Owen easily overtook him; he stopped at the line and took the stones he had collected from his pockets and was already throwing when Edryd got there.

'One, two, three, four, five, six,' he counted as he threw. Edryd skirted round him, and ran around the rock, appearing over the top of it.

'You really do look quite daft,' Edryd said, sitting down on the rock.

Owen stood up, the sap rising within him. He considered how

easy Edryd would be to fell.

'I didn't mean throw stones literally. What I meant was, throwing verbal stones, such as: Miss Roberts, are you aware that your nose appears to have three equal sides and not just two? Or, Headmaster, when you are relieving yourself are you thinking about how many helpings of steamed pudding you will be able to put away at lunchtime?'

Owen began to smile.

'Your turn,' Edryd said, getting up. He stamped his heel against the rock surface. 'Yes the surface of the skull is very thick,' Edryd stamped again. 'And seems to be numb. Nevertheless the walrus needs further insulting—he insulted you did he not?'

Owen felt his anger diminishing in the glow of Edryd's apparent solidarity. The rain had stopped and the sun lit up the sky in the east all the brighter for it being dark with charcoal trimmed cloud in the west.

'Your arse would lose the cane if you were to get it,' Edryd said addressing the rock that stood in for schoolmaster. 'For reasons of ugliness—AND VASTNESS.'

'And your face swallows itself when you shout,' Owen said.

'And everything else,' Edryd said.

'Yes, and here's a stone for looking and acting, the part—of—' Owen said.

'Of an arse,' Edryd finished.

The boys laughed for some time before verbally pasting more teachers, and one or two pupils on the rock, after which Owen gathered his stones and began skipping them over the water. Edryd sat down and watched. The mockery Owen expected did not come. He threw a stone that landed at Edryd's feet.

'Come on, there's a smooth one,' Owen used the toe of his boot to point out a flattish pebble.

'No thanks.'

'Come on. Let's see if your wrists are as good as your brains.'

'I can tell you they're not.' Edryd, his arms folded, looked across the lake. The mountain was perfectly mirrored in the lake, its twinned peaks formed a rugged diamond.

'Well try it.'

Edryd picked up the stone and tried skipping it across the

water. It plopped. Owen laughed.

'Did your father never teach you to skip stones?'

'No he did not.'

Owen stopped laughing. 'Why not?' He kicked at a long tuft of bronzy grass.

Edryd picked up another stone from the clear shallow water, and tried again. 'I suppose he's been too busy shaping me into being the politician he wants me to be,' the stone plopped again.

'Does he do other things with you?'

Owen showed him how to hold the stone and flick his wrist. Edryd tried again with limited success.

'He does schoolwork with me and he teaches me about politics.'

'You will have to practise.' Owen said. 'For many years,' he added skipping a stone over the water so it skipped six times.

'I have better things to do,' Edryd said, picking up his satchel.

'Nothing can be better than skipping stones on a warm afternoon, especially when you beat your own record.'

Edryd laughed as he began to walk. 'I am sure I can think of better things but I will take your word for it.'

Owen wiped his hands on his shorts, picked up his own satchel and ran towards the road after Edryd. At the marshy area they stopped to look at the rams; at first they appeared to have gone, but then they noticed a ram horn sticking up through the water.

'It's drowned,' Owen said, splashing into the water. He turned the ram over. Its glassy eyes rolled up to the now waterless sky.

'Help me pull it out,' he said.

'Why? It's dead.'

Owen stared at him. 'So? Would you leave him to rot?'

'I suppose not,' Edryd said, walking round to where the horns stuck up through the marsh grass.

'Grab his horns and I'll push,' Owen said.

Edryd grabbed the horns and Owen, up to his knees in water, pushed the ram from the rear. The upper part of the ram's body appeared above the water line and then sploshed back in.

'Take him under the forelegs,' Owen said.

'I'd rather not take him at all.'

'Take him nevertheless,' Owen said. 'Are you not used to animals?'

Edryd did as he was told and before long the sheep lay on his side on the grass, its broken neck flung back awkwardly.

'Poor bastard,' Edryd said.

Owen began thinking of tea, cake and the welcoming fire at home.

'Do you want to know about Victor Hugo then?' Edryd said.

Owen glared at him, his lip curled up in exasperation.

'You don't like being found out do you?' Edryd said.

'Are your fists as good as your comments? Does your father coach you in that too?' As soon as he said the second part he felt bad for taking the rise and saying it, since he liked Edryd's father.

'Why bring my father into the fray?'

'The fray? Why not use *it*. Why do you always make a show of yourself,'

Owen kicked at a smallish rock that was half submerged in the water, dislodging it and causing a miniature world of turmoil as black silt exploded into the clear water disrupting the habitat of millions of microscopic beasts. A tiny snail shell floated to the surface of the water.

'*It* is not specific,' Edryd said ignoring him. '*It* has no real meaning.'

'It does if *it* is being referred to,' Owen crouched to pick up the snail shell; the snail was curled into a dark ball within.

'I suppose. Wales must be an *it* to England.'

'Why do we return to Wales all the time, do you ever just talk?' Owen said, running to keep up with Edryd who was walking quickly up the wet sand towards the track.

'We will always return to Wales if we are Welsh. I hear you have won the scholarship,' Edryd said. 'So you will be the second one from the district to get in.'

'The first will be last and the last will be first.' Owen said catching up with Edryd. 'How did you know?'

'Word travels fast in small places. People must find things to talk about.'

'You're not very kind about your own people.'

'I'm kind enough.'

They were reaching the fork in the road where the track went over the mountain to the smallholding or down the mountain road to the town.

'Well if you make it come down to the football and meet some of the lads,' Edryd said, 'some of them are town boys from school.' Edryd walked off, leaving Owen wondering if he had made a new friend or not. He did not think he liked Edryd and he was beginning to feel uncomfortable for mocking some of the denser boys at school, though not Headmaster. His mother would have hated what Edryd had said about Miss Roberts, and now Owen felt bad for laughing at Edryd's words about her. As he pondered these things, Edryd turned and said, 'What do you mean the first will be last? I was the first, so how can I be last?'

'It's from the Bible,' Owen said. 'My father taught it to me.'

Edryd paused, but said nothing; then he continued on his way. Owen watched Edryd walk down the hill to the town where he lived in a little terraced house with his father and their landlady. He thought of him sitting in one of the little front rooms being taught by his father who hadn't thought to teach him to skim stones. The rain stopped as he walked home across the track and a bank of cloud shifted; the lake gleamed in the sudden sunlight made sharper for the dark clouds that rode the mountains behind them. It was not until he was sitting eating his mother's bread with freshly churned butter and blackberry jam that he remembered Edryd had invited him to football. He was not sure he wanted to go now anyway. He realised too that Edryd had put him through some kind of test. Owen decided that perhaps he just wanted to go to the football because everyone else seemed to. Well now he thought he would not follow the stream but swim the other way.

Chapter 19

Owen, Huw and Robert were walking on Porth Neigwl on the Llŷn Peninsula, where Robert had a family cottage on Rhiw Mountain. They were there with Anwen, Bethan and Eilwen, so that the women could pray and practise together for the upcoming revival meetings. Jacob was travelling to Caernarfon with Martyn and Seth, who were stirring up expectation for revival, by relating the testimonies of people that they had documented who had already been touched by God, as well as with the power of their passionate preaching: the message they felt they were all hearing from the Holy Spirit was: unity amongst all Christians regardless of denomination, class or creed, and also concerning intimacy with God leading to purity of heart and mind. The hunger for preachers who spoke with power was increasing in the north given that a flow had begun in the south, with reports of hundreds of converts coming in daily. The newspapers enthusiastically reported on all the meetings and on the supernatural phenomena that often precipitated, accompanied or followed these events; they published daily figures of those that had been saved by experiencing the joy of the new birth. A London reporter that had contacted Jacob to arrange to interview him said that he had been following the story of Rhys Davies, who had apparently had a dramatic supernatural encounter where he had told a reporter that Jesus had appeared at his bedside one night and told him that he was "The Way, The Truth and The Life." The family had been astonished: *Revival must come now!* Anwen had said, following a visit to Mary's house. *The toughest nut has been cracked!* Huw joked.

The surf was up and the sandy beach was vast. The August sky was vividly blue with great upsweeps of cloud that mirrored the crashing surf below. Owen picked up pebbles and with Huw, competed skip sequences on the waves with them, while Robert, deep in contemplation, walked a little ahead of them. The men were dressed casually in shirts, with their trousers rolled up to the knees. They sat on the beach laughing and talking, six bare feet dug into the sand. Robert had his copy of the King James Bible in his top pocket, already battered from fevered thumbing, every now and again his hand went up to it as if he was going to take it out to read, but he did not. Since his first encounter with Huw at the public house, Robert had been devouring the word of God. *I just can't get enough of it. I'm rapacious for it. Each scripture is like a rare pearl, with shade upon shade of divine colour in it.* The three sat looking out to sea, discussing the clouds, the science of them, and the divine artistry behind them. Soon they began to see different cloud faces and patterns in them, taking childish delight in pointing these out: elephants, men's faces and so on.

'Could that be Balfour over there? Lecturing, as he does?' Huw said.

'Ah yes, the high pate, hair and whiskers, I see the likeness now. Balfour—he is done for,' said Robert.

Owen looked surprised, but then said, 'Oh yes, The Education Reform Act—Mother was not pleased about that,' said Owen.

'Yes, Mother is convinced that next election, the Liberals will be in, and Balfour, will be out, or as you elegantly put it my friend, will indeed be done for—all things—or should I say, all men being equal.'

'It is possible to respect authority while believing in something higher. One can respect and still question, Owen,' Robert said, interpreting Owen's expression for him.

'Yes brother,' Huw said. 'Whatever you do,' and here Huw shoved his brother's shoulder. 'Do not get too serious,' about anything or anyone, least of all oneself.'

'I know. Mother and Father have a lot of respect for Balfour though they may not like all his policies,' Owen felt slightly annoyed. 'Especially his mining policies.' He did not mean to come across as too serious and he had hoped to keep up with the banter and now he began to feel foolish for trying too hard.

'Apart from God,' Huw and Robert said this simultaneously, drowning Owen's comment. 'About whom, we are perfectly serious.' This last was also said in unison and was accompanied by great gales of laughter and finished off with a tickling of Owen by Huw such as he had not received since he was a much younger boy, which really was the icing on the soggy cake.

'God is not religious, Owen,' Huw said. 'It is man who perceives him this way.'

'I know,' said Owen. 'He told me this Himself.'

The men laughed.

'I am perfectly serious,' Owen said, trickling sand through his fingers.

The men laughed again. 'As God is—perfectly serious, perfectly dense, as in beyond our comprehension, yet perfectly light—a lightness of being—considering He is one serious creator,' Huw said.

A lightness of being—exactly how I felt after chapel, Owen thought.

'A vivid vivisection indeed good fellow,' Robert said laughingly to his friend. Owen dug his fingers into the sand. 'Robert, what is darkness?' he asked.

'The absence of light.' Robert sat up and circled his arms around his shins, 'Jesus is the light, but not the light from the sun as some primitive people supposed.'

'The light shined in the darkness but the darkness had not understood it,' Huw said quoting the first chapter of John.

'Unless Jesus shines his light on someone, they cannot understand him and they will remain in the futility of their own thinking, Owen,' Robert said, digging in the sand with a shell. 'Jesus has to appear to us as the light in some capacity or another in order for us to understand. When he shines in our hearts or minds, the darkness flees, the veil is lifted, and we see that He is the Truth. He is the living word. This is why when someone like Rhys Davies states that Jesus is The Way, The Truth and The Life, people believe him, because the light of truth has shone on him and this light has become part of him so he reflects it and people perceive that truth with their own spirits though they cannot fathom it.' Robert emphasised his words by making a circle with his hands and tapping his thumb and fingertips together. 'Or you could look at it this way. Jesus The Word, The Living Word, as he is described in the Bible, has appeared and become flesh and dwelt amongst us.' Robert picked up handfuls of sand and allowed it to trickle through his fingers as he spoke. 'The person who has experienced the living word assimilates that word and it becomes flesh to them, life to them—part of their own body. So it is with communion, we partake of the cup and the bread and by faith we are transformed by Christ's death and by the wonder of his resurrection. *We are being transformed from Glory to Glory*—isn't that amazing? If we take communion in faith and understand what we are doing, Owen, we will be like him as his sons and daughters!'

'Well that very much depends on your theological bent,' Huw said.

'Or whether you believe in its power,' Robert said.

'You are describing a process?' Owen asked. 'How do people recognise these truths?'

'It is a process, spiritually discerned,' Huw said. 'You see with the eyes of your heart,' he said, tapping the Bible in Robert's breast pocket. 'How wonderful that you are not hampered by denominational theology and you have reached your own, unique, and I am sure, Holy Spirit inspired, conclusions.' Huw jumped to his feet.

'But why some and not others?' Owen said, insisting.

'Here are matters for debate,' Huw said. 'How much is process and how much is given through faith? Here is a conundrum: what does the Bible mean when it says: *Many are called but few are chosen?*'

'I understand it to mean that we are all called by God, but only some of us accept the invitation or choose to hear,' Robert said.

'A sticky denominational web that one,' Huw said, wriggling his toes in the sand.

'But does not God give us all ears to hear?' Owen said.

'I think he does,' said Huw, but some choose not to. In their own wisdom, they have better things to do.'

'Yes,' said Robert. 'They are their own gods or their god is their mind—or their stomach—'

'Or their wife,' said Huw.

They laughed, but Owen was serious.

'How can we be sure of anything?' Owen asked. He thought of the increase in the visions he had seen and of what he had felt at Heledd Jones' and more recently, while watching the quarrymen sing, and now wondered whether he had experienced powerful imagining.

'We can't,' said Huw.

'We can be sure of God,' said Robert, 'what we cannot be sure of we can trust to Him. But we must be sure to examine the facts—and there is a place for the mind here as well as the heart—I consider true religion, to use that word carefully, to be weighed up by the mind as well as the heart—human logic and understanding coupled with spiritual experience—something that transcends understanding—faith.'

Robert saw his young friend battling in his mind.

'Oh furrowed brow,' he pushed Owen playfully. 'Jesus would not have asked us—his disciples—to go out on the highways and the byways and preach the gospel to all men, if some of us were already condemned, or if He was not going to equip us—therefore we can trust Him to help us truly understand the simplicity and the complexity of the Gospel' Robert said.

'But He knows the end from the beginning?' Owen ran his hand through his hair several times. One of his crossed legs was beating up and down.

'Yes, I believe He does.'

'Well then?'

'None of us have all the answers Owen,' Robert said.

'But He does,' said Huw pointing upwards. 'Thank God,' Huw put his hand on Owen's knee and Owen stopped shaking it; instead he repeatedly ran his hand through his hair.

'Yes,' said Robert. 'Thank God.'

'Cake,' said Huw, dusting sand from his feet and reaching for his boots.

'Huw's God calls,' Robert said, also getting up.

'I will come along in a while,' said Owen, still running both hands through his hair. Huw nudged him with his shoulder as he got up, 'Don't pull your brains out.'

For a long while Owen sat on the beach and did exactly that. But no amount of brain pulling helped him reach any conclusions. As he watched the figures of his brother and Robert walking up the beach path he boxed at the notion of *free* will. Huw had his jacket slung over one shoulder, and Robert had one arm loosely draped over his friend's shoulder; they seemed so relaxed about everything, but he wrestled with the idea of grace and he verbally expressed his frustration at the notion of predestination and pulled and pulled at the thought of God knowing everything in the first place so why bother with anything at all? Eventually he decided to go and eat cake.

The house was set above the bay of Porth Neigwl and the view of the curve of the bay was spectacular when viewed from the window of the front of the house that was perched on the edge of the hill; a sloping field of grazing sheep separated the house from the cliff and the winding coastal path to the beach. The sky was pink and the ladies were bathed in the golden light of late afternoon sun as they brought their practise session to a close and began to talk of tea as Owen came in from the beach. Robert was writing at the long polished dining room table and Eilwen was playing softly on her violin near the window of the dining room, where many summers had bleached the parquet floors a caramel colour. One knee on the cushions that curved around the window bench, Bethan stood gazing out to sea through the telescope that stood by the window, wondering where the ship she could see on the horizon had been.

'Sometimes I wish I was a man. I could travel the world over without a care in the world. My goodness what am I saying! I will travel as a woman by hook or by crook.'

'Or by book,' Eilwen said, raising her Bible and shaking it in Bethan's general direction.

'All men have cares, darling Bethan,' Anwen said, coming into the room with a plate of gammon sandwiches and placing them on the dining table next to slices of bara brith and butter. 'Of course, you could always dress as a Shakespearean boy and take your chances,' Anwen laughed, but as you well know: 'There is neither Jew nor Greek, there is neither slave nor free man, there is neither male nor female; for you are all one in Christ Jesus.'

'Yes, thank you Saint Paul, or should I say Saint Paulina?'

'Say nothing,' said Robert, 'You are a Galatian, roundly, lectured.'

'You should stay with Saint Paul seeing as there is no man nor woman,' Owen said, helping himself to a glass of water from the jug on the table.

'Very good indeed, Owen,' Eilwen said, pointing her bow at Owen. 'And not bad Robert,' she said as she tucked her violin under her chin.

Robert glanced up at them and smiled, before going back to his writing.

'Take your chances with whom?' Huw asked, coming up behind his mother and pinching a triangle of sandwich. 'Very elegant,' he said of the sandwich before popping the whole into his mouth; chewing vigorously, he winked at Bethan. Bethan smiled and left the window-seat; she took up her drum and leaning against the wall at the far end of the window, began drumming with her fingers in response to Eilwen who had begun playing. Owen sat down at the table with a sigh.

'Still vexed my young friend?' Robert said. 'Take it to God in prayer and then wait for the answers. Trust him for the timing of them.'

'What are you doing?' Owen asked Robert.

'I feel Owen, that I have to document every thought, every feeling, every notion. We are about to embark on a journey so magnificent, that I know I must have it in black and white for the future,' he leaned across the table. 'Centuries hence Owen, people will read of the happenings we have seen and will yet see and marvel at them to the point that they will hunger for these things themselves and cry out to God afresh.'

'What if this is the last one?'

'The last revival? I don't think so. The impression I have formed from studying the book of Daniel and the book of Revelation is that there is much to come, before the time of the great harvests—perhaps they will become more sustained until Christ himself returns. But Owen, let us live this well and finish the race we are to run well. And let it be documented.'

'Most men do not tackle Daniel and Revelation at first, but Robert is a swimmer of the deep blue sea,' Huw said, performing a comedy diving motion. 'No doubt he has already fished up some revelation for his next preach.' He clapped his friend on the back. 'Which I look forward to hearing.'

'You too are called to preach, Huw,' his friend said. 'Also you forget that I was raised a good Anglican. I know the scriptures very well. It is just that now, they have become alive to me whereas before they were—well to be honest—texts. Now each one is illuminated. Where once they were simply black and white, now they are in splendid colour. I am consumed with them.'

'So we see,' Huw said, popping another sandwich into his mouth. 'And to our benefit of course,' he winked at Owen.

Robert went back to writing.

'Nothing like the zeal of the newly converted,' Huw said.

Owen caught sight of Bethan staring at Huw from the window. He felt again a mixture of jealousy and fondness laced with the excitement of having seen something he perhaps should not have. He relived in his mind, the events of the day before: the sight of Bethan, her head thrown back against the stone wall of the cottage orchard, and the sight of his brother kissing her face and throat, his arms up around her arched back. Owen, who had been sitting on the top of the pillar of the gate to the orchard, had mostly been obscured by the apple trees and the fading light; he had considered flinging a ripe fruit at them to make his presence known, as he had seen them enter the orchard and lean up against the wall a little way along and below him, but the sight of his brother unexpectedly kissing Bethan had held him transfixed and frightened at the same time: bringing to him feelings and sensations that were perhaps, arrested, though he reasoned they were natural; he was annoyed with them both for giving rise to these feelings at a time when there were enough battles going on in his mind already. He was worried about having to go to school in town; mostly he was worried about his writing:

174

left-handed, he had, after plenty of rappings on his knuckles by the metre ruler of various teachers and his headmaster, come to write right-handed, but he was self-conscious of his writing, that had been deemed 'spidery' by his teacher. The stems of his letters had been mockingly dismissed as 'reaching towards the heavens.' Owen felt sure that his teachers, who already saw him as too big for his boots, would somehow pass on their sneers and there would be nothing but laughter and mockery awaiting him when he arrived. He did not see how he would fit in either, as there were only a few boys from the village that went to the town school and they were all older than him. Owen wondered how the boys from the town houses would take to him, and whether he would have any friends. Would the other boys laugh at him as he walked to school? He imagined Edryd priming his friends with Owen's weaknesses, real and exaggerated, and felt sick at the thought; perhaps he would prefer to stay with his schoolmaster and headmaster, but then his mind turned over and he resolved to fight: Edryd and the imaginary boys who mocked him, the teachers and the English language that he would be taught in. In his imagination, he felled them all and took all the prizes as he so often had for art or poetry or literature in the many literature festivals and Eisteddfods that were held at the chapel. He thought about the pennies he had earned and the books, and the smile on his mother's face when he won them, and of the general recompense to be had in winning, and thus comforted in advance, he felt better about life in general, until that is, he felt guilty for his pride, swiftly followed by the usual annoyance at having to be exposed to these spiritual matters, so riddled with meaning and feeling, when so young. Annoyed and in turmoil, he started to build the fire for the evening. After he had built the fire, he helped himself to cake and sandwiches and then lay propped up on one arm eating them as he listened to Eilwen play a tune that he did not recognise, but one whose tendrils seemed to curl around the heart, and whose melody magnetised the memory; before long his thoughts had lost the power to take him on journeys of their choosing, and he was completely drawn in by the sounds. Robert got up with his notebook and stood by Eilwen showing her something he had written inspired by her music.

'Sing the phrases,' she said

Anwen began to echo the words and provide harmonies; Bethan's clear voice draped itself over the top of Anwen's powerful, fluid tones. Owen felt an echo of the emotion he had felt when the quarrymen had sung, rising up through his chest. He could see the sky from where he lay, and as he watched the kaleidoscopic spectrum of colour before the sea subsumed the red sun, he thought about all the peoples of the world and their rising and setting suns. What about all the other people and their religions, he thought, are they all wrong? As he thought this, he saw the middle-east section of the globe of the world, as on a map, with a sun rising at the centre; the rays of the sun extended across the dark continents of the globe, lighting them up. Owen understood that the rays of light were the gospel that was capable of extending and reaching everyone, one way or another. The music and the vision made him feel emotional and afraid that his tears might spill, he jumped up to tend to the fire. The tears did come as he threw peat and wood and once the flames had gathered, lavender, on the fire. The tears were partly born of frustration: tears at having been unable to find the answers to the thoughts that he wrestled with; tears of powerful attraction to the things of God, but also of the complexity of not knowing: not knowing God, despite the visions, and the sense of love and beauty he had experienced in the gatherings, but wanting to; tears of doubt: doubting the spiritual world, doubting his own sanity. But when he focussed on the lyrics that Robert had written: *Now is the time of prophesy, now is the time to be all you have created us to be, now is the time of understanding, who are we and who are we created to be...* and the music, he was drawn once again into a world of beautiful strangeness. A world where he felt he could get lost and found at the same time, a world where thoughts interacted with emotion and feeling in such a way that they nullified negative feeling and brought only warmth and a sense of understanding even though there did not seem to be any conclusive answers for him at that moment in time. Owen decided that it did not matter that he did not have all the answers. At that moment he pictured himself embarking on a journey of faith that would take him away from the land of his physical life across waters so wild and meaningful, that when he disembarked, that land would be more like the land of heaven from which it sprung.

September

Chapter 20

That autumn, Owen started school in town and after a few days
of walking the several miles there and back on his own, he was
invited by Edryd and his friends to walk with them, and so he
settled into a group of three or four, who he perhaps might not
have chosen, but liked well enough; he liked Edryd most of all,
particularly now that he was not trying to prove anything to
Owen and was just being himself. Owen appreciated his quick
wittedness and his regional solidarity. As was predicted, Owen
was doing well at school, though at first he had found it hard to
get to grips with the level of English that was required; he was
enjoying sharpening his brain on the keen wheel of History and
Literature; his favourite subjects. He had already won the Literature prize, and on the day that he did, Cerys Jones, a girl who
had also won a scholarship in town and whom he had noticed on
account of her spectacles and two blonde braids, as well as her
studious replies to questions in class, came over to congratulate
him with her mother, who knew his mother. Sometimes, when
he could not remember English words for things in class, she
whispered them to him from her seat behind him. She seemed
aware that she should not talk to Owen when he was with the
boys, for which Owen was grateful, but as Owen grew in confi-
dence and given his aptitude for his lessons, and his popularity
with the boys, he began to talk to Cerys during recess. During
these breaks from lessons, where they would sit against the back
school wall, he discovered that her father had run off to Australia,
leaving Cerys and her mother to fend for themselves; a fact that

made him feel more protective towards Cerys; his feelings softened further when he looked at her blue eyes and imagined her
long blonde hair uncoiled from the complicated ropes that were
pressed to her skull, that looked as though they hurt. Most of
the boys came from families in town that were better off than his,
apart from Edryd, which helped him form a kinship with Cerys,
but for the first time Owen began to feel a slight shame about the
fact that although his brother had ambitions for the ministry, he
worked in the quarry, and their smallholding was humble com-
pared to one or two of the houses he had been invited to that
had various floors and bathrooms with porcelain tubs and basins
rather than the tin tub that was filled and used in front of the
range at home. He found himself speaking of home less and less
and was not always keen on his family coming to school func-
tions, because he could not abide the provocative questions of
some of his peers, though he made excuses about these feelings,
even to himself.

Cerys was unusual in that her mother followed the Catholic faith
due to her Irish father. She wore a gold cross under her shirt.
Some weeks after their conversations had begun, Owen was sitting with her near the school orchard that was alive with butterflies due to the warmth of the day and the ripe plums. They had
picked blackberries and tipped handfuls of them onto the grass.
Cerys pulled the little cross out from between her buttons and
let Owen look at it. A tiny Jesus in a loincloth, his arms outstretched, hung on the cross. Owen was fascinated. The crosses
that he had previously seen were wooden or made of reeds and
here was this ornate work of art. Cerys did not keep her cross
out for long, she tucked it under her blouse and Owen wondered
what it might be like to nestle there between her warm skin and
her cool shirt; but he was left staring at a tiny stain of blackberry
juice on her white blouse.

   'When I am afraid in bed at night and think that I will never
see my father again I take hold of my cross and think of my
heavenly father and then the world is alright and I am no longer
aware of its turning,' Cerys said, leaning back on her hands and
tilting her face to the sun.

'What do you mean its turning?' Owen asked, popping another blackberry into his mouth, his mind still on the image he had in his mind of Cerys in her white nightgown, her hand on her cross, eyes raised to the ceiling in the manner of a Whistler painting, a cascade of golden hair falling from her head and all over her bedclothes.

'Time spinning like the globe frightens me,' she said, picking at the small wild daisies that grew through the grass they were sitting on. 'It takes me further from my father and further into the future. 'I don't want to get old and weep like my mother.'

'God is outside time,' Owen said. 'He is eternal. Time only exists on earth. We will be free of it when we leave for heaven,' Owen ate another blackberry.

Cerys jumped up. 'Oh please don't. Please don't speak like that,' she put her hands to her temples. 'I can't bear it. I can't contain it.'

'Alright,' Owen said, slightly annoyed but fascinated at the same time. She was like the liquid mercury that the science master had spilled onto the examining table. 'I shall say no more of time if you sit down immediately. If not, I shall remind you that it is time for Latin class,' Owen smiled.

Cerys sat down. 'Do you ever wonder how God managed to make so many millions of people look different? And only tiny spaces between the facial features—it's a wonder,' she said, her face flushed and beautiful as a peach.

To Owen, Cerys was a wonder. And a sign: of the future.

December

Chapter 21

From the end of September, Jacob, Martyn and Seth ran chapel
meetings every night up until a few days before Christmas. By
the third night of prayer meetings, the Atheist Society began
picketing them, trying to cause disruption by shouting through
the windows. Anwen, Bethan and Eilwen responded by singing
all the louder. One evening, Eilwen stopped singing and went to
the window: *We will not tolerate attacks from the Kingdom of
Darkness* she said. The men began to jeer. *Take out your sword
then missy, one of them mocked.* Eilwen began to sing scriptures
until they slunk away one by one, and then she shouted through
the window after them: *How does the sword of truth feel as it
slips in! Repent and be saved!* The following night two of the
atheists were converted at one of Jacob's meetings. With each
successive meeting, it seemed that the tension in the air had built
to bursting as people became hungrier and hungrier for spiritual
food and Jacob, Martyn and Seth were preaching that a thorough
breaking of the Holy Spirit was imminent. The meetings would
begin with Jacob or Martyn giving a testimony from the south,
or one of them would read a newspaper account from the valleys.
This would spark someone off praying and then another would
start up. Soon a woman might begin to sing a hymn or a man
read a passage from the Bible. One evening a child came in and
asked God very simply to save his father before he drank himself
dead. This set grown men off weeping for the man's salvation
and the next night the man appeared, gave his life over to Jesus
and the following night he brought his whole family who did the

same. Each night the pressure in the atmosphere built further and the testimonies were *like steps to heaven* as Gwyneth Hughes said one evening, as more and more people began to give their lives over to Jesus and to the wild abandonment of freedom of heart and soul to say nothing of spirit, that followed, which was often expressed in passionate prayer for loved ones and neighbours with singing, dancing laughing and weeping even from the dourest of people.

The district was full of expectation because the men who had left to work in the coal mines in South Wales following the lockout, were coming home for Christmas and it was rumoured that some of them had been touched by the revival in the south and were keen to pass it on. Following his encounter with Jesus, Rhys had begun to hold revival meetings in the coalmines, or in train carriages, outside the courts of justice, and wherever he went. His reputation as a fighter and a gambler had followed him from the quarries to the mines, making his conversion even more remarkable, but as Jacob said to his own stunned family when he gave them the news: each hardened soul saved from themselves is its own miracle. According to the press, hundreds had responded to Rhys' simple message that Jesus was The Way, The Truth and The Life, with witnesses reporting that when Rhys uttered the words people would fall to the floor under the power of God only to rise up with the same power, just like when the apostles in the book of Acts laid hands on people and the power of God for miracles was transferred. The community was stunned at this news, and all were clamouring to see this new Rhys with their own eyes. According to the journalist who had attended the meetings in the mines, hardy miners would fall to the floor weeping and crying out to God to save the lost. Another article concerned a man who said he had been accosted on the way to work at the mine by an angel who told him not to go to work that day, but to make plans to go and preach in England instead. That day there was an accident in the mineshaft where he worked. And so the testimonies from the south *came like a flood that would soon engulf us* as Seth put it. Anwen had prophesied that it would be *one of ours who struck the rock that caused the water to flow.*

There had been spurts of Holy Spirit activity as witnessed by Owen and the Evans family; and so the time came for the living water that had become a trickle to flow in the mountains.

Chapter 22

On a clear night in December, Owen stood in front of the vast red doors of the chapel, gazing down the mountain. His mother was rehearsing inside with Bethan and Eilwen and the quarrymen's choir for the evening meeting. Snow lay waist deep in the valleys, surfaces sparkling as if composed of crushed diamonds, emitting a blue aura as if it were a living being. By contrast, the sky was already punctuated with stars: the evening star seduced the eye, and the moon was ripe. Owen was looking at a tree, the stripped upper branches of which were bent backwards as if in an attempt to prop up a sky that seemed somehow heavier than usual. He focussed on the silence; the atmosphere was so companionable that he hoped that it would last for as long as possible; he felt as though he were the only person present in the world and as if the stillness was a being in its own right. As he stared at it the snow seemed to pull him into its glittering whiteness and he began to experience the revelation that the whiteness was starker because of the darkness. Was darkness necessary to prove the light? Robert's words rang in Owen's mind and he was so focussed on pondering these things, that for a while the golden light that he could see shining way down the mountain path did not register with him; as he came into a state of awareness, he thought at first that it must be someone coming to the meeting, holding a lantern aloft, but the light grew and grew, and as it did, Owen became more and more unsettled in his spirit: the light had begun to take the shape of a man and Owen began to shake with fear and with the proximity of holiness. As the man of gold advanced towards him, he wondered whether he should go in, he could hear his mother's voice as she warmed up; sporadic voices were beginning to warm up too. Owen began to see smaller, whiter lights moving up the mountain, followed by figures. He realised that these were the worshippers coming to chapel, but the gold man seemed to be leading them. Owen noticed that the bright gold of the form of the man did not blur as light from a lantern would, but rather the light was contained sharply and geometrically. Owen turned and glanced at the doors of the chapel, as he turned back, he expected the figure to be gone, but it had moved further up the mountain, as had the people who were advancing behind him. The golden man stood two or three feet above the heads of the tallest men that were advancing. Now Owen could see a second gold being that appeared to be a woman. Another trail of people followed before a third gold being could be seen. Owen understood that these ones must be heavenly beings. The primal fear that Owen felt, riveted him, and he began to pray that someone would come out to share this experience with him and to convince him that he was not losing his mind; as he thought this, his mother appeared on the steps behind him.

'I had the strangest feeling that we were going to have a visitation tonight—Owen can you sense it? It is so taut out there, as if the heavens are about to tear and spill their contents. Do you take my meaning Owen?'

Owen stared at his mother and nodded.

'Look, they are coming up the mountain already. They have come prepared for a long vigil—don't the lanterns look pretty? They lend an exquisite beauty to the aspect don't they—moving along like that?'

'You don't see them mother do you?'

'Of course I do, they're beautiful,' Anwen put her arm around her son.

'The gold ones?'

'They look white to me,' Anwen said.

Owen realised Anwen was seeing the lanterns, but she could not see the gold beings, the first of whom was now so close that Owen's legs began to shake. She gave Owen a sideways hug before going back inside. The gold one stood a few yards away from him, but Owen felt engulfed by his presence; he had long hair that reached down below his shoulder blades that was billowing as if in the wind, though there was not a breath of wind; unlike human hair, his seemed to be alive beyond the roots, like the angel Owen had seen in his dream. He wore a white tunic with a white sash that had gold fringes. Gold inscriptions were written on his belt in a script that Owen was not familiar with. He smiled at Owen and said. 'Do not be afraid. We have been sent to bring what you prayed for.' He handed Owen a scroll about the size of Owen's hand and commanded him to eat it. Owen did as he was told and the scroll melted like wafer beneath his tongue.

'This is your earthly assignment. It will become clear to you at the proper time.'

Owen felt his knees begin to buckle. 'Strength!' the gold being said.

Immediately, Owen felt the muscles in his legs tauten and strengthen; he had the peculiar sensation that his muscles had grown.

'Your spirit muscles have been strengthened to carry what you will see. Tell no one of your visions before time or you will be throwing pearls to swine. Pray for strength and it will come.'

Owen nodded. The gold one walked into the chapel where Anwen had begun to lead the worshippers in song, *Here is love, vast as the ocean, loving kindness as a flood, when the prince of peace our ransom, shed for us, his precious blood...*

Owen realised the gold being had walked straight through the oak doors. He had hardly digested this notion when the second gold being, the woman, moved past the people who were now only yards from Owen; she called out to him in greeting. Her hair was fashioned into a mass of elaborately patterned braids; she was more beautiful than Owen had ever seen beauty. The skin on her face, forearms and hands was gold as was her dress that was fashioned out of a crumply gold material, heavily embroidered with a thicker material at the large hanging cuffs, in the style of mediaeval dresses and around the edges of the dress and train. As she approached, Owen was filled with such peace and love, that he wanted to melt into her arms. 'My name is

Peace,' she said. Peace raised her hands and placed them either side of Owen's head. 'The peace of Jesus to guard your heart and mind,' she said. Then she took a step towards him and blew on him; her breath was fragrant with scents that Owen had never encountered.

'Safe passage to travel in and out of the veil,' she said.

As Anwen sang, the second gold one began to sing with her. *Grace and love, like mighty rivers, poured incessant from above...*

'I love this hymn,' the womanly being said. 'It is one of our favourites, we love William.'

Owen thought she was speaking of William Rees who had written the hymn the previous century.

'Your eyes will be fully opened to see into the heavenly realms,' she said. She licked the tips of her fingers and touched them to his eyes. Owen's eyes fizzed as though hot coals had seared them, but he did not feel any pain; then she touched Owen in his stomach and he doubled over as heat resonated through his body.

'Streams of living water will flow through you,' she said, as if answering the question that had barely formulated in Owen's mind. He realised that the beings could read his thoughts.

Owen felt such a sense of peace that he might have melted and become liquid gold himself. He stood there for a moment as wave upon wave of peace flooded his body.

'Increase!' she said, as she too walked towards the doors. Owen felt the peace and the delicious, unearthly fragrance increase until he wanted to remain in that euphoric state for eternity, but the third being was coming towards him. Owen began to tremble again. This being had a flowing beard and hair and appeared to be ancient and young at the same time; he was wearing a long blue cloak, the inside of which was red and had inscriptions embroidered in white. As he approached Owen he held him in a gaze that Owen found so unfathomable and petrifying that he could not stand. He was carrying a vast sword that seemed to be of similar height to his own; as he approached, he raised the sword above Owen. Owen shrank in fear, but the being commanded, 'Strength!' and again, Owen straightened up and had the odd sense that he had increased in stature. As Owen wondered at this, the being plunged the sword into Owen's chest. Owen gasped. He felt as though molten metal had invaded his chest cavity and he should prepare to die. The being said in a loud voice, 'You shall not die but live to proclaim the glory of the Lord!'

Owen recognised the words from Psalm 118 verse 17.

As he said this, Owen's body relaxed and the heat in him cooled; the terror dissipated.

'Take off your boots, this is holy ground!' the being commanded. Owen knelt to take off his boots. He felt ashamed. 'You will not suffer shame,' the being said. 'Our Lord took your shame. Do not insult him by holding onto what he suffered and died for.'

Owen tried to pull himself together; he had never known such terror.

'There is strength in humility,' the being said. 'Our God opposes the proud, but he gives grace to the humble.'

Owen's hands were having difficulty with the laces of his boots, the cold had made his fingers inoperable, but the words of the being seemed to pass into Owen and take root in him. Even as Owen looked down he felt himself to be at the entrance of a raging hot furnace, behind which a mighty army stood. He looked up. The being was waiting. As Owen stood, his toes numb with cold, the golden being pulled the edge of his cloak and swept it over Owen. 'Know the fear of the Lord!'

The sound of the being's voice was like concentrated thunder rumbling through the mountains. Owen felt himself being thrown backwards over the big boots of the quarrymen that stood in rows against the doors. He understood that he never wanted to be on the wrong side of the power that came out of the being that had now also disappeared through the doors. He became aware of his mother's voice as she continued singing, *Who his love will not remember, who shall cease to sing His praise...* and then a man was helping Owen up.

'Are you all right my boy? You seemed to stumble backwards quite forcefully over the boots. It looked most un-natural. Can I get you something or someone?'

Owen shook his head and assured the man that he was fine and that he just wanted to sit for a little while. People of all ages were streaming into the chapel now. Owen walked down the steps and into the graveyard that stood to the side of the chapel. He walked round and round pulling at his hair with his hands, trying to contain what was happening to him, but he found he could not form any thoughts. He considered calling his mother and asking her to take him to the hospital. Part of him thought that he could not live with what had happened; he felt as though he were being asked to do something that he did not have the strength for. As he thought this he heard again the command *Strength*! and he found himself grow stronger; a moment later he remembered the command for peace and felt peace grow in his mind and body like a living thing; he began to laugh with relief as he remembered the words from Ephesians 4 verse 8 *And he gave gifts to men.* God had given him the gifts that the angels had communicated to him.

'What are you doing out there dancing on the graves?'

Huw stood at the little wrought iron gate with Bethan. 'Come inside you fruitcake,' he said.

Bethan was laughing. 'Straighten your silly hat Bethan,' Huw said, straightening her hat, that was, in truth, silly with its feather and fruit fashioned from felt.

'It's chapel time,' Huw said, theatrically, raising his own imaginary hat. Bethan lifted a hand to straighten her straw hat and began laughing some more. Huw was holding his arm out to Owen. They linked arms either side of Bethan and walked up the chapel steps and through the red doors that looked unmarked and innocent enough despite what they had witnessed.

'Next time I will wear your hat.' Huw said to Bethan.

'You will wear it now!' Bethan said, taking the hat from her head and planting it on Huw's head.

'So I will,' Huw said pulling it down a bit. He went in wearing the hat, but soon placed it back on Bethan's head.

As Owen entered the chapel, he saw the three beings standing behind the big chair that the minister was supposed to sit in, though these days, Jacob never sat there except to pray; he preferred to speak walking up and down the front or amongst the people. Now however, Jacob was sitting there, deep in conversation with Martyn who was kneeling on the floor next to him and Seth who was standing next to them. The three men began to pray. Huw, Bethan and Owen made their way up the side steps to the gallery, as there was no room in the pews nor on the floor or even in the aisles in the main chapel. Up in the balcony the pews were packed with young people. Owen recognised Robert and other friends of Huw's.

'Why are you not singing tonight?' Owen asked Bethan.

'She needs to look after her hat,' Huw said. 'It demands a great deal of care and attention.'

Bethan began to giggle and Owen responded to Robert's wave from across the room.

'He is a joker isn't he?' Bethan said, watching Huw.

They sat down in the pew a few rows from the back of the balcony. Owen stood up for a moment to look over the balcony. The angels were still there; as he looked, they looked up simultaneously and said:

'Praise the Lord who gives gifts to men! May they grow in character so that they can be properly utilised!'

Owen jumped and Bethan asked if he was all right. 'Yes,' Owen said. 'I had a kind of hiccup.' Owen realised that only he could hear as well as see the heavenly beings.

'People! Martyn, Seth and I have had some time in prayer and we feel that the Holy Spirit will not come if there is anything in our hearts that will hinder him. Men and women, children even, is there anything that you feel you have in your hearts and minds that would hinder a move of the spirit of God?' Jacob said.

The people began to murmur. Some fell to their knees in prayer. A young woman with a tiny baby in her arms went up to the front and began to call out to God for forgiveness. 'I have not served you even though I felt you call me. I preferred the world and the ways of this world and went too far into them. I preferred to drink and to forget my cares, even with this little one at my breast I preferred to drink! Rescue me now Lord!'

The woman fell onto the floor still clutching her baby and Anwen and Eilwen rushed to help her up; they took her to one side, and while Eilwen held the baby, Anwen prayed with the young woman. The effect of the woman's confession was that many others began to do the same, while others began shouting out in thankfulness and praise until Jacob called for silence as Rhys came rushing through the crowds accompanied by three other men. 'People!' Jacob said. 'This is Rhys Davies and he has something to say!' Jacob, Martyn and Seth knelt briefly with them in prayer. A hush came over the room as Rhys rose to speak.

'I have much to say, but I pray you will hear my young daughter first, she is yet twelve.'

There was silence as Catrin, her hair tied in a ribbon, stepped out of the front pew and took her place on the platform in front of her father.

'Until recently, I was an unhappy child, like. My mother was unhappy and my father was unhappy,' Catrin said in a strong, clear voice, glancing briefly at her father who placed his hands lightly on her shoulders. 'One day, a friend visited with his mother—I cannot name him as I have not asked his leave—and he gave me a drink of water, and he also said to me, that his mother had food that would never run out. That night, I went to bed and said my prayers. As I did so, Jesus came into the room. He was shining white. He showed me His marks on His hands and then He said He was the bread of life and that I could have the living water, which is the Spirit of God flowing through me. Then He went, and I went to bed. The next day, when I woke up, I was full of joy unspeakable, and I had no shame. I became bold because now I knew who I was—a daughter of God—and I had purpose—to find other sons and daughters of God and rescue them from the darkness that was trying to take them though they knew this not.'

The crowd of people that had swelled the chapel further since Catrin had begun speaking, began to applaud and praise God, but Rhys held up his hand to silence them and Catrin continued. 'Also I knew in my heart that my father was going to be saved by Jesus and all my family too. And here is the proof of it,' Catrin looked up at her father who looked as though he might cry, but instead he began to speak in a voice that sounded like Rhys's voice, but was so full of authority and kindness that Owen, who was still struggling to take in all that Catrin had said, closed his eyes and took the sides of his head in his hands in an effort to contain all that had been happening. Owen knew that this was the man who had insulted his father and caused the clash between the dissenters and the quarrymen, but his transformation was complete. A woman next to him smiled at him and putting her hands between his shoulders, prayed briefly for him. Owen, embarrassed, kept his eyes closed but as he began to feel calm and clear minded again, he looked up to thank her, but the woman had gone.

'We have come from South Wales to ask forgiveness from our brothers who returned to the quarries. Brothers! Will you come and receive our forgiveness,' one of Rhys's companions said.

Members of the quarrymen's choir made their way to the front. Soon the men were embracing and begging each other for forgiveness and then they burst into song. This went on for some time until Rhys went up to the big ministry seat at the front and leapt onto it. As he stood, he shouted out, 'Jesus is The Way, The Truth and The Life!' With the utterance of the words, an eerie event took place: a wind came into the building and swirled amongst the people; the wind caused many to fall to the floor and others to weep. People, finding themselves labouring under the unexpected conviction of sin in the sudden presence of a Holy God, began to fall on their knees and cry out for forgiveness. No one seemed concerned that Rhys had had the temerity to stand on the big seat, least of all Jacob who was on his knees beside it, his face raised in wonder.

'Do you feel the wind of the Holy Spirit?' Jacob shouted. People began to shout out for salvation, others that they were healed. Jacob, Seth, Martyn and Rhys moved through the crowd, laying their hands on people's arms, heads, shoulders and uttering words of encouragement. Jacob called for Robert, Huw, Eilwen and Anwen to do the same. An elderly man threw away his sticks and danced a jig with his wife. Outside, people began to push in through the doors; some were even trying to climb in through the windows as the crush to get in became overwhelming.

'People we must make way for others. As the Spirit moves your heart, if you have had your touch from God, spill forth onto the streets and pass it on to your fellow man and woman so that others may come in. Lay hands on people—the gift of the Holy Spirit is transferrable!' Seth and Martyn opened the door at the back of the building and people began to make their way out.

The meeting lasted until the early hours of the morning, after which further groups of chapel people made their way down the mountain and onto the streets singing and laughing and sharing the gospel with anyone who was awake enough to listen. Owen and his family walked home through the snow, Jacob holding the lantern aloft. They were as silent as their footsteps. There was no possible way to describe the events of that evening. Owen watched his boots press into the snow until they were covered in white and disappeared.

Chapter 23

Owen did not tell anyone about the heavenly beings as he did not know how to, or whether he had leave to; besides, he was not sure that anyone would believe him; he was not sure if *he* believed him. He was experiencing mixed feelings about all that had happened, but his confusion had caused him to turn to the Bible in a new way. He began reading about the men and women who saw angels and visions in the Old and New Testaments and was comforted, until he began to understand what was demanded of them in exchange for the gift and then he would begin his vexing all over again. He had not even discussed his experiences with his mother, though he had asked her about angels and she had spoken to him about Gideon, Jacob, Mary and Joseph and other Biblical figures that had had angelic encounters, and once he could connect himself with a broader spiritual narrative he began to feel better about what he had experienced. He had half a mind to speak to Catrin, who seemed so clear about everything, but did not know how to approach her, given his muddled emotions, and he did not want to suffer the embarrassment of having his mother arrange a meeting. As the revival gathered momentum, more and more people began to experience supernatural phenomena, and reports began to be made known about strange lights in the sky, visions and other mystical experiences as well as healings of the emotions and the body. The overwhelming sense that Owen was experiencing however, was that something had been impressed upon him that he had not asked for. He knew he should feel grateful for being singled out for these experiences which often left him feeling so spiritually uplifted and full of love as to not want to come down again, as at Heledd's house, but then before long he became confused and resentful again, wanting to be left to explore the usual physical maps of his youth, only to be taken up again by the wonder of it all, as in the recent meetings, and to leave the meeting and the state of wonderment, before questioning all over again. As he battled with his mixed feelings he heard these words in his spirit: *There are two kingdoms. Both are doing battle for you*; he thought of the two rams he had seen with Edryd by the lake and he knew it was a battle of life and death.

Chapter 24

The journalist for the London paper placed his top hat on a pile of Jacob's sermon notes, before taking out his notebook and sitting down. Anwen and Owen sat at the dining room table, facing Jacob's desk, looking like spectators at the races. Jacob was smiling and laughing at the good-natured pleasantries that the reporter was making. Owen noticed that the reporter had a large balding head and a beard wide enough for a family of swallows to nest in; he sniggered slightly as he made this observation and, Anwen slapped him lightly on the leg. After a moment or so more of preamble, the reporter became serious and taking up his pen and notebook, he asked Jacob if he was ready to begin. Jacob composed himself in a way familiar to Anwen and Owen by crossing his right leg over his left and leaning back in his chair as if attempting to view something from a great distance.

'You look very bright for a man who was taking a chapel meeting until two am this morning.'

'I like to think I am not dull, and when The Spirit is moving, you move with Him,' Jacob said, smiling at his wife across the room.

'What would you say to accusations that you are stirring people into a frenzy. Some of the parents in these parts are not happy about their young people being up so late and being stirred to passion and emotionalism?'

'I am not responsible for a *frenzy* as you put it. We make way for The Spirit and we trust His work. Jesus is passionate and He was emotional on earth—he was angry at injustice for instance, and when the sacred was made profane—as when he overturned the tables of people who had turned the temple into a marketplace—he wept with compassion at the death of Lazarus. Having made these points, I will say that sometimes the flesh comes out at the meetings, but as I always say, better out than in,' Jacob smiled, 'and God can heal. We work as a team—men and women—to support people who are experiencing the Spirit in a powerful and often unsettling, way, though He is always good, *'And we know that all things work together for good to them that love God, to them who are the called according to his purpose.'*

'Romans 8 verse 28,' Anwen whispered to Owen. 'One of my favourites.'

'Very liberating, I am sure,' the reporter said. 'It is clear you were born to preach,' he smiled. 'Tell me sir, about this fellow Twym, whom have now seen quite cured, as was confirmed at the hospital. Is it true that this fourteen year old was *completely* deaf from infancy and now he can hear and utter sounds?'

'Yes. You knew that didn't you? He was as deaf as a post and now he is as cured as a kipper!' Jacob, slapped his thigh and winked at Anwen, which Owen found embarrassing.

Owen could not suppress a groan. The reporter smiled and examined a plump, white hand as if expecting his next question to spring from his fingertips.

'You seem to have a special dispensation in this area do you not?' the reporter said.

Jacob laughed loudly. 'You mean Gwyndaf? Yes, the Lord has been gracious to me. I have badgered Him so much that he is trying to prove a point: He hears me and so does everyone else.' Jacob laughed so much that the reporter became impatient.

'You would be forgiven sir, for thinking that some kind of conspiracy was afoot.'

'Yes, that would be understandable,' Jacob said, leaning forwards conspiratorially in his chair.

Anwen suppressed her amusement. Ever since she had had her encounter with the Holy Spirit she giggled far more than usual.

'After all we are not speaking of natural matters here, but rather su-per-natural, matters of the spi-rit,' Jacob drew the words out. 'Have you read the New Testament?'

'I have received a classical education sir.'

'Well, there you have it. A little knowledge is a dangerous thing! There is knowledge and then there is *understanding*,' Jacob said, his foot going up and down, to Owen's distraction.

'Have you read the New Testament with understanding—with the revelation that only the spi-rit can give? Have you prayed before reading and asked the spirit—the Holy Spirit of God to guide you?'

'No I have not—I think—I do not,' the reporter said, shifting his chair backwards slightly.

'Indeed we must remedy that.'

'Yes, well, perhaps at the end of the interview.'

'As you like. But let us hope in holy fear that the world does not end before then as I am not sure where you will be bound!'

The reporter stared at Jacob.

'By heaven I am only sporting with you man,' Jacob rubbed his hands together. 'Be at peace! The Lord will provide the opportunity!' Jacob roared with laughter and winked again at Anwen who smiled and nodded and said 'indeed.'

'Mother,' Owen pleaded.

Anwen put her arm around her son and squeezed his shoulder. 'Don't be so serious my Owen,' she said.

'Without further ado,' the reporter said, taking up his fancy pen, 'Would you like to describe what happened to Twym, Mr Evans.'

Owen thought the reporter something of a dandy and imagined him preening like a peacock in front of the mirror in his undergarments and top hat, which temporarily suspended him from being embarrassed by his parents in his presence.

'Jacob. Please call me Jacob. It is my name and I am blessed to have it.'

Jacob grew serious.

'It was a meeting like many others we have been having of late—by this I mean, we started with some beautiful worship—the women from the district who love the Lord Jesus with all their hearts sing as beautifully as angels and are not afraid to show themselves to be so—'

The reporter nodded and tapped his foot, which gave him an air of impatience and annoyed Owen.

'After a time, I felt the presence of the Holy Spirit enter the chapel and I stated this fact. Shortly afterwards, I announced His presence I felt my hands heating up—'

'What do you mean sir—heating up?' the reporter interrupted.

'I mean sir, that my hands were so hot that they felt as though they were on fire—as if they had been thrust into a furnace—and I knew then I needed to lay hands on the sick and that they would be made well—just as the Lord told the disciples in the New Testament.'

The reporter nodded, 'Go on.'

'I called for healing, and the people rushed to the front like sheep let forth from a pen. I began laying hands on the people. Some fell to the floor with the force of it—'

'What do you mean sir?'

Jacob leaned forwards again. 'I mean sir, that when the Holy Spirit—the power of God—the primal power that created you and me and the whole universe is present—most people cannot stand, they fall over, they shake, they weep at the sudden revelation of their sinfulness, they cry out for forgiveness, they sob and beg and plead to be given eternal life through the blood of Jesus for the world to come.'

'And all this was happening—when?' the reporter looked up at Jacob without lifting his chin, raising his brows as he did so.

'Initially—during worship—God alights on our praises. All this and more.'

'Such as?' The reporter's pen was poised in the air like a question mark.

'Praying for salvation and casting out demons—'

'Casting out demons?' the reporter stroked his beard and frowned. 'Can you elaborate sir?'

Jacob leaned back again in his chair and crossed his arms. 'Do you think sir, that demons only needed to be cast out in the days that our Lord Jesus Christ walked the earth?'

The reporter stared at Jacob.

'Well sir, *many* are afflicted today, but today those suffering under the influence go to a doctor or to hospital or even prison. They try to rationalise these impulses, to apply science—'

The reporter smiled before speaking again.

'I have heard accounts of men coming to your meetings and never being able to touch a drop thereafter. I have interviewed the local publican. He is by no means pleased.'

Jacob laughed. 'Indeed we are putting him out of business!' Jacob winked at Owen who raised his brows and smiled.

'So would you say they have been delivered of a drinking spirit?'

'Well sir, they are delivered of drinking spirits!' Jacob leaned forward to deliver his joke and then roared with laughter.

'And their wives and children are better off for it!' Anwen said.

Jacob laughed and said 'indeed,' and now the reporter laughed too and said 'indeed' as well.

'What are demons and how do they operate?' the reporter asked.

'Demons are *spi-rits*—fallen angels—who chose Lucifer when he fell because of his pride. Their aim is to take as many people as they can to hell with them. One of their chief activities is to cause double mindedness or confusion about the things of God so that people will go their own way—which in the end is his way.'

'How does this happen?' the reporter said, scribbling in his notebook.

'In the mind—a thought deposited by a demon in the service of Satan will often seem to be an innocuous thought no different to any other, though of course some might be obviously evil suggestions—his oldest trick is to get a person to doubt the existence and supreme authority of God.'

'As with Eve?

'Exactly,' Jacob said.

'And in the mind—can wrong thinking lead to madness?' the reporter asked without looking up.

'It could,' Jacob said. 'There now, I see where you are going,' Jacob said, uncrossing and then crossing his legs again. 'The battle is for the mind, therefore as St Paul tells us in his second letter to the Corinthians, *we need to cast down imaginations, and*

*every high thing that exalts itself against the knowledge of God,
and bring into captivity every thought to the obedience of Christ.'*

'How does one differentiate between thoughts from God and
thoughts from demons?' the reporter put down his pen and
looked directly at Jacob. 'How can you prove that this revival
comes from God and not from some other source.'

'One needs to know the one who is Truth and to recognise
His voice—Jesus Christ of Nazareth. Secondly, there is the fruit
of it, which is love, forgiveness, healing, joy,' the enemy of God
is a corrupter of fruit, he seeks to destroy, not to edify.'

'And what of the person's own thoughts? Surely he is not
just a tool in the service of Satan—or indeed God.'

'Indeed not. A man needs to be transformed by the renewing
of his mind once he has accepted Christ, it is his responsibility to
crush the voice of Satan in his mind and plant the word of God
instead.'

'What takes place when the demon is cast out?'

'The Lord reveals to me, what the demon spirit is. I simply
command it to come out in the name of Jesus Christ—he is the
authority, I am the ambassador—the power is in His resurrected
blood that overcame death—not of myself.'

'And then the person is free?'

'They are free, but they need the Holy Spirit of God to take
up habitation within them, in all His fullness, lest the demons
return, as Christ warned, in Matthew 12, with more like them.'

'Why must they accept Christ? Surely, in kindness—'

'A person who does not legally belong to Christ, through faith
in his birth, death and resurrection, is an open house as it were.
I could deliver him but he may end up in a worse condition when
the demon or indeed demons come back as with Legion in the
Bible—these people are often very violent and can speak in many
voices—a demon can imitate whomever or whatever it might—
say a man's voice in the prettiest of women.'

The journalist shuddered. 'As in a séance?'

Jacob pursed his lips and nodded.

'I have found this—teaching of yours—fascinating Mr Evans,
if a little disturbing, and I should like to know more, but I have
come to interview you chiefly about the boy Twym for whom I

have evidence from the hospital regarding his healing—could you explain what happened exactly?'

'His mother brought him to the front and stood behind him while I prayed, her hands on his shoulders.'

'How did you pray?'

'I placed my hands over his ears like so,' Jacob cupped his hands.

'Were they still hot as you said before?' the reporter asked.

'They were still hot,' Jacob said. 'I commanded him to be healed in the name of Jesus of Nazareth and then I began to click my fingers—his head turned to the sounds.'

The journalist tapped his pen on his notebook. 'By this you mean?'

'He had been completely deaf and dumb, unable to make a sound. I then began to utter the name Jesus and he repeated it.'

'How did his mother react?' the journalist asked, without looking up from his notebook.

'She wept,' Jacob swung his leg up and down with enthusiasm.

'My colleague, Cadfael, who it seems has been so taken up with this revival that he has been attending your—' the journalist coughed into his right fist, 'and your wife and son's meetings—it seems qualification for the ministry is less important in these moves of God,' he coughed again.

'I consider myself qualified by the Holy Spirit,' Anwen said, getting up to fill the kettle.

'Yes, indeed, I am sure,' the journalist said. 'And self possessed.'

Jacob and the journalist laughed. Owen did not like the reporter's interest in his mother and so remained impassive.

'Possessed of The Spirit I hope, though myself is alive and well too,' Anwen said as she went into the scullery. 'And it all began in a barn,' she said as she reached for the tap.

'I think you are not sure of anything,' Jacob said to the journalist.'The things of God must be experienced or they can be dismissed as nonsense, which is very grave indeed.'

'My colleague tells me Gwilt's father has been writing off his customer's debts, and one or two of them have returned to his shop with monies for accidental overpayments.'

'Indeed,' said Jacob putting out his hand in response to the journalist's. 'Miracles are happening left and right.'

'Could you give me some names and addresses of other witnesses to the healing of Twym Gwilt?' the reporter tapped his pen on his notebook.

'Indeed there is one here. Owen, my boy.'

Owen joined his father and the reporter at Jacob's desk.

'Well young sir, what did you make of the healing of Twym?' the journalist stood and picked up his hat from Jacob's desk. 'Did you see him healed?' he straightened his hat with the fingertips of both his hands.

Owen ran his fingers through his hair as he pictured the inside of the chapel: he saw the stunned expression on the face of Twym Gwilt, the son of the village storekeeper, who had never made a sound; his lips pursed and his breath pushing out the name of Jesus; he saw again his weeping mother and his incredulous father, who was only there at his wife's urging. He knew it was true but he could still barely believe it now.

'I saw him sir.'

'And?'

'At the time I was not sure that I could believe it. But I believe it now,' he said.

'It is most particularly hard to believe young sir. Many are the events that are occurring of late that are difficult to believe though the witnesses are many,' the reporter said, closing his notebook.

'What I mean sir,' Owen said. 'Is that it takes a while for our minds to catch up with these things,' Owen said.

'There are mysteries upon mysteries happening,' Anwen, who was placing a plate of round cakes on the table said. 'They need to be experienced to be believed.

'Why not come and see for yourself?' Jacob asked standing up and handing the reporter the notebook he had left on his desk. 'Some need to see with their eyes before they believe—even then, some, as in the days of our Lord—do not believe.'

The reporter politely declined Anwen's offer of tea. 'I think I might just do that,' he shook Owen's and Jacob's hands, before going to Anwen and taking her hand; he bowed slightly, 'I shall certainly do that.'

On the front doorstep the journalist turned and asked: 'Why revival?'

'God is the same yesterday, today and forever. He created us for a vital and living relationship with Him.' Jacob said. 'He is infinitely loving and merciful but we are quick to forget Him. Sometimes heaven needs to come to earth to remind us. Then heaven retreats and we must seek it again. The more we seek the more we find—He longs for true relationship with us—thus the onus is on us.'

The journalist smiled and tipped his hat and his parents said goodbye and closed the front door. From his chair at the table, Owen watched the journalist walk down the garden path towards the lower field, through the front window. At the sheep gate he paused and looked towards the house again as if he wanted to return to ask another question, but then he let himself out of the gate and walked down the road that lead towards the sea.

Chapter 25

Lloyd George said that the revival was "Rocking the Welsh people like a great earthquake," and so it was. The Evans group, as they came to be known, held meetings day and night at chapel, sometimes until two or three in the morning; besides Jacob, Seth and Martyn, often Huw or Robert would preach and occasionally Anwen too. Anwen, Bethan and Eilwen would sing at the meetings along with many other women, some of them young girls on the cusp of adulthood, who had become so passionate about the gospel message that they sang and sometimes spontaneously preached with great boldness in the power of The Spirit. Catrin began to accompany her father to the south and led meetings with him amongst the miners, many of whom 'came out of the darkness and into the light.' Soon pit and quarry meetings began with prayer and even children began or took part in meetings. The Women's Suffrage Movement praised the revivalists for freeing women to speak and preach alongside the 'big men' of the revival. Anwen appeared in their literature after being interviewed by them along with a well-known Lady who had been converted one evening when Huw was preaching. The police thanked the revivalists for 'putting them out of work,' as crime became almost non-existent. Football clubs closed down as players preferred to attend chapel meetings rather than play matches, much to Edryd's disgust, *cloudheads*, he called them. The thing that Eilwen found most extraordinary of all was that people were *kind* to each other again.

As the river of revival flowed and began to burst its banks and spread all over the country, there was some fervent opposition to the revival as reported in the newspapers by ministers of religion from various parts of Wales and from as far away as England who, though they had never been to the meetings, nonetheless condemned Jacob and the group, with one minister referring to the group in a letter to a newspaper as Jacob and 'his women.' *How sad that brother should turn on brother at such a time as this!* Jacob said. Regarding the outbreaks of joy and laughter and the speaking in unknown tongues in the meetings, there were some who scorned the notion that God might have a sense of humour and dismissed the unknown tongues as 'quackery' and remained stony-hearted in their resolution to refuse meetings and the 'general nonsense' that continued to interrupt their ordered lives. Gryff, *tired of beating his head against the stone wall of revival*, left for America for a time. Medical journals published articles denouncing the revival as hype and hysteria. The Humanist Society declared it 'foolishness and trickery' and accused people of having gone mad. *There is advancement of the Kingdom of Light and there is attack from the Kingdom of Darkness,* Anwen said one evening as she preached from Romans 14 verse 11, *but one day every knee shall bow and declare that Jesus Christ is Lord,* while Jacob was often heard to say: *those of us that know, know.*

Chapter 26

Snow piled up under the windows, rubbing out the paths, and burying the fields and sometimes the sheep too, in white. Owen sat in the back pew of the chapel waiting for the revival meeting to begin; he had decided that he was going to observe this meeting with cold clarity of mind to see whether he could control himself, and therefore come to some conclusions regarding the visions and the meetings. His mother, Eilwen and Bethan, mindful of not becoming exhausted and thereby open to satanic schemes, were resting and not singing that evening. Several young women gospel singers were visiting from South Wales with Martyn's friend, and they had offered to sing to give the three women a break. One of them was a renowned Soprano who had given up the stage for the chapel. Owen's current feeling was that if it all became too much for him he could escape. People were still streaming into the chapel, even though all the pew space was taken. Men, women and children began to line the walls. He recognised many people from the community, but there were others as well, many of these were young men and women who came night after night; some of them appeared to be very well to do and spoke other languages. People were coming from all over Europe to experience the revival personally, and to *carry back the fire* to their own churches. Owen read in their faces a kind of fervour, and saw coming off them a heat and a glow. Determined to control himself, Owen stared at his hands clasped in front of him in the pew and listened to the noise of the chapel filling still further. The sound of murmuring grew louder as people struggled to contain themselves in the now confined spaces. When he next looked up, he saw that the people who lined the walls were now three deep and the space between the first pew and the altar was crammed with young men and women, who lolled around chatting. On the balcony a mother raised her baby to coo at him; for a moment the child was suspended in the air above the balcony that ran all the way round the walls except for the part of the wall above the altar. A woman in the balcony above the child's head smiled down and alerted her friend to the baby below and they began to wave and smile at the child, delighted with it; but the child's fat red face sickened Owen for some reason. There was something about its blubbery helplessness that repulsed him; perhaps he identified with its hopeless flesh. The man next to him smiled. 'To think we were once like that,' he said.

Owen felt a sense of despair and wondered whether the man had been reading his mind. Half a dozen women appeared on the dais at the front of the chapel, one of them, a teenaged girl, in a large black hat began to speak: 'I am Maisie—'

'And we are her gospel singers!' another young girl announced. She too had an elaborate black hat with plenty of netting.

'And we love the Lord Jesus Christ with all that we are and all that we have!' a slim girl cried, her head tipped back to the ceiling, her arms thrusting up from her white shirt. She looked to be not much older than Owen.

You can refuse it all and go your own way, the voice in his thoughts said. *Choose this night what you will do.* Owen ran his fingers through his hair in despair. 'Yes alright!' he said. He realised he had spoken aloud but his voice was drowned in the eruption that greeted the girl's extraordinary singing: *Here is love vast as the ocean. . . loving kindness as the flood. . . when the Prince of Life, our ransom, shed for us His precious blood. . .*

People began crying out as the young women sang, their words creating the change in the atmosphere, that ushered in the Holy Spirit and that Owen was now becoming accustomed to. 'I can see heaven above me,' a woman shouted out. 'I can see the angels!' a child shouted. Owen began to experience something unprecedented: it felt as though the physical world was being pushed downwards by the heaviness of the spiritual realm above. He pictured Samson pushing the pillars of the temple apart and felt the forces around him in a visceral way. At the same time he pictured the demons that he had seen at Anna's; except that he saw them trying to enter the atmosphere above the chapel and being flung away by an invisible vortex above them, that was expanding with the prayer and worship of the people; they screamed as they were sent spinning into the outer darkness. Owen was afraid: 'I choose you Lord! He said out loud. Voices were tossed up as on an invisible sea:

'We love you Lord!'

'Forgive us for our arrogance in assuming we have the answers to life!'

'I did not know until now that I needed a saviour—save me and my family—save us all!'

The atmosphere in the room increased. There was a crash as two men appeared to fall over the back pews. Owen recognised Cadfael from The North Wales Press, who had recently interviewed Anwen and had now become friendly with her; he had taken to dropping by the cottage for regular conversations with Jacob and Anwen. The other man was also a journalist. The men tipped their heads back and laughed. Cadfael threw his notebook up in the air; it landed near the wall across from the back pews, just as the London reporter who had interviewed Jacob came in through the chapel doors at the back. Owen began to laugh. The London journalist caught sight of Owen and tipped his hat, before crouching down next to his dazed fellow journalists to take notes. All around him people continued to weep and cry out. He glanced behind him and saw a man on his knees near the back doors weeping and rocking. 'Forgive me Lord! Forgive me! I have gone my own way!'

At first Owen did not realise that this was his schoolmaster; it was so unlikely to Owen that he should see him splayed on the floor in such a humble position that Owen felt acutely embarrassed for him, as well as a desire to bolt, but at the same time he found himself fascinated by the spectacle, this was followed by pity: here was a man in pieces on the floor; though a man who would no doubt be put back together in quite a different way.

Jacob began thanking and praising God for the saved and for the miracles in advance. People shouted their responses, 'Amen! Halleluiah! More Lord!' Jacob continued to thank and praise the Lord, 'You are the living God, the God of Abraham, Isaac and Jacob! You are the same yesterday, today and forever! You are the only way Jesus! You are the way the truth and the life!' These shouts and exclamations went on for a while until Owen grew impatient and wondered why Jacob was telling God whom He was. Surely he knew? Owen began to amuse himself with thoughts such as these and before long he found himself looking around the room at the spectacle with increasing amusement. That woman over there did not realise that the flowers drooping from her hat were dangling in front of her nose; that man over there was showing the crack of dawn as he knelt and keened; that old woman dancing in the corner looked like the old fool from the travelling circus that had rolled into town recently; lost in these amusements, he did not notice the atmosphere drop in the room until he heard the music die down and his father's voice boom as he pointed to the ceiling.

'There are mocking spirits up there in the spiritual atmosphere that are causing people in this room to mock with them. There are people in this room that find the scene before them amusing. I would ask you to *consider* that at this very *moment* some of the people that you *mock*, are in the *process* of giving themselves to Christ. They are *walking* through the gates of *heaven*. Soon they will be *seated* with Him in heavenly *places*. Would you *hinder* them?' Jacob's voice cracked with emotion.

As he took in his father's words, Owen pictured the demons again. Though they had been spun out of the atmosphere above them by the prayers and worship of the people in the chapel, they continued their attacks from the periphery. He saw a vortex of swirling light above the women who were singing; in the swirls of white and yellow gold he saw the shapes of heavenly beings of various forms and description that he did not have words for, the forms were connected in a circular pattern. He heard the words from Psalm 133: *Behold, how good and how pleasant it is for brethren to dwell together in unity!*

The atmosphere became intense again as people began crying out once more. Again Owen felt a melding of fear and thrill mixed with shame for falling prey to mocking spirits, his former annoyance was banished as he realised that he had been a pawn, and what he thought of as his own cleverness was in fact, a weakness and a form of enslavement. He thought too of how easily he had slipped from feeling awe to giving way to mockery and it frightened him. *Enter ye in at the strait gate: for wide is the gate, and broad is the way, that leadeth to destruction, and many there be which go in thereat* he thought of the words from Matthew 7 verse 13. There was an ever more palpable presence in the room and as the women began to sing with more passion so the presence increased: *On the mount of crucifixion. . . fountains opened deep and wide. . . through the floodgates of God's mercy. . . flowed a vast and gracious tide. . . grace and love like mighty rivers. . . poured incessant from above. . .* Owen felt the hair on the back of his neck begin to prickle. His gaze was drawn upwards as he began to go into a vision with his external eyes: vast pillars of pearl appeared before him like a mirage; a glance at a man next to him proved to Owen that others did not see these pillars. Owen jolted with shock. The pillars seemed to be swirling with life, he saw sheens of colour in the pearl that he was familiar with, but he also saw other colours in the pillars that he did not have the language to describe. He found himself inwardly begging to see more. A voice in his thoughts said, *Repent for allowing your previous thoughts and I will show you more.* He immediately began apologising inwardly for his mockery. As soon as he did so, vast gates, higher than anything he had ever seen and glowing with vivid gold, rose up before his eyes, dwarfing the altar and the singers that he knew were behind the vision, and that he could hear but no longer see. Beyond the gates, Owen saw striking white flashes of a liquid so pure and bright that he could not look for long; he covered his face with his arm. *I have removed the veil*, the voice in his head spoke again. Owen looked up again and found that he could see through the closed gates, even though the gold that they were made of seemed solid; he saw a river that appeared to be composed of liquid crystal and as Owen gazed at it, he saw that the river had what appeared to be exquisitely thin, gold sheets mingling in it; as Owen stared at the river, it began to flow through the gates towards him, so that he felt himself pulling back in his seat as he felt heat in his face. *The river of life*, Owen thought; simultaneously, the river came rushing towards him and went right through his solar plexus. Owen gasped and began to shake so hard that he was aware that he was convulsing under the power of what felt like volts of electricity coursing through him, he felt as if the river and the electricity that seemed to flow through it was coming up through his chest and threatening to gush forth from his mouth, so that he felt as though he should prepare for his own death or surrender completely to the river; as he thought this he inwardly said: *I surrender*, and the convulsions died down; he heard the word peace and looked up and saw the angel named Peace above him. Now her massively powerful, yet somehow delicate gold wings, outstretched as they were, completely engulfed the space of the chapel above his head. He began to experience wave upon wave of peace, so that he felt that he had become like the gentle final waves that fizz on the shore after having been engulfed in the roar of mighty surf. Slowly, he became aware of hands on his shoulders and he drew strength from them; another hand was laid at the back of his neck. After a while the electricity calmed and he was able to look up at the two who had laid hands on him. A young man stood in the pew behind him. 'What was happening to you? The strength of the power here has been phenomenal.'

The young woman next to him spoke, 'Do not feel you need to tell us unless Holy Spirit directs you,' she said. 'Sometimes the things of heaven are too precious to be shared unless for a given purpose. You must ask leave from Holy Spirit first.'

Owen stared at them, unable to speak.

'Are you Jacob's son?' the young man asked. 'Perhaps you are born to be a mighty preacher like him?'

'He is born to be a prophet,' Owen turned to see Anna standing in the aisle across from him; she came and sat down next to him.

The young man and woman who had been praying for him began singing and worshipping again.

'You have dreamt since you were small, of things that have come to pass and of things too fantastic to describe because they concern the future, is this not so?,' Anna said.

Owen nodded.

His father's voice continued to thank and praise God, and the presence in the room began to increase again.

'You have had angels appear to you in your dreams and visions have you not?'

Owen nodded again.

'Then you are a seer prophet, are you not?'

Owen nodded yet again.

'I am going to lay hands on you and impart to you what I have, and to commission you to prophesy, if you are willing,' she said. 'The Lord has asked me to do this, though it will be your choice to do so. Are you willing?'

Owen nodded. He stood there as she prayed, unable to take in completely what she said and afterwards he could not remember her words either, or what had happened to him when she had prayed, though he wondered whether he had been transported somewhere for a time, nevertheless he felt the power and authority in them.

'Now,' she said. 'Get up quietly and go home. When you arrive, go upstairs and examine your face in the looking glass. Try not to encounter anyone on the way home and in the house when you arrive. Is that possible?'

Owen thought of his mother, who would be in bed, and of Huw who was upstairs in the balcony with his friends.

'I will tell your father that you have gone,' she said.

Owen nodded and looked into her eyes; while they were kind, they burned with a strength and intensity that Owen found intimidating and defied her almost century of age. Owen wondered for a moment how she had got there. As he stood up he heard her say, 'Don't worry, it's a gift, there's nothing you can do about that, you received it before you were born into this realm, but if you want to grow in the gift you must have the character of Jesus. This is the salvation from the self. I assume you are born again?'

Owen, still dazed, nodded.

'Then you have entrance to the kingdom, but if you want to operate to capacity in the kingdom, you will need to take up your cross and crucify your own desires in order to take on His. Only then will the fire come.'

Owen nodded.

'I see you understand,' she said. 'The choice is yours. Our Lord so honours choice,' her eyes glistened with emotion. 'And he is faithful.'

Owen stood up. 'Off you go,' she smiled at him.

He ran through the high red doors, tripping over the rows of miner's boots that stood on the steps in front of him; he ran headlong down the road his head tipped back and his arms splaying out behind him. The stone houses were dark and quiet, their occupants enraptured by the presence that had suspended their lives in the chapel. He let himself in quietly through the back door; the fire was low in the grate. In the scullery, he looked into the mirror. His face was covered in gold flecks. Owen stared; he looked away and looked back, the flecks were still there. Then he looked at his hands; they were covered with a gold sheen. He stood there staring for a long time; the gold on his hands seemed to contain green and red and blue sparkles as he moved his hands this way and that; he sat down on the floor and looked at his hands again, his forearms were also covered with the gold dust. Owen crept out of the washroom and into his bedroom. He opened his curtain so that he could see the silver pathway across the sea to the moon. In the darkness the gold was not visible. He pulled the covers beneath his chin and fell into a deep dreamless sleep.

January 1905

Chapter 27

Owen was woken by Huw appearing over his ladder with a bowl of oatmeal and buttermilk. 'Are you coming with us Owen? We are going to take revival fire to the university. Mother, Bethan and Eilwen are coming. Hurry up!'

Owen looked out of the window. It was only just getting light. He bolted his oatmeal before climbing down his ladder to go to the outhouse.

'Coming down!' he shouted.

'Avert your eye ladies!' Huw said. 'Long johns appearing from above!'

'Yes, and they may crack off with the cold at any moment,' Owen said.

The women laughed as Owen made his way outside. 'A fine pair of legs in the making,' Eilwen said.

Huw was preparing Rosie. 'I've done your chores for you. Spend what you need to. I can't do that for you.'

Standing over his stream in the outhouse, Owen had second thoughts. Would he rather spend the day idling at home while the others were out? He thought of all the reading and drawing he could do; or of the idling in town, with Edryd and the lads. Perhaps he could walk past the Matthews place in the hopes of seeing Cerys? He was expected to go; he was sick of expectations, of family, of school, and in his darker moments—of God. He saw his life stretching ahead of him a long way ahead: miles and miles of expectations. A knock on the door from his brother silenced his thoughts.

'Come on brother! We are loading up!'

The women sat in the back of the cart swathed in scarves and shawls against the biting cold, the tips of their noses red and in Eilwen's case, dripping. Their instruments were piled up under sacks in the back of the cart. Anwen handed round blankets and bottles of tea from her basket before getting into the cart with the ladies under the blankets. Owen put sacks over them to keep the snow off before huddling up with his own blanket at the rear of the cart with the instruments. Huw took the reins. They sang all the hours to the city. *Guide me, O thou great Redeemer, pilgrim through this barren land; I am weak, but thou art mighty; hold me with Thy powerful hand: bread of heaven, bread of heaven, feed me till I want no more, feed me till I want no more...* The ladies tried to get Owen and Huw to join in with their harmonising, but they refused. 'Sing to the valleys ladies. Sing to the mountains. The trees of the fields will clap their hands,' Huw said, clamping the words from Isaiah to his final suggestion. The women laughed and sang all the louder. Rosie's hooves rang sharply on the unfamiliar hard roads. They passed the Golden Tup, and the butchers with the sign that squeaked when the wind blew it, sending the bull with the ring in his nose skywards. Owen always thought of the head as severed, the eyes of the bull all glassy and dead. In the doorway, the butcher, Mr Awbrey took the pipe that he was puffing from his mouth and waved it at them from his sausage-fingered hand as they went by, his bullish frame engulfed by his striped apron.

They were still singing as they arrived on the outskirts of the city: *Open thou the crystal fountain, whence the healing stream shall flow; let the fiery, cloudy pillar, lead me all my journey through: strong deliverer, strong deliverer, be Thou still my strength and shield, be thou still my strength and shield...* men raised their caps at them from the sides of the road, a mother wheeling her two babies in a pram pointed to them and the elder baby waved her lace cap; a group of young men on the steps of the town hall jeered and asked to clamber aboard, but nothing could dampen the expectations of the group. At the university they were met in the entrance courtyard by Robert, who was in a state of great excitement.

'The Saturday Society is meeting at the moment in the smoking room. See the windows are just there,' Robert indicated. 'I have a feeling that if you ladies begin to sing, you will break into the atmosphere and bring heaven to earth. Owen, tether Rosie—there under those trees,' Robert indicated a copse of plane trees to Owen.

'Anwen,' Robert continued, helping her off the cart, 'these men are the most intellectually proud in the university. They take great pride in their achievements, and give no credit to God for creating them! Let us see what God does in them given many of them have been saying that religion is excess emotionalism for the feeble minded.' Robert was clasping his hands together in excitement. 'You begin ladies,' he smiled at Eilwen and Bethan as he began to walk backwards in his haste to return to the smoking room, 'and I will see if I can arrange for us to speak,' Robert dashed off in his black gown.

Eilwen began to play her violin beneath the windows that Robert had pointed out, and Bethan began to play on her mouth organ as Anwen sang, *Here is love vast as the ocean, loving kindness as a flood, when the prince of peace our ransom, shed for us his precious blood, who his love cannot remember, who can cease to sing his praise...* People passing by began to gather, and Owen became aware of the students in the building looking out of the window; some were throwing comments, but others were listening intently as the revival hymn pulled open their hearts: *On the mount of crucifixion, fountains opened deep and wide; through the floodgates of God's mercy, flowed a vast and gracious tide. Grace and love, like mighty rivers, poured incessant from above, and Heav'n's peace and perfect justice, kissed a guilty world in love.* Soon a shift in the atmosphere became perceptible and Owen began to get shaky, but this was a different kind of tremor to what he was used to, not fear, but excitement; he looked up and saw a dark haired woman staring down at them; immediately Owen knew the battle going on in her; her chest was bursting with the knowledge that Jesus was who he said he was, and that she felt she had to give this knowledge utterance in some way, but her father was a professor and a humanist and she feared his rejection of her; Owen almost called up to her, but

220

he did not want to embarrass her, nor himself either, though the shakes were building so much that it seemed that he might get beyond the point of embarrassment soon. After a while, Robert came out and said that Huw was to come inside to speak to the philosophy students.

'All of you come!' Robert said. 'The women too, though women aren't usually invited!' Robert laughed.

They followed Robert over a red carpet into a cavernous hall lined with busts of important looking men attached to pillars, up a grand staircase towards a landing where a larger than life sized portrait of an important looking man loomed over them, and then up another brief flight of stairs and through one of the imposing wooden doors that ran around an open corridor on the first floor. The room was filled with smoke and young men sitting on chairs facing a lectern. Robert slammed the door shut behind them before jumping onto the podium. 'This is the man I was speaking to you about—the man that was in my testimony. Huw, some of the men want to hear about salvation. Tell them how.'

'You simply give over your lives to Jesus,' Huw said.

'How do you do that?' a man shouted. His friend whispered something to him and they both laughed loudly.

Owen looked around the room. Most of the men were laughing and joshing. He felt bad for Robert in the face of the mockery, but Robert did not seem to mind. 'Perhaps he sees the end from the beginning,' Owen whispered to Eilwen, who was perched on the end of the low stage that the lectern was part of.

'He is a rare bird,' Eilwen laughed.

The men began firing questions. 'You mean you cease to exist as a thinking being in your own right?'

'Do you ask Jesus whether to have ale or beer in the pub?'

'Is he there in your marriage bed with you?'

There was great hilarity now; Huw too, was laughing and it seemed as though the opportunity had been lost. Remembering the activity of the demons in the chapel before he saw the river, Owen began to pray inwardly that the mockery would stop, and as Owen watched the faces of the students, he went into a vision and he saw a screen transposed over some of the men in the room on which scenes of their lives were being played out. Eilwen began to play again, which brought the change in atmosphere that they had experienced outside. Some of the men were still laughing, though a little more uncomfortably: there was more coughing. The door opened and the dark haired woman that had been watching them from the window slipped inside and went and stood near the back. Anwen noticed her and went over to befriend her.

'What is happening to the boy? He seems to be in some kind of trance!' A young man called out.

Huw shook Owen gently by the shoulders, Owen was experiencing the peculiar taste and texture of the scroll that the angel had made him eat outside the chapel: *This is your earthly assignment. It will become clear to you at the proper time.*

'Would you like to share what is happening with us?'

Owen became aware that his head was moving from side to side as he watched the visions over the men; he deliberately turned his head to focus on Huw. 'I was seeing what would happen to some of the men.'

'Was it all good?' Huw whispered in his brother's ear.

'I think so.'

'If it will encourage them would you like to tell them?'

Owen prayed inwardly for strength as the angel had commanded him to, and as he did so, he had the curious sensation of his spine hardening as if molten metal had been poured into it. He felt again Anna's firm hands on his shoulders as she commissioned him to prophesy the effect of which made him feel very calm; he nodded. The noise in the room had begun to quieten. Huw whispered in Robert's ear.

'The boy has had some visions which he would like to share with the men concerned,' Robert said.

One of the sceptics shouted out, 'Come on boy! Make it up as you go along and make it dramatic. I am growing weary of these scenes of hysteria.'

As the man spoke, Owen began to see scenes from his life playing out in his mind like a film, rather than in the open vision he had experienced with his physical eyes before. He began to speak them out.

'God is showing me that you had no intention of studying

medicine. You wanted to move to London and become a writer. You are studying medicine because your father is a doctor and he has laughed at your ambitions and torn up your poems. But God is saying he made you to be a writer and you have it in you to become one of the greatest writers in Wales. He is saying that you must follow your heart and your head will follow.'

The man was on the point of weeping. 'Did Robert tell you about my father?' he ran his hands through his hair. 'No I have told no one.' The man ran from the room.

Owen called out the names of three men who stood up. Robert sunk to his knees in reverence to the Holy Spirit moving in Owen, through his prophetic gift. Bethan went and sat next to Huw on the podium; she caught Anwen's eye and saw that her friend was weeping at the sight of her son moving in the calling that God had given him.

'Did Robert give you their names?' a man called out.

Robert held up his hand. 'Let the boy speak.'

Owen began by speaking of events in their former lives and then prophesied over their futures. All three of them would become missionaries, one to China, another to India and another to South Africa. The men trembled or wept under the power of God. The atmosphere in the room became thick with the presence of the Holy Spirit, and some of the men began to laugh, but this time the laughter was not of the mocking kind.

'I feel quite drunk though I have not drunk for at least three days!' the man who spoke clung to the arm of his friend who also began to laugh. 'And I have not drunk since at least our last cadaver!' the man doubled over with laughter and the students around him seemed to catch the laughing bug and began laughing also.

'Praise God! This is the joy of the Lord!' Robert said. 'Streams of living water are flowing! God sits on His throne and laughs with joy!'

The dark haired girl was weeping and shaking her head, but not unhappily. Anwen put her arm around her. 'I am so happy,' she said through her tears. Anwen laughed and pushed a wet tendril of dark hair from her face.

Huw whispered in Robert's ear again.

'Please do not speak of the boy's second sight without his permission. He deserves his right to privacy,' Huw said.

'Wait!' A man said. 'Tell us again what we need to do to get saved.'

'Well, you say a prayer like this,' Huw said. 'Dear Lord, through faith, I accept that you died on the cross for me to freely bear the sins that would have resulted in my eternal death. I am sorry for going my own way when you created me for relationship with you. I realise you gave me the freedom to choose life with you or life without you. I chose the former, now I choose the latter. Come in Holy Spirit to dwell in me, and give me the power that I need to walk out this life with true meaning and purpose. Today I choose life. Today I choose a new adventure in the spirit through close communion and relationship with you. Today I choose to be guided by you and not by my vain thoughts. Today I acknowledge that your ways are higher than mine and your thoughts are beyond mine! I choose to enter in to the mind of Christ!'

'Today it is then,' a young man said as he pulled the contents of his pockets, which included a sheaf of banknotes and some coins, onto the table. 'Today I choose God instead of filthy lucre!'

Owen watched in fascination as most of the men repeated Huw's words that, as had become usual, slipped from prayer into preaching.

Anwen and the dark haired woman came over to accompany Owen outside; on the way downstairs Owen quietly shared with the woman what he had seen as she looked down from the window; she began to weep on Anwen's shoulder.

'You are a true prophet,' she said.

The men were milling in the corridor laughing and chatting loudly. Doors began to open, and as they did so, the men began to speak of what had happened to them. They did not need to say much as people just seemed to catch what they had: students, men and women, appeared through the doorways and were simply asked to follow, which they did. Outside, Anwen began preaching to the crowd as Huw, Bethan and Eilwen moved amongst the people, praying with the ones who asked. Robert moved among the crowd laying hands on people and praying for their ailments. An uproar of prayer ensued as people began crying out for healing. Every now and again Bethan or Eilwen would interrupt Anwen, who was preaching the gospel, with a testimony: 'This woman had a withered arm since birth,' Bethan held the woman's arm up, 'but it became perfect before our eyes!' Bethan said.

The woman was clutching Bethan by the arm and blathering with excitement.

'This man tells us that he has been suffering from arthritis, but all the pain has gone from his hip and the swelling disappeared from his hand joints as we watched!' Robert called out.

The crowd that had grown larger and larger would erupt after each testimony, with people praising or singing snatches of hymns.

'The person of the Holy Spirit is healing thanks to Christ's death and resurrection!' Anwen called out. 'If you need a touch from heaven for your ailments or for those of your family, raise your hands to heaven now!'

Owen was sitting on the pavement. He felt euphoric, but exhausted, and content to watch the others. *You must learn to steward the gift and to rest in the Lord,* he heard the Holy Spirit warn him in his thoughts, *So that you will not be enticed from the narrow path.*

The testimonies continued, and the dark haired woman, whose name was Margaret, began going through the crowd and writing them down.

'She is the editor of the student newspaper,' Robert told Anwen.

Men and women began coming up to Robert and Huw asking how they could be saved. Like Bethan and Eilwen, they began kneeling with groups of students as well as men and women and some children of various ages and social background. Anwen called Owen over to help, and he too began to pray with seemingly countless people; at one point Owen looked up at the sky as a flock of starlings took off and flew south; he was gripped by a sudden pain in his chest, but he knew that the physical pain that he felt did not signify sickness but rather momentarily heart sickness at the knowledge of something dreadful to come that would take him and many others away from the spiritual beauty that surrounded him. Anna's words came back to him: *He is The Way and the destination.*

Later that day the group went to the boarding house with groups of students. There they knelt amongst the cigarette butts on the floor and spoke to people that were bedding down for the night because they had nowhere else to go. Prostitutes who had rented rooms were converted along with sailors and others who were in the rooms for the evening. Students who were converted in the morning were preaching the gospel by the evening. Late into the night, after singing hymns in the town square with the newly converted, the party drove home, arriving in time to do the first morning's milking. They found that Jacob had milked the cows, fed the livestock and begun the fire in the grate. Jacob was on his face on the floor in front of the fire. Anwen screamed and ran towards him. As she did so, Jacob began to get up.

'Don't worry Annie, my love. He came. He finally came.' Jacob pulled his wife to him. 'Though I had to repent of my bitterness to Him for taking Samuel,' his voice sobbed over the name Samuel. 'I did not realise I harboured a grievance until he showed me. Oh, the human heart can be deceptive Annie,' Jacob said to his wife. 'We so need the Holy Spirit to illuminate matters for us.' Anwen hugged him again. Jacob reached out his hand out to his firstborn son. 'Huw. I asked forgiveness for trying to change you. For trying to make you into something you are not—into something more like me. I love you for who you are Huw. You are a most remarkable person. I am so proud of you,' Jacob put his hand on his son's shoulder.

'Thank you Father,' Huw said. 'I always felt bad for coming after Samuel.'

Anwen began to weep. 'Oh no my son, oh no, how awful,' Anwen had her hand on her chest as she walked over to Huw. 'My heart is breaking. You are each of you irreplaceable, and we are so grateful for having had two more when the doctor had told us we never would,' Anwen wiped her tears with the middle finger of her left hand; she put an arm around Huw and gestured for Owen to come to her with her other arm. Jacob too was crying.

226

'I have been holding on to the old ways of doing things for too long. I want you and Robert to preach more often and take more meetings, Huw. Ah yes, I almost forgot to tell you Huw—and you too Owen, William—your schoolmaster came earlier to apologise for his ill treatment of you. Huw, he asked if he could take you for a pint of ale by way of apology for his rudeness to you. He told me he admired you for your defence of your brother, which he now understood was the right thing. The revival has turned him inside out,' Jacob laughed. He is running all over town making amends with people.'

The family laughed as they huddled together, in what Owen jokingly referred to as a scrum. For the first time his brother, who had died suddenly at nine months, and who was never mentioned, except as a sudden silence, seemed truly alive to him, which was strangely comforting. He watched his family weeping and saw that this experience had tightened and strengthened them all. Owen began to feel deep repentance for allowing a sense of shame to creep into his heart regarding his family; he felt a renewed love for them that seemed even greater than what he had known before.

In bed, Owen looked out the window as the dawn became noisy with sounds; he felt ecstatic that there were no chores to be done and that he would be left to sleep for hours, all day if he wanted.

Epilogue

Looking back, Owen was to call those days of revival 'shining days,' his mother called them simply 'days of heaven,' but the white heat of the revival fire became a glow by 1906, and soon afterwards, Owen had a dream, where he saw newspaper litter blowing amongst autumn leaves of red and brown; he saw the number twenty-eight on one of the newspaper pages, and he heard the sound of marching boots; the boots marched over the sea from mainland Europe over the island of Great Britain; as they marched, they drained the colour from the landscape until everything appeared in shades of grey or black. He also saw Cerys, holding her hands up so that he could look at them: the skin on her palms was canary yellow. Owen woke sweating with fear. It took him a while to shake the tangible presence of evil that he knew would soon begin. He began to repeat Psalm 91, over and over again until he actually felt he had entered the secret, untouchable place of the fortress of the Lord: *Thou shalt not be afraid for the terror by night; nor for the arrow that flieth by day; nor for the pestilence that walketh in darkness; nor for the destruction that wasteth at noonday. A thousand shall fall at thy side, and ten thousand at thy right hand; but it shall not come nigh thee... Because thou hast made the* LORD, *which is my refuge, even the Most High, thy habitation; there shall no evil befall thee...* Eventually a pale dawn outside his window brought him peace. Owen continued to prophesy on occasion as the Spirit moved him, but his parents remained careful that he should have his youth and maintain balance in his life and so they protected him from the many people that would come to chapel seeking a word from the Lord from Him. *Better they seek God's face for themselves*, Jacob was heard to say after Owen had been kept later than usual at the chapel attending to a line of people that had asked for Owen to pray for them specifically. After a few years, Owen did not prophesy again in public, though he continued to see many things that he had been told by The Spirit not to speak of *until the time is right*. His parents came to think of his gift as a pearl that continued to develop in the deep waters of his spirit; they continued to encourage it by saying nothing.

Bibliography

Chapter 8

"Calon Lân" ("A Pure Heart")
Words: Daniel James (1848–1920).

Chapter 12

"Be Thou My Vision" ("Bydd yn Welediad fy nghalon a'm byw")
Words: Ancient Irish hymn; trans. Mary Byrne, 1905, and versified by Eleanor Hull, 1912

Chapter 17

"Llef" ("A Cry")
Words: David Charles (1762–1834).

Chapter 21, 23, 24

"Dyma gariad fel y moroedd" ("Here is Love Vast as the Ocean")
Words: William Rees (1802–1883), verses 1–2. William Williams possibly wrote verses 3–4; translated from Welsh to English by William Edwards in *The Baptist Book of Praise*, 1900.

Chapter 24

"Arglwydd, arwain trwy'r anialwch" ("Guide Me, O Thou Great Jehovah")
Words: William Williams (1717–1791).

Acknowledgments

For the purposes of this book, I engaged in extensive study at the British Library, but there is one book I relied on for personal and eyewitness accounts of the Revival and that is "Voices from the Revival" by Brynmor P. Jones, Bryntirion Press (Feb 1995). I also found "Carriers of the Fire" by Karen Lowe, Shedhead Productions (March 2004), informative and inspiring: in particular her relating the accounts of the supernatural Egryn Lights as investigated and witnessed by journalists from the Mirror and the Mail.

www.emilybarroso.com